Region 6

Region 6

WHAT IF THE ALLIES HAD LOST?

IAN JAMES KRENDER

Matador
9 Priory Business Park,
Wistow Road, Kibworth Beauchamp,
Leicestershire LE8 0RX
Tel: 0116 279 2299
Email: books@troubador.co.uk
Web: www.troubador.co.uk/matador
Twitter: @matadorbooks

ISBN 978 1789017 359

British Library Cataloguing in Publication Data.
A catalogue record for this book is available from the British Library.

Printed and bound in the UK by T J International, Padstow, Cornwall
Typeset in 11pt Minion Pro by Troubador Publishing Ltd, Leicester, UK

Matador is an imprint of Troubador Publishing Ltd

For Craig

1

21st June 1983
Ost-Bereich;
the East End of London

THOMAS JORDAN

The late-night knock on our door came a week after my fifteenth birthday. It was not in response to any particular event, just one of the regular purges that occurred every few years around here. We just put up with them now. They were a part of life.

My parents and I were held at gunpoint in the front garden during a house search, which uncovered our short-wave radio. We were taken to a concentration camp and interrogated.

They took my mugshot and prints, then, after an hour of questioning and a bit of roughing up, I spent most of my two-week detention grafting in fields near to the camp. It was like they had to go through the motions to justify why they had arrested me. I did not see my parents during those two weeks. I reckoned they were fruit picking like me, but in another section.

It was back-breaking work, in hot, humid weather. They gave us meagre rations, and I spent my evenings exhausted and hungry. Me and the other prisoners tried to keep up our spirits, and there was some good banter in what passed as a canteen. No matter how bad the situation, you have got to stay positive. *Life ain't a rehearsal*, my old man used to say to me.

I slept on a bunk in one of the hundreds of unheated cattle sheds arranged around the camp. I say sleep; it was restless due to the bloke on the bed next to me snoring all night, then there were the guards patrolling outside, who talked loudly. I always remember the clack of the guard's boots against the wooden floor as he patrolled our shed and the orange glow of his cigarette against the blackness. The smell of his tobacco smoke masked the stench of stale sweat and the foul odour from the cesspit. Some nights, the screams from the interrogation building kept me awake, or there would be gunfire. I switched my mind off to all of it. I had to, or I would have gone mad.

I reckoned the collective farms needed extra labour during harvest, and that was the real reason for my arrest. I learned that we were being held at Hastings Concentration Camp. We all knew of it, and its reputation. I wondered if I would just waste away here, but no, eventually, I was released with a caution.

As I queued at the camp gate for the lorry that would return me to Ost-Bereich, I noticed that my parents were not in my group. I waited patiently, my stomach churning with worry, hoping they would appear. One by one we were processed and, after signing my release papers, I was allowed to pass through the camp gates, beyond the barbed wire and electric fences, to the lorry transports.

Still, I could not see my parents. I felt anxious, but when I looked back at the camp, I was relieved to see them in a line of people walking towards a squat building with bricked-up windows and a large chimney that was giving off a sickly-sweet smell. A wooden sign hung above the door – *Camp Bakery*. I was oblivious to the irony.

"Mum," I shouted desperately.

My mother looked up at me, squinting. She fell out of line, but a guard struck her, bellowing in a Yorkshire accent.

"Get back in line."

"My son," she pleaded. "Just let me say goodbye to my son."

He pushed her roughly towards the building.

"He's fifteen," she begged.

"Move forward."

My mother looked like shit. Her hair was matted with blood, and her eyes were swollen, but they were still full of love. She ignored the guard and started running towards me.

"Tom," she shouted desperately. I noticed how emaciated she looked, yet she was full of determination.

I started to run through the gate leading back inside the camp. A tall bloke called Mick held me back. I lunged forward, struggling in his grip. The guard raised his pistol and shot my mother in the back. She fell forward, still alive. I saw her battered face. She looked at me, the life draining from her, her right hand outstretched.

"I love you," she cried out weakly.

The guard approached her. He looked up at me. I froze. In the corner of my eye, I could see my father being held back by another prisoner. He was in tears, shouting, "Murdering bastards". I had never seen my father cry before. I shook with both fear and anger. The guard reached my mother and, with cold eyes, looked directly at me. He smiled as he pointed the gun at the back of her neck.

"No, please," I shouted.

He ignored my cries and shot her in the skull. Her head fell forward, blood gushing from the back, staining the grass red.

"No," I shouted in disbelief.

"Keep quiet, son," said Mick. "There ain't nothing you can do."

"They… They killed her," I stuttered.

"And if you carry on like that, you'll join her," he said.

It dawned on me that I had caused my mother's death. Why did I call out to her? I started to cry uncontrollably, pouring out my grief in front of the other prisoners and the SS guards. The officers were devoid of pity. If anything, it seemed they were enjoying the spectacle. I saw one of them snigger. Momentarily, I felt anger, but this soon dissolved, to be replaced by fear. I felt my stomach wrenching, like a flannel being wrung. My heart raced and my breathing was asthmatic. My knees felt weak as the painful reality of my mum's death sunk in.

I watched Dad being ushered inside the bakery. I had lost Mum, but at least it was some comfort that my old man was all right. No doubt he and the other prisoners would be put to work baking bread for the towns around the region. Why did Mum run? Why disobey an SS soldier?

"What did she do wrong?" I wailed.

An elderly female prisoner with long grey hair and liver spots comforted me, putting her arms around my back. I cried into her bony shoulder.

"It's all my fault," I sobbed.

"There's nothing you could have done," she said soothingly. "Just remember her last words to you – *I love you*."

"I loved her too. I never had the chance to tell her."

"She knew," said the old woman. "All mothers know."

A Stormtrooper with heavily pockmarked skin, wearing round glasses, came over and pulled us apart. "No contact."

"When will I see my dad?"

"Work brings freedom," he said.

"What does that mean?"

The guard smiled before he walked away.

We were ordered onto a white lorry and driven back to Ost-Bereich. I sat cross-legged in the back as we drove, feeling numb. There was an awkward silence in the cargo bay, as my fellow captives came to terms with their own losses. I could not accept what had just happened in front of my eyes. My mind could not process it. The lack of respect for human life. The sheer cruelty of it. What had my mother ever done to them? I felt angry, yet powerless, weak and desperately miserable.

✠

When I got back to Stepney, or Ost-Bereich 15 as the Krauts called it, I found out that my home had been reallocated to another family, so I moved into the box room in my uncle's house. The new tenants had kindly packed away my belongings, including my dad's record player and his LP collection. They were decent people, who helped me carry all my stuff to my new home.

A standard letter from the SS arrived a few days later, informing me that Dad had been *voluntarily* sent to Aberystwyth, for a *two-year re-education course*. I never saw or heard from him again.

The SS usually kept one member of a family unit alive, and it turned out that was me. The messenger – the one who went back to tell family and friends about the horrors of what happened when you stepped out of line. Terror was the key to their power. Their tentacles were everywhere, in every part of life. You never knew who to trust, who was an informer or who was a genuine friend. I had no idea why I was released instead of my parents; they probably tossed a coin for all I know.

My cuts and bruises may have healed in the months that followed, but the emotional scars were to stay with me for a lifetime. I was grateful for them. They were responsible for the person that I became.

2

1979–1986
St Albans, Hertfordshire

STEPHEN TALBOT

The 1980s was an awesome decade to grow up in. My childhood was a time of carefree laughter and happiness. We lived in St Albans, which was a well-integrated town, where German expatriates mixed freely with the local population and often socialised with them.

Germans took possession of the grandest houses in the town, but Father's work for the government had its associated benefits, and we were allocated a lovely eighteenth-century terraced cottage, close to the ancient city centre, which we rented from the Völker Wohnungsbaugesellschaft. It was one of those characterful properties in which, if you were tall, you had to duck your head in some rooms, but it was cosy, with inglenook fireplaces, exposed oak beams and a lovely kitchen with an Aga.

It was during the 1980s that we enjoyed some of the greatest leaps in living standards, thanks to the economic miracle engineered by the National Socialist German Workers' Party. Hunger and poverty had been abolished. I remember feeling an innate optimism as a child. There was a collective sense of purpose, a common goal to which we all strived. I remember the surges of national pride during school assemblies, as we sang the anthem pledging loyalty to the Third Reich. We would swear allegiance to our Eternal Führer, whose body lay embalmed in a mausoleum next to the Great Hall in Welthauptstadt Germania – the capital of the Third Reich. Here, he ruled from beyond the grave.

Society felt immense gratitude to the German Army for liberating us from the brutal rule of the aristocrats. We were part of a powerful military alliance that protected us from the communist tyranny in China and the decadent capitalism of America.

I have so many happy memories of growing up. As my father progressed in his career, we took expensive holidays abroad. We skied in Austria, we sunbathed on the beaches of Crimea, and sailed in the Mediterranean. I remember the pride we all felt when he returned from work in a new BMW 5 Series. I can still hear the burbling V8 engine now and smell the sweet scent of leather and wood. Father and I used to spend Sunday afternoons polishing it so thoroughly that you could see your reflection in the gleaming black paint.

While my childhood could generally be described as idyllic, there were times when it was tainted. My father had a successful career in the Gestapo, the division of the SS responsible for internal security and compliance. This made my family enemies, including some of our own relatives. Mother used to say that there was a lot of ignorance and jealousy in the world.

There were other hiccups too. I remember when I lost my best friend, Helmut, at prep school. He vanished along with his family. All traces of his existence were removed – he disappeared from class photographs, and if you asked teachers what had happened to him, you were greeted with silence.

My father's career put a wedge between him and my grandfather, who hated the Gestapo. The tension came to a head one afternoon. I remember hiding in Grandfather's kitchen, listening to the two them having a massive row in the lounge. I was eight at the time.

"You're a traitor," said Grandfather angrily. "Like anybody who puts on that uniform."

"You're stuck in the past," argued Father. "Clinging to rose-tinted memories of a world that never existed."

"We were free men."

"You're deluding yourself. We were slaves to the bourgeoisie."

"The winning side writes the history books. You're too young to remember the days before German rule. You could jump on a train without needing a permit. You could sit in a pub and moan about the government or the King without being arrested. That was freedom."

"Those who respect the law are free."

"As free as the leash that you're attached to."

"Do you want to go back to the 1930s, have your grandson mopping factory floors for tuppence a day?"

"You believe the propaganda? The Nazis own all the media. All we ever get is their twisted view of the world."

"What other views are there? The communists', the Yanks'? Whose side are you on?"

"The side of a million people exterminated when the atomic bomb exploded over Kent. The two million that disappeared when they took over."

"Enemies of peace."

"Including children, the elderly? Where are the Jews? Where did they go?"

"They have their own land in the East," said Father, reciting the official history books.

"What's this land called? I never hear of it."

"You ask too many questions."

"I thought I'd taught you right from wrong," said Grandfather sadly. "I lived through the social cleansing at the end of the war. I witnessed what men did to their fellows."

"Nobody is saying that the *Sozial Reinigung* was easy. It was ghastly but necessary."

"I watched our culture go up in smoke to chants of *Sieg Heil*. If you could have seen the destruction. Jewish businesses and synagogues razed, millions of books incinerated. They erased our heritage in weeks."

"They brought us hope."

"Hope?" said Grandfather incredulously. "You think what happened in 1944 brought us hope?"

"I know we paid a heavy price for losing the war, but we rose from the ashes. The Germans helped rebuild our industry. We enjoy undreamed-of living standards. I was destined to be a lifelong factory worker. Now look at me."

"I liked you better as a factory worker. At least you did an honest day's graft."

"Region 6 is—"

"Region 6," growled my grandfather. "We live in Great Britain, not Region 6. The country that started the Industrial Revolution. The nation of innovation, invention, discovery, philosophy, the birthplace of democracy... It took them less than two generations to erase our identity."

"We're going around in circles."

"I know you won't change your career, but I'm begging you to take Stephen out of that school. They're changing him, indoctrinating him with their vile ideology. I can't believe what comes out of his mouth sometimes."

"He's becoming a National Socialist, like his father."

"He's becoming a racist bigot."

"Watch what you say."

"Are you threatening me?"

"I'm just pointing out that you don't know who could be listening."

"I've long been anticipating that knock on the door, in this free world of yours," said Grandfather sarcastically.

"I get that you won't accept my choice of career, but let's be civil. Think of Stephen; he loves you."

"Don't use your son to blackmail me," snapped Grandfather. "Our relationship ended when you signed those recruitment papers."

"We're your family."

"My family? Is that what you told Maisie when you took her to the clinic?"

"Careful," warned Father. "Stephen might overhear you."

"Don't you think he deserves to know the truth?"

"We'll tell him when he's old enough to understand."

"Who's Maisie?" I said, walking into the room.

"Never mind," said Father. "Go back into the kitchen."

"I'm sorry, Stephen," said Grandfather. He crouched down on his knees and gave me a kiss on the forehead. "I'll always love you. Never forget that."

He started sobbing. I did not understand why he was so sad.

"Come on, Stephen." My father beckoned.

My grandfather looked at me tearfully. I gazed into his sad eyes, not really understanding what was happening. It was as though he knew that he was never going to see me again. He tousled my hair and patted me gently on the back.

"You must go now," he said. "Your future doesn't lie with an old man like me."

I walked towards our car, where my father was waiting. My grandfather closed his front door, and I heard him turning the multitude of locks, bolts and chains in the misguided belief that they would somehow protect him from the outside world.

Grandfather used to tell me about life before the war. He described a world that was very different to the one I knew. Even at that young age, I knew that it was all a fantasy. Nostalgia was a powerful narcotic for the elderly.

My father, on the other hand, was an enthusiastic supporter of the New Order, and the peace it brought to Europe. They disagreed openly on many occasions, but this row somehow felt different. It had a permanency to it, as though an irreversible red line had been crossed.

From that day, my father forbade me from having further contact with my grandfather. Understandably upset, I told my teacher at school about their quarrel. He listened intently, and reassured me that I was right to confide in him. I was an impressionable and naive child, who had no comprehension of the consequences of this conversation.

My grandfather was old, and not a threat, but dissent was not tolerated in any form. He was taken to one of the re-education camps located on Dartmoor, where he passed away. I had a postcard from him, a few days before he died, saying that he was suffering from pneumonia, but that he was being cared for by a professional team of doctors and nurses in the camp's hospital wing. His writing was spidery. Clearly, he was weak, but it definitely was *his* writing, I recognised it from birthday cards. He signed his postcard, uncharacteristically, *Heil Hitler, Grandpops X.*

I was sad that he was gravely ill, and perhaps harboured some resentment towards my father for not letting me see him for the last few weeks of his life, but I knew that he was in the best possible place. The free national healthcare that we received from the cradle to the grave under Chancellor Helmut Goebbels' benevolent leadership was second to none, and the re-education camp hospitals were no exception. The infirmary sent us his ashes two weeks later in a small china urn. We scattered them in Verulamium Park in our home town of St Albans, where he used to spend hours feeding the ducks.

✠

A few years later, when I was eleven, my parents sat me down at the kitchen table and told me about Maisie. The only time I had heard that name before was during Father's argument with Grandfather. My mother spent most of the conversation crying, while my father explained what had happened.

He took out a photograph of a baby girl in a cot in the spare room of our house.

"This was your little sister, Maisie," he said.

"My sister?" I said, surprised.

My father stood up and gazed out of the French windows into the garden. "Sometimes life presents us with tough decisions. I want you to know that this was the most difficult choice that your mother and I have ever had to make."

He came back to the table and sat down. He held my hand.

"Maisie was born with a condition called spina bifida."

"What's that?"

"It's a very serious illness. She had a deformed spine, which meant she would have suffered all her life."

"What happened to her?"

"We couldn't bear to think of our little girl in pain. I know that you have been taught about the Eugenics and Blood Purity programme at school."

"Yes," I said, beginning to quote from the textbook. "The disabled and diseased cannot be allowed to place a burden on the rest of society; it isn't humane to condemn them to a life of suffering, or risk the health of the remainder of the nation should we be contaminated with their defective genes... Something like that, anyway."

"Exactly. Those words make complete sense. Nobody is a greater supporter of Social Darwinism than me, but when suddenly the policy affects you so directly, when it's your own flesh and blood, you realise how brave the parents are who have been faced with this situation."

"What are you saying?"

"Taking Maisie to the Viktor Brack Clinic was the hardest thing that we have ever done. I looked at her tiny body, wondering how I could live with myself, but I knew if we did not do this, we would be hypocrites."

Mother blew her nose loudly.

"I want you to know that she never suffered," said Father. "It was like she just went to sleep, but didn't wake up."

"The doctors and nurses were marvellous," sobbed Mother. "So caring."

"It was the kindest thing to do," I said. "I understand."

"You're so grown-up," said Mother, drying her eyes.

I gave my mother a big hug. My father patted me on the back. I felt immense respect for my parents. They had made the ultimate sacrifice, for the good of society. Of course, I felt a little sad, but I was too young to remember this little girl, so I could not grieve for somebody I never knew.

After that conversation, Maisie was never mentioned again. I never asked my parents why they did not try for another baby. Indeed, the government encouraged party members to procreate with generous benefits. Population growth amongst those with superior bloodlines was seen as a demographic weapon against the rival superpowers. Land liberated by the Nazis in the former Soviet Union, under the highly successful Lebensraum policy, needed to be repopulated. Yet, I had no siblings. I was unsure of my mother and father's reasons. Perhaps the memories of Maisie were too painful for them. It did mean that I gained exclusive access to my parents' attention.

✠

Shortly after my thirteenth birthday, I passed my common entrance exam to the Heinrich Himmler Academy, an elite school in St Albans. It was next to the spectacular cathedral ruins in the otherwise well-preserved conservation area, which had survived mostly intact from wartime bombing, and was a ten-minute walk from home.

A boys-only school, it prided itself on strict discipline. We were required to keep our uniforms neatly pressed, our blazers buttoned, and our shoes polished, enduring a military-style playground inspection each morning, whatever the weather.

Steeped in tradition, parts of the flint-fronted school building dated back to the tenth century. Formerly it served as a monastery, and latterly as a private school for the bourgeoisie. We excelled in sports as well as lessons. I loved school; I made great friends, had immense respect for my teachers and enjoyed learning. By all accounts, it was an idyllic childhood.

3

Summer 1985

THOMAS JORDAN

I was in my family home on Ibbot Straβe, Stepney, moaning about my second-hand school uniform.

"It doesn't fit," I complained. My trousers were an inch too short and my jacket was three sizes too big.

"Like it or lump it," snapped Mum.

My parents were standing in our galley kitchen, drinking mugs of tea. Dad wore his bus conductor's uniform, and Mum was in factory overalls. She worked at the Ziegler AG Foundry, a copper smelting plant in Ost-Bereich 11, or Barking. It played havoc with her asthma.

As usual, Mum had laid out some cereal on the counter. I helped myself to some Weetabix and sat on a stool.

I wolfed down my Weetabix, grabbed my satchel and headed towards the front door.

"Have a good day," said Mum cheerfully. I loved her smile.

"And behave yourself," said Dad. "I don't want to be paying any more visits to your school."

I went out the front door and mounted my bike. I got to the end of the road, which was on a hill, and the East End of London stretched out in front of me. Soulless concrete tower blocks and rows of Victorian terraced houses, many of them reduced to rubble in the war and never rebuilt. Beyond the residential zone, there were hundreds of factories. They stretched as far as you could see, disappearing into the smog. It was not a scenic view, but it was all I had ever known.

I pedalled to the school gates and started to chain up my bike on the rack outside the leaky Portakabin which served as my classroom.

My surroundings blurred and vanished, and I suddenly found myself on Stepney High Street. It was market day, and Big Jim was shouting, "Two Reichsmarks a punnet of strawberries" from his fruit and veg stall.

Big Jim bent down and gave me a punnet. "On the house," he said. "They're the bruised ones; I saved them specially. They're still tasty."

"Thanks, sir," I said gratefully, snatching them from him.

"Give my love to your mum and dad."

I skipped along the High Street excitedly, past the launderette, the pie and mash shop, and the bricked-up Mile End Underground Station, eager to share the fruit with Mum and Dad.

The pavement collapsed beneath me, and I felt dizzy as I spun around in the darkness. Suddenly, I was seventeen again, and in a boxing ring in my gym in Bethnal Green. My opponent was dripping with blood, and I was punching him repeatedly. He fell to the floor. The referee started counting to ten. Then I heard the bell ring. I raised my gloved hand triumphantly. In the baying crowd, I saw my dad look on proudly.

"Get in there, my son," he shouted.

The bell kept ringing and grew louder. He faded from view. My bedroom came into focus. I turned over sleepily and groaned as I looked at my bedside clock. It was 07.00. I pressed down the button on top and silenced the alarm.

I yawned, trying to remember my dream, before climbing out of bed and going to the bathroom. I took a long piss, then tried to take a shower. Chance would be a fine thing; it was always hit or miss whether you would get running water. My uncle never put money in the meter, but then why would he; he never washed, the dirty bastard, until I nagged him when he got too stinky. I think he thought washing was for poofters.

I managed to coax a cold dribble from the sink tap, so I flannelled myself down.

I remember Dad moaning at me after boxing practice when I dared to have the luxury of four minutes of warm water. He was always shoving twenty-pfennig coins into the meter to pay for the immersion heater. *Costs me a fiver every time you have a bleeding shower*, he used to holler up the stairs.

Two years on and I miss him like crazy. I wish he could have seen how well I had done with my boxing. After the SS murdered my family, I kept up with the sport, channelling my hatred of the Nazis to good effect. Our gym was a proper man's gym, not one of those posh health clubs that the elite classes used, with their personal trainers, plunge pools, and poncey aerobics classes. Bill Watson, who owned the gym, said all you needed were a few punchbags, a boxing ring and a bench press.

I progressed from welterweight to heavyweight, when, of course, the fights got harder. I think I was hooked on the adrenaline, the noise from the crowd, the smell of blood, sweat and testosterone. Bill took over as my trainer from my dad. He was a massively built cockney skinhead, a little overweight and covered in tattoos. He had always been a close family friend and became like a substitute father to me. Don't get me wrong, nobody could ever replace my dad, but I loved and respected Bill. He was harsh and pushed me to my limit, but his military routine – and believe me, he was like a sergeant major – saw me win twelve fights in a row.

The cash from the fights came in handy too. I bought myself a second-hand telly, had the roof fixed, and suddenly we could afford fresh meat twice a week. Not that my uncle appreciated it.

Today was Saturday. My working week at the Schwebke television factory had finished the day before, but all under-twenty-ones had to do 'voluntary' work in the morning, I suppose it was like community service. They called it *zivildienst*. Mine involved crossing the *zwischenwand*, the nine-metre-high wall which segregated London. The racially inferior, intelligentsia and anyone else the Nazis did not approve of, like me, were kept separate from the Krauts and their collaborators.

Aware that I was running late, I ran towards the Aldgate checkpoint. The wall was an ugly concrete thing topped with barbed wire, and I always felt fearful whenever I got near it. As I approached, one of the guards in a watchtower shouted, "Halt."

I stopped in my tracks. I looked down at the red laser dot on my chest. I shut my eyes, trembling. So-called accidents happened all the time. The shot never came. I just heard his jeering. I walked nervously towards the checkpoint, wondering if the guard still had his gun trained on my back.

The checkpoint guards were arseholes too. I handed over my papers, trying to ignore the snarling Alsatians. Once through the border inspection, I got onto a minibus, and we drove to Speer Park, not far from Buckingham Palace.

We were weeding flower beds today. It was a sunny day, and there were worse places to spend the morning. I looked jealously at the well-dressed citizens of the West, mingling with soldiers, their privileged children playing in the short grass, blissfully unaware of life on the other side of the wall.

There was always that carrot dangling in front of you: that one day, somehow, you would obtain a new classification and be able to move to the west side. I started talking to a co-worker about West Ham's latest fortunes, but our supervisor bollocked us, so we continued in silence. In the middle of this particular flower bed, there was a granite statue of Hitler, our so-called Eternal Führer. They claimed that he ruled from beyond the grave. Apparently, we were a *necrocracy*.

My family's fate had been sealed due to our distant Jewish ancestry. We were classified as Type 5 undesirables by the Sozialplanungsministerium. Blame my great-grandmother, who fortunately for us had married out of the faith. It meant that the pollution of our bloodline was at the lower end of the Mengele scale.

Nobody really knew what had happened to the Jews. They told us they were resettled in Siberia, part of Region 3 – the former Soviet Union. I remember my dad saying that this was a lie, and they had all been killed. I thought that was a bit far-fetched, but the fact was that you never heard anything about them.

Sadly, the only realistic way I could get my categorisation changed was if I joined the army. My parents would turn in their graves if they thought I had even considered it.

When I got back home, I would usually sit and watch the footy on Channel Two with my uncle, who was, more often than not, pissed. There were only two channels: Channel Two was entertainment and sport, and RT – Reich Today – was the twenty-four-hour news channel. RT was a class act – slickly dressed newsreaders in ultra-modern studios made the news, which I knew was just propaganda, seem credible. America was portrayed as a crumbling anarchy where gun-toting schoolchildren massacred their classmates. It was the only news we had access to, aside from the American short-wave broadcasts from the Atlantic, but they were usually jammed, and I knew only too well the risks of being caught.

My Saturday evenings were more often than not spent with my mates down the local boozer – The Black Horse, a typical spit-and-sawdust East End pub that served London Pride alongside German lagers and was the scene of many a punch-up. In fact, it was unusual for something not to kick off on Saturday nights, but despite the aggro, I loved it.

For some reason there would be a sprinkling of Kraut soldiers in there too, the ones unlucky enough to be stationed over on the east side of the *zwischenwand*, usually in Hackney Barracks. They did not really mix with us, but I knew the landlord, Trevor, was grateful for their money.

The East End was a far cry from the glittering Nazi utopia in the western sector, but I still loved it. The people were real. It was where I lived out my childhood. The ruined streets were our playground. I played football with my mates, and the bombed-out houses and rubble were make-believe mountains that we climbed. Yes, my job was beyond dull, my wages were paltry and I lived in a shithole, but it was still my home, and I had always believed that life was what you made of it. Even if I had to live with the bitterness over my parents.

However, over time my attitude gradually changed. As I grew into a young adult, I wanted more than a life of servitude. I started to question my state-determined fate. My resentment festered over time – I began to think dangerous thoughts. Why should we just accept occupation as a done deal? Why trade in our freedoms so readily, for subsidised rent, trains that ran on time and food in the fridge?

We had been subjected to four decades of brainwashing. German rule was welcomed by most people. Democracy was a distant memory associated with a time of disorder, war and inequality. The public lapped up the lies like blind cats licking cream. My parents had taught me right from wrong, taught me real history as opposed to the bullshit we were fed at school, but I knew that people like me were in the minority.

Life was hard, but people celebrated forty years of peace in Europe, even if that peace was born out of terror. There was almost no crime, justice was swift and merciless, and there was full employment. Germans had given us autobahns, world-class transport, free healthcare, spectacular monuments, and education for all. We were part of the Third Reich; one big, happy family.

Nobody knew what was normal any more. The state would accept nothing short of blind devotion to its leaders. Our national identity had been taken away, to the point that in a couple of generations, most of us knew little or nothing about our real past. The royal family were traitors; the ruling classes of the past were *bourgeois exploiters*. Propaganda posters were pasted on every available billboard. It was mandatory for every household to keep portraits of Hitler and Chancellor Helmut Goebbels polished and hung on the wall. They watched over us, day and night. You never forgot that they were in charge, and strangely, you believed that they were somehow watching over you. God, I hated them.

4

13th June 1986

STEPHEN TALBOT

It was a week after my sixteenth birthday, and our class was excited about a two-day trip to London. It was a warm, sunny day, and I sweated in my school uniform.

We waited in an orderly queue in the school car park to board our coach. The driver, a Romanian Untermensch, loaded our suitcases into the luggage compartment, while Mrs Turner ticked our names off on the register as we boarded.

Thankfully, the coach interior was air-conditioned. I took a window seat next to my best friend, Phillip. Once everybody had boarded, Mrs Turner stood at the front and gave our class the customary Nazi salute.

"Remember," she said. "You are representing the school. Anybody who misbehaves or brings our reputation into disrepute will be dealt with severely. Heil Hitler."

"Heil Hitler," the class replied in unison.

She sat down behind the driver, next to Mr Haines, our history teacher.

The coach departed, crunching through the gears as it drove along Fishpool Straβe and then onto the main road out of St Albans. In ten minutes, we had joined Autobahn 1. As we approached the North London checkpoint at

Hampstead, the traffic became heavier, filtering into twelve lanes. Senior Nazis, the SS, military and Gestapo had their own priority lane which flowed freely; we mere mortals had to be patient.

A Metropolitan Police constable boarded the coach at the barrier and walked through the aisle, checking our travel permits and swiping our identification cards into a portable scanner. After he had finished, a sign displaying *Vorgehen/Proceed* illuminated, the barrier rose, and we rejoined Autobahn 1.

"You're chatty," I said to Phillip, who was listening to some music on his Walkman.

"Uh," he grunted.

I gazed out of the tinted window. A work detail of Polish Untermenschen were digging up a coned-off section of the road, identifiable by the mandatory red-and-white flags embroidered on their overalls.

After forty-five minutes, we reached the Hitler Youth Hostel on Great Russell Straβe, a brutalist, high-rise building draped in five-storey swastika banners, built on the site of the bombed British Museum.

I stepped off the coach. The city air was polluted and thick with soot. Red buses thundered past us with Ministry of Enlightenment advertisements pasted on their sides, black cabs honked their horns, and civilians shared the pavements with soldiers. It was all so busy.

We checked in, unpacked, then met in reception for a walking tour. We caught a Tube train from Tottenham Court Road to Westminster on the spotlessly clean London Underground. Under the 1953 National Socialist Affordable Travel Act, a twenty-four-hour off-peak travelcard cost only one Reichsmark. This also allowed you to use the buses, trams, and monorail system. I wondered why anybody would bother with a cab.

As we emerged from Westminster Station, I saw the Houses of Parliament for the first time in real life. The building stood proudly as a symbol of our friendship with Germany, with dozens of elongated swastika banners draped from poles on the roof, extending to the lower floors. I took some pictures with my Instamatic. Mr Haines had a monotonous voice, and I did not really follow what he was reading from the Education Ministry notes. Something about the building being restored as a goodwill gift from our Eternal Führer. He was droning on about how many Reichsmarks it had cost and other boring statistics.

We walked on.

Mr Haines pointed towards the Arch of National Socialist Victory.

"Based on the former site of the Admiralty Arch, this was another gift bequeathed to Londoners by the German government, in 1949. Designed by the chief architect of the Third Reich, Albert Speer, it measures nearly ninety metres in height. It is an eighty per cent scale replica of the original in Germania."

I squinted at the gold eagle on top, its wings outstretched majestically, perched on a swastika. It glinted in the summer sun.

Phillip started pulling stupid faces at me, doing an impression of Mr Haines, who was possibly the most boring teacher in the world. I giggled.

"Talbot, pay attention," shouted Mr Haines.

"Sorry, sir," I said.

"Since you seem to have better things to do than listening to me, you must know all about this already. Can you tell me how many German soldiers gave their lives to liberate us?"

"I can't remember, sir," I said.

"Can anybody else enlighten us?" said Mr Haines, looking around the group.

A swotty lad called Marcus raised his hand.

"Smith," said Mr Haines.

"Twenty-three thousand, four hundred and twenty-nine," he said.

"Correct," replied Mr Haines. "Two house points. The name of each one of those brave men is engraved on the granite walls."

There was a bronze torch underneath the arch, with a tall flame that burned perpetually in memory of the dead.

We walked along Adolf Hitler Straβe, towards Buckingham Palace, where Governor General Hans Müller resided. Phillip took a picture of me with one of the guards in ceremonial Reich uniform, stationed in wooden huts at intervals along the road. He was standing to attention with his bayonetted rifle pointing to the sky. We tried to provoke a reaction from him by sticking out our tongues, but he stood there impassively, staring into space, undistracted by our juvenile antics.

Eventually, we got bored and caught up with the rest of the class, who had continued walking towards the palace. It loomed large in front of us, swathed in twenty-metre-long swastika banners.

Mrs Turner opened her Education Ministry booklet, and leafed through the pages to the relevant section.

"In front of you stands Buckingham Palace, originally commissioned by the Duke of Buckingham in 1703 at an equivalent cost of tens of millions of Reichsmarks, while much of the country languished in poverty. Children suffered from now-eliminated diseases such as polio and typhoid. Hunger and starvation were widespread. Meanwhile, the upper classes lavished money upon themselves, building increasingly ostentatious homes, which they filled with degenerate art and other vulgar displays of wealth."

"What's a duke?" asked one of my classmates.

"Good question, Turnbull. It's an old aristocratic title…" said Mr Haines, pausing as he was drowned out by an electrically powered Lufthansa Zeppelin descending towards Euston Airport. He resumed: "A title given to social-climbing sycophants of the royal family, and abolished by the National Socialists. Now the palace serves as the Governor General's residence and administration centre."

Despite a restoration, the palace's stone facade still bore the scars of war. We spent a few minutes admiring the building. A short bus journey took us to Trafalgar Platz, where we took turns to salute Hitler's Column, reaffirming our oath of allegiance. Then we went to the National Gallery, overlooking the square, where there was an exhibition of Renaissance paintings on loan from the Führer Museum and Art Gallery in Linz.

It was an exhausting day. We arrived back at the hostel in the evening, ate dinner in the canteen and went to bed at around 21.00.

✠

The next morning, we attended the National Socialist Enlightenment Chamber for a lecture from the Junior Sports Minister, where we mingled with pupils from several other all-boys schools.

We had the afternoon free to explore the city on our own before our coach returned to St Albans. However, I was staying behind to meet my parents later for a trip to the opera. A group of four of us decided to head to bustling Oxford Straße, the main shopping street of London. There were fashionable boutiques, international chains, and department stores, staffed mainly by Slavs. I bought a snow globe of the Arch of National Socialist Victory as a present for my mother, from a market stall.

After an hour of browsing shops, we returned to the hostel. I waved off my school friends, who boarded the coach back to St Albans, and caught a Number 73 tram to King's Cross to meet my parents.

I waited for them on the concourse. The train had arrived, and I could see them queuing up at the security gate to have their travel permits and tickets checked by guards with Alsatians. My mother looked elegant in a black ballgown, which matched her long dark hair. She was slim and beautiful, with polished red nails and immaculately applied Chanel make-up. She wore the pearl necklace and matching earrings that my father had bought for her fortieth birthday. Father was wearing his dress uniform.

"You look beautiful, Mum," I said.

She gave me a hug. "How was your school trip?" she asked.

"Brilliant – I bought you this," I said, handing my mother the snow globe, wrapped in some tissue paper.

"It's lovely," she said, unwrapping it.

"How was your journey?" I asked Father.

"Apart from being delayed at the Cricklewood checkpoint for fifteen minutes, fine," he said gruffly. "Bloody people who don't get their travel permits stamped."

Mother rolled her eyes. "You look very smart, dear," she said, admiring my neatly pressed school uniform and polished shoes. She straightened my tie, neatened my blond hair and, to my horror, gave my face a spit wash.

"Mum, I'm not ten years old," I said in disgust.

"You're still my baby."

We exited the *Bahnhof* via the main entrance and Father hailed a black cab, which drove us to South Kensington to the Adolf Hitler Opera House, to see Richard Wagner's *Die Walküre*.

The opera house replaced the Royal Albert Hall, which was destroyed during the Blitz. An Albert Speer building, it paid homage to the original Victorian design, itself inspired by the Colosseum in Rome. Speer's construction was twice the size, and built from concrete, decorated with Nordic-inspired statues and imagery.

We entered the echoey hall, a cavernous marble chamber dominated by a statue of the Führer. An usher showed us to our seats in the upper circle. This was supposed to be a treat, but within twenty minutes of the performance beginning, I realised that I loathed opera, and I gritted my teeth until the end. At least the dialogue was in German so I could understand the plot, but it was genuinely torturous.

It was a pleasant, balmy evening with a gibbous moon when we left, so we took a stroll to nearby Speer Park. A gentle breeze carried the hum of traffic from the main road, but the smell of freshly cut grass masked the pollution. It seemed that others had the same idea as us, as there were many couples and small groups enjoying the summer weather.

As we walked around Serpentine Lake, my parents discussed the performance enthusiastically, while I pretended that I had liked it. I did not want to appear ungrateful as the seats were expensive.

We left Speer Park and continued onwards, passing by the Ritz Hotel.

"Wow, look at that, Dad – it's a Bugatti Type 60," I said, pointing at a car parked outside.

"You don't see many of those," he said. "I'd rather have a Maybach, though."

"Nah, Maybachs are for old men."

I stood there wistfully, admiring the curvaceous lines and the bright chrome trim against the black paintwork, the purposeful, overly long bonnet housing a monstrous V12 quad-turbo engine. I wondered if I would ever be able to afford one. I doubted it, but it did not stop me dreaming.

A Routemaster waited at the bus stop opposite us, belching out diesel fumes. The advertisement on the side depicted Chancellor Helmut Goebbels beaming, handing an excited family the keys to an apartment in one of the new tower blocks that were springing up all over the country.

We reached Piccadilly Circus, where we found a little café and I enjoyed a hot chocolate and a teacake, seated at one of the tables arranged outside around the Statue of Eros.

Even though it was 23.00, the whole area was bustling with pedestrians, businessmen, soldiers and traffic. The night sky was lit up by colossal neon signs advertising German multinational companies such as BASF and Mercedes, but it was the massive television screen that caught your attention. It curved around the corner of Shaftesbury Avenue and Regent Straße, showing the Reich Today twenty-four-hour news channel. The headlines scrolled underneath, along an LED crawler.

"We'll finish these drinks, and catch a black cab to King's Cross," said Father. "We've still got an hour left on our travel permits."

On the opposite side of the café, in front of the statue of Eros, in the cordoned-off area reserved for Germans and their families, a group of junior SS officers were drunk, and behaving obnoxiously towards the waitress. They were rowdy and disrespectful, groping her and making inappropriate comments.

I felt sorry for the poor creature. She was young and beautiful, but she wore an obligatory identifying badge sewn onto her uniform, in this case a yellow-and-blue striped flag, indicating that she was Ukrainian. Even though she was subhuman, their treatment of her was unnecessary.

She looked exasperated as though she were suppressing the urge to punch them, an unfortunate act that would almost inevitably result in summary execution. I could see that my mother was uncomfortable too.

"Can't you say something, Edward?" she murmured.

"It's not worth it," my father replied. "She's only a Slav; she's not worth getting into an argument over."

"I don't like their language."

"They're just drunken men in high spirits."

"But they're in uniform. Aren't they supposed to have standards of conduct? Don't you outrank them?"

"I don't like it either, but I'm not about to create an incident. They're German." Then he quickly added, "It's just not worth the hassle, believe me; the paperwork alone would take me days. Let's just finish our drinks, and we'll go home. We've had a lovely family evening – I'm not going to let this spoil it."

I took a different view to my father's dismissiveness of the girl's racial heritage. It was not fair to treat anybody like that, regardless of their inferior bloodline. I thought the SS officers were like a pack of wild animals, and they made me feel uncomfortable.

Ignoring their lewd behaviour, I took a sip of creamy hot chocolate, which tasted delicious. I glanced up and saw one of the SS officers trying to reach inside the waitress' blouse. It seemed that finally, they had pushed her too far. She snapped and slapped him across the face. He stood up angrily and started to shout at her in German. I saw her reach into her waistcoat. She smiled and closed her eyes, as if in a trance. I saw her pull on something.

5

14th June 1986

THOMAS JORDAN

I winced as I nicked my chin with my blunt razor. Blades were scarce, even on the black market, so I made them last for a few months. I had a quick shower and towelled off, making a mental note to get my hair clipped sooner rather than later.

My boxing workouts had given me a muscular body. I weighed in at ninety-two kilos. My physique gave me confidence, though some people found my size intimidating.

I turned eighteen today. It was three years since I lost my parents. It was on birthdays and public holidays that I missed them most. How great it would have been to have gone to The Black Horse and enjoyed a stein of London Pride with my old man, but the Nazis had robbed me of that chance.

Dad told me stories of how polite the German officers were when they first arrived. People had feared them, but they spent money in shops and restaurants, and everyone was glad that the war was over, even if we had lost. Children, like my dad, played football on the streets with German troops. They gave him and his friends chocolate and took them for rides in their tanks. He told me that they were kind. They talked about their own children back in Germany. It did not seem too bad.

King George VI fled to Canada with his family, and Edward VIII became King again. Dad said that everything seemed different but strangely normal at first. Nobody knew what was to come.

Everything changed when the Butcher of Britain, Dr Franz Six, arrived in London and set up the SS death squads. Millions were tortured and killed. Concentration camps were built along the South Coast; the social cleansing started. Dad told me his Jewish friends disappeared first, then others followed – Freemasons, Jehovah's Witnesses and the toffs listed in Schellenberg's Black Book.

My grandpa's blood was tainted with Jewish genes from his mother. The family were rounded up. My dad was spared and sent to a state orphanage, which he hated, but at least he lived.

Life had been shit since the 1940s, but the Nazis needed cheap labour. So that was where I fitted into their plan, working in the Schwebke AG factory, the largest television maker in the Reich. I soldered circuit boards on an assembly line. Our television sets were the best in the world, far better than the crap the Japs made, but I would never be able to afford one.

My job was chosen for me by the Arbeitszuweisung Ministerium. I had no say. It would be my job for life unless I joined the army. People like me accepted our fate, and part of me was grateful for a secure job and the promise of a decent pension at sixty-five.

Yet, I felt that I was destined for something more. The boredom of working on a production line drove me crazy. There were few breaks, and it was only twenty Reichsmarks for a ten-hour shift.

Most of our goods were exported to Germany via the Docklands, but some were sent across the *zwischenwand* to stock the posh department stores used by the Germans and their collaborators. A lot of people in Region 6 had done well under the Occupation. If you licked the right arses, you could get on in life.

I had organised a piss-up at The Black Horse with some mates to celebrate my birthday. I was already a regular there. One of the few good things the Nazis did was lower the legal drinking age to sixteen. Probably to let us all drown our sorrows.

I walked across the landing to my bedroom with a towel wrapped around my waist. I glanced at the photo of my parents that I kept on my bedside table. I was starting to look uncannily like my old man. That was not a bad thing; he was a good-looking bloke, muscular, square-jawed like me, with a determined but trustworthy face. He grew his hair long, though, unlike my number-two crop.

It was 21.00, and only just starting to get dark. I loved the summer. Like my parents had, my uncle lived in an old Victorian house on one of the terraces that survived the Blitz. There were brown patches on the ceiling where the roof leaked. My furniture was all pre-war, old-fashioned dark wood, but it was solidly built, unlike the mass-produced junk they make today.

The government was building tower blocks to replace the substandard housing in Ost-Bereich. *Fruits of the economic miracle*, they told us. They looked like giant grey tombstones and many said they were crappily built, but people would pay hefty bribes to get an apartment in one.

I heard my uncle come in through the front door and walk upstairs. He gave me a knock.

"Tom?" he said. "You in there?"

I opened the door.

"Happy birthday," he said gruffly, handing me a card.

"Cheers, Uncle John," I said, taking the envelope. As usual, he stank of alcohol.

"Are you going to open it, then?"

I opened the card. Inside there was a crinkled ten-Reichsmark note. "Wow."

"Have a good night out on me."

"Thanks. This is a lot of money. You didn't have to."

"I wanted to. You're only eighteen once. Besides, you're my favourite nephew."

"I'm your only nephew."

"I know," he replied, giving me a wink.

There was an awkward moment when perhaps we should have given each other a hug. Instead, my uncle patted me clumsily on the shoulder, avoiding eye contact, and went back downstairs. He did not do emotion.

There was a strained love between us. I was his only link to his brother, but I think that he resented having to raise me after my parents were murdered. Likewise, he reminded me of my father. They looked different, but their mannerisms were identical. He was a hopeless alcoholic, though, who had never married. Unlike my old man, who scrubbed up well, he was grubby, had a heavy drinker's complexion, and was painfully thin with long, greasy hair and a straggly grey beard. He was perpetually grumpy, but for all his faults, I thought the world of him.

I put the money in my wallet and dressed. It was a hot day, so I wore a pair of jeans and a white T-shirt. My uncle was now sitting in his armchair, wearing his work overalls, drinking whisky and smoking a roll-up.

"I wish you'd cut down," I said. "If you're gonna get pissed, why don't you come down the pub with me?"

"My days of drinking in bars ended a long time ago," he said in his gravelly voice.

"The booze will kill you in the end."

"You gotta die of something," he slurred. "If this is all life is, bring it on."

I sighed and headed off to the pub, leaving him to wallow in his own self-pity. I had tried to help him dry out so many times, but it was hopeless. He was best left alone to get on with it.

My friends were already propping up the bar. There were eight of us. We all knew each other from Bill's gym. We looked like a bunch of hard nuts, but we were as good as gold.

"Get this down your neck," said Derek, handing me a stein of London Pride.

"Cheers," I said, taking a sip.

My friends all downed their drinks in one gulp and looked at me expectantly.

"Okay," I said. "I get it. It's one of those nights."

"It's your eighteenth, mate," said Pete. "If you're not throwing up by midnight, we've not done our job."

Within an hour, I was drunk, as an endless supply of beer and whisky flowed from the bar. It was strictly a lads' night out until a group of nice-looking girls walked into the pub.

Me and Derek walked over to them, full of drunken bravado.

"I'm Del," said Derek. "This is Tom. It's his birthday."

"Of course it is," said the most attractive of the girls. She had long blonde hair and wore a lot of make-up. She did not look impressed.

"Nah," I said, pointing at the *18 today* badge on my T-shirt. "It really is."

"Can we buy you birds a drink?" said Derek. "You can come over and join us."

"No thanks," she said icily. "We're only staying for one."

We rejoined our group, glancing over at the girls, knowing that they were out of our league.

"She's gagging for it," said Derek. "That type always are."

"Yes, Derek," I said sarcastically. "What girl could ever resist you?"

"I reckon they're all lezzers."

"Or frigid," agreed Pete. "Got to be."

Ten minutes later, the girls left, and our behaviour got worse again.

"Guys, watch the language," warned the landlord. "There's other customers in here too."

"Soz, Trev," said Pete.

There was an old jukebox in the corner of the pub, which we loaded with five-pfennig coins and decided to sing along to the tunes, thinking we had great voices. The bar rapidly emptied.

It was an evening of teenage fun. For a while, we could forget about the Occupation. It did not matter that we lived in a police state, trapped on the wrong side of the wall.

I saw Trevor, the obese landlord, move over to the jukebox and unplug it. The pub became abruptly silent.

"Come on, Trev, don't be a spoilsport," I slurred. "We've got ages until closing."

"Shush," he replied. "You need to watch this."

Trevor stood on a chair and reached up to a shelf to switch on the television. He thumped the top to stabilise the picture.

Maria Thorpe, an elegant newsreader, looked grim as she read from an autocue.

"We're going to stay with this story. If you've just joined us, at 23.25 tonight, London suffered a major terrorist attack.

"In a new low for the anti-democracy terrorists, CCTV footage seems to indicate that the bomb was concealed within a person's clothing. It appears that the perpetrator blew herself up in the process.

"This so-called suicide bombing is a new kind of tactic. The bomb has caused devastation to Piccadilly Circus and damage to buildings up to two hundred metres away. At least twenty-five people have been killed with many more injured, some seriously.

We're going across to our correspondent at the incident, David Austin. I warn you, there are some shocking scenes."

David Austin appeared on screen, in front of what was barely recognisable as Piccadilly Circus. The famous neon billboards and giant television screen were shattered; there was wreckage around the streets. You could scarcely hear the correspondent above the wails of car and burglar alarms. A fire was raging in a café, fought by a crew of firemen, risking their own lives attempting to rescue trapped people from the flats above.

There were dozens of Metropolitan Police cars, fire engines, and ambulances. Their blue lights strobed in the darkness. In the background, you could see bodies being carried away on stretchers.

"As you can observe," Austin said, *"apocalyptic scenes here in Piccadilly Circus, as fire and ambulance crews search for survivors. Though small enough to be concealed on a person, this was a powerful bomb, designed to maim and injure innocent people. No warning was given; it was a pleasant summer evening, the cafés and pubs were busy, and we're a short walk from Theatreland."*

A helicopter equipped with a searchlight passed overhead, drowning out his commentary.

He shouted over the din, *"The entire area has been sealed off, and anti-terrorist police are conducting thorough searches with sniffer dogs, to see if there are any more explosive devices. If you work or intend to travel to Central London tomorrow, the advice is do not try. All travel permits are rescinded until further notice and London is on the highest security alert."*

An SS officer started to usher the news reporter away from the scene.

"I think we may have outstayed our welcome," Austin said hurriedly. *"I'll keep you posted on the latest developments on the ground. In the meantime, thank you for watching."*

"That was David Austin at the scene," said Maria Thorpe. *"Now, just bear with me a second."* She fumbled with her earpiece. *"Okay, we're just going over to Downing Straβe where the Prime Minister is about to make a statement."*

The picture changed to show some journalists standing outside 10 Downing Straβe. The Prime Minister emerged from the familiar black door and walked towards a lectern on the pavement in front of them. He cleared his throat and spoke into the microphone.

"Once again, our capital city has been the target of a cowardly and pointless attack by terrorists, aimed at undermining our way of life. The communist resistance has claimed responsibility for this outrage.

"While the primary perpetrator has escaped justice, please rest assured that we will *capture her fellow conspirators, and they* will *be made to suffer tenfold for the misery they have caused the families of the brave heroes that have perished tonight.*

"I have had a lengthy discussion with the Governor General, and he agrees that the imposition of martial law is appropriate at this time. We hope that this will be temporary, but I trust the public will accept that our safety takes absolute priority. This will come into effect from 02.00 for a minimum period of one month. Full details will be published in tomorrow's newspapers and on Reich Today."

There were flashes and questions from journalists.

"Gentlemen, I hope you will understand that I cannot take questions at this time. I need to prepare for an emergency Cabinet meeting shortly; my press secretary will keep you posted with any developments."

"It's time you all went home," said Trevor.

I nodded silently. "Come on, lads, it's been a great night. Thanks for celebrating it with me."

"Bit of a downer, though – the news, I mean," said Pete.

"There'll be a crackdown here, that's for sure," said Derek.

"Fucking Nazi bastards," said Pete.

"There's no point moaning," said Derek. "There's fuck all we can do about it."

"Well, I'm sick of it," said Pete angrily. "What's it all got to do with us?"

"Hurry up, lads," urged Trevor. "I need to lock up."

He switched off the television. The picture shrank to a small dot in the centre of the screen.

We left the pub, and I walked home, feeling sullen. I was drunk, but the shock of the attack had snapped me into alertness, albeit a groggy one. These events usually had severe consequences for our community. We knew what was coming next. Revenge.

I had mixed feelings about the attack. I admired the resistance for their bravery, but I did not think it was fair to punish innocents. However, to sacrifice your own life for a cause must have taken some courage. I did not believe that I could do it.

The Chinese-backed communists were the most ruthless of the resistance factions. Apart from the Americans, the Chinese were the only power capable of stopping the Nazis spreading. It was only nuclear weapons that prevented us all from going to war. We lived in what they called the Cold War, an uneasy truce.

Spying was widespread, there were proxy wars in Africa and all parties sponsored paramilitary groups in each other's territories. The Chinese hated the Nazis as much as the rest of the world, but they needed their oil. The Japanese loathed the Chinese and the Nazis equally, but had stayed neutral since their surrender at the end of the Pacific War, after the Americans dropped atomic bombs on Hiroshima and Nagasaki in 1945.

If only the Americans had won the race to build an atomic bomb, the war would have ended very differently, but the Nazis got there first. The Soviets, who were winning the Battle of Stalingrad, gradually regaining their territory, were defeated in weeks after they were nuked. Hitler refused to share the secret of the atom bomb with Japan, leading to a split in the Axis.

Fortunately, American scientists succeeded in producing their own atomic bomb, albeit with the help of the infamous defector Werner Heisenberg – the Nazis' chief nuclear scientist. This protected America from invasion and established it as a beacon of hope for the world. As it was, the globe was divided into three major powers, locked in a stalemate, and people like me were at the bottom of the pile.

6

28th June 1986

STEPHEN TALBOT

I could see a harsh fluorescent light above me. Everything was blurry, but gradually my surroundings came into focus. I blinked. I was lying in a hospital bed with a thumping headache.

"Stephen?" said a male voice. It sounded distant, as if the person was standing at the end of a tunnel.

I adjusted myself to see the man talking to me. I realised that my arm was in a cast, and I was in considerable pain.

"Phillip?" I said. "Is that you?"

"Yes. Welcome back, mate."

"Speak up. I can't hear you."

"Is that better?" he said, raising his voice.

"Yes. Where am I?"

"Hospital."

"What happened?"

"Do you remember anything?"

"Only that I was with my parents in a café in… my parents, oh my God, where are my parents?"

"It's okay, dude," he reassured me. "They're both all right."

"Thank God for that. Where are they? I need to see them."

"Your father is at work. Region 6 is under martial law; he's part of the big operation tracking down the terrorists who did this to you."

"They're not hurt?"

"Your father suffered a few cuts and bruises," he said. "Your mother… What can I say? She was badly hurt, but you came off worst. She's been here every day by your bedside. I'm here so she could go home and get some rest."

I groaned. "How long have I been in here?"

"Two weeks."

"Two weeks," I said, shocked. "What happened exactly?"

"There was a terrorist attack in Piccadilly Circus. Some Ukrainian bitch blew herself up. They're calling it a suicide bombing. She had explosives under her clothes and detonated them. She killed dozens – not just a load of soldiers, but women and children too."

"Bloody hell. I recall her vaguely. She was so young."

"Apparently, you were thrown from your chair and hit your head on the pavement. You had a lot of swelling on your brain, so they kept you in an induced coma."

"I remember I felt sorry for her. She was being hassled by some soldiers. I wish they'd shot her now. What kind of vermin would do something like that? I mean blowing yourself up along with everyone else."

"She was an Untermensch. They don't value life in the same way that we do."

"Even so – it revolts me. How can you be so full of hatred that you'd not only end your own life, but kill innocents?"

"These people don't think like us. They've been radicalised. They'll do anything to further their cause, no matter who gets hurt."

"They're scum."

"I agree. But they'll never win. They'll never destroy our way of life."

"I'm so proud of my father," I said angrily. "I hope he hunts them all down and makes them suffer."

"Your mother will be disappointed that she wasn't here to see you wake up."

"Is there a payphone anywhere? I want to call her."

"She'll be on her way back here by now. But travelling anywhere is a nightmare at the moment. The whole country is on lockdown."

A nurse came into the room.

"Good to have you back, Mr Talbot," she said. Her voice sounded muffled. "We've all been worried about you."

"Why can't I hear you properly?"

"The blast damaged your eardrums," she said.

"Will my hearing recover?"

"I'm not a doctor, I'm afraid. You can ask him yourself; he should be along shortly."

She adjusted the pillow behind my back and handed me some pills and a glass of water.

"Painkillers," she said.

I put the tablets on my tongue and swallowed them.

"They may make you drowsy," she said. "I'll be back soon."

The nurse left the room.

"Which hospital is this?" I asked.

"Barnet General," said Phillip. "You were in Charing Cross, but they moved you outside of Zone Alpha so you could receive visitors. It's only an hour on the bus from St Albans. At least, it would be if it weren't for all the security checkpoints. You can forget about travelling into Central London unless you're a senior party official."

"So which resistance group did that Ukrainian belong to?" I asked.

"The commies," said Phillip.

"Fucking bastards."

"Don't worry, they've been rounding them all up. There's been a massive clean-up in Ost-Bereich. That's usually where the trouble starts. Cockney twats."

"I suppose I was lucky."

"You were; a lot of people died or lost limbs. That crowd of soldiers you mentioned – most of them died. They told me you were saved by the statue of Eros."

"I remember we sat beside it."

"It shielded you from the worst of the blast."

"I guess the Germans wouldn't have had that protection in their section of the café."

"Better them than you."

I shuddered. "Maybe."

"I don't know what I'd have done if I'd lost you."

I looked at Phillip. He had a tear in his eye. I stretched out my unbandaged hand. He clasped it for a few seconds.

"I've got to go," he said awkwardly. He leant forward, gave me a peck on the forehead and hurried out.

The medication began to take effect. My various pains subsided, and I suddenly felt very sleepy. At some point, I was woken up by a doctor in a white coat, shining a torch in my eye.

"Splendid," he said. "Normal reflexes."

"Who are you?" I asked politely.

"Dr Waters," he replied. "Nice to see you awake. You're a fighter, that's for sure. Someone's here to see you."

"Hello, darling," said Mother, leaning forward to give me a sloppy kiss on the cheek. "How are you?"

"I've felt better," I croaked, wiping her saliva from my face with my good hand.

"We're very pleased with you," said Dr Waters. "You've made an excellent recovery."

"When can I get out?"

"I see no reason why you can't go home in the next couple of days. We've just a few more tests to do, just to make sure you're okay. We can disconnect all this, though."

He removed the drip and the pads on my chest.

"At least you're free to move around now," he said.

I looked at my mother, who was wearing an eyepatch. She had applied more make-up than usual, but I could see a graze on her cheek through the foundation, and her arm had a nasty bruise on it.

"What about my hearing, Doctor?"

"It's too early to tell if there's any permanent damage, but we're hopeful."

I breathed a sigh of relief.

"I'm sure that you two have some catching up to do," he said. "I'll be doing my rounds again in a couple of hours."

Mother stood up and hugged me. I winced.

"I can't wait to tell your father that you're awake," she said. "The last couple of weeks have been hell, you've no idea. He's been working so hard that he's not been around to support me."

"I'm sorry to have put you through this."

"You've nothing to be sorry about. It's not your fault. By the way, your friend Phillip – he's been an absolute rock. I don't know what I would have done without him. He's a real friend to you."

"I know he is. What's the story with your eye?"

Mother sighed. "There was nothing they could do."

"You mean..."

"It was perforated by a shard of glass. The surgeon extracted it, but the eyeball was too damaged."

"You've lost an eye?"

"It's not the end of the world. My other eye is fine. We have health insurance. The ophthalmologist says that they'll be able to make a glass one that will make it much less noticeable."

"Oh, Mum," I said, distressed. "Come here."

We hugged.

"I hate those fucking commie bastards."

"Watch your language," chided Mother.

"Sorry. Mum, can you do me a favour?"

"Of course."

"Is there a television in the hospital anywhere?"

"There's a sitting room on the next ward that has a TV."

"Will you help me there? I feel a bit dizzy with all the medication. I just want to see the news."

"Let me see if I can borrow a wheelchair."

She came back with a wheelchair and pushed me along the corridor to the television lounge, an austere room that smelled of antiseptic, full of those ghastly plastic wing-backed chairs that they have in old people's homes. A few patients were leafing through out-of-date magazines. The television was showing the news.

The terrorist attack still dominated the headlines. There had been many arrests. It was hard to comprehend that I had been there, in the thick of it.

The Gestapo had found most of those responsible. Their trials would be in less than six weeks. How dare they believe it was justifiable to blow up innocents in such a callous and indiscriminate way? How dare they permanently disfigure my beautiful, kind mother?

I watched the news channel for nearly an hour before somebody asked if they could change to Channel Two, to watch *Family Fortunes*. Mother wheeled me back to my private room.

"I need to go home to cook your father's dinner," she said. "He's coming to visit you tomorrow."

"Tell him I'm looking forward to seeing him."

"The Gestapo will want to interview you now that you're conscious. It's just routine."

"I'm surprised they're not here already."

"They know there's not much you can tell them. They've already interviewed me, and your father has made a lengthy statement."

"I could do without it," I sighed. "But it's my duty as a citizen."

"Just concentrate on getting better. You've got your whole life ahead."

✠

The day before I was discharged from the hospital, a plain-clothes *kriminaloberassistent* from the Gestapo took a statement. He was an amiable man, and I warmed to him. He told me that there had been an operation in Ost-Bereich. Apparently, they had uncovered houses full of weapons, and forbidden literature such as Chairman Mao's *Little Red Book* and the Hebrew *Tanakh*. The communists were in league with Jewish sympathisers.

Despite all the security in the capital, there was a nasty little wasps' nest hidden in our midst. They fed on us like parasites, enjoying all the benefits of living in the great Reich, but secretly hating us and plotting ways to hurt us. Perhaps it was appropriate to reintroduce the greater racial segregation that they had in the 1950s. It was justifiable if it saved lives. We had been treating Slavs far too well in the last few decades; almost as if they had the same rights as us. If this liberalist infection continued to fester, they would be breeding with us before long.

The following morning, the doctor declared me fit enough to return home to convalesce, handing me a carrier bag full of painkillers. My parents collected me, and we drove to St Albans. It felt good to be home.

7

15th June 1986

THOMAS JORDAN

It was 03.00 when four SS officers barged their way into the house. I was still pissed from the previous night's birthday celebrations, sweaty, with a banging headache, and my muscles ached. The Stormtroopers rounded up the entire street at gunpoint and herded us like sheep to a white lorry with the jagged SS insignia painted on the side. Anybody lagging was pistol-whipped, kicked or, in one case, shot dead. Children cried, comforted in vain by their mothers in nightdresses. I was reliving the nightmare of three years ago.

The lorry doors were slammed shut behind us, and I heard a bolt being slid across. Inside it was pitch black; the only light came from the faint glow of someone's watch. We were packed in tightly, and there was standing room only. It was soon sweltering, and difficult to breathe.

We had no idea where they were taking us, but it was not going to be anywhere good. Wherever it was, the journey was bloody horrible. The roads were twisty, and we were thrown around as there was nothing to hold on to for support.

An hour into the journey, sunlight shone through the narrow gap around the doors. I guessed we had been travelling for three hours when we finally stopped.

Stormtroopers ordered us out of the lorries, with machine guns trained on us. The sky was covered with dark grey storm clouds, and the air was muggy. While we were waiting to be processed, a thunderstorm started. In minutes, we were soaked by torrential rain, while thunder rumbled in the distance. I looked up at the sky, opening my mouth in an attempt to swallow some water. The rain washed away my alcohol-laden sweat, and I combed it through my clipped hair with my fingers.

There were tannoys mounted on fence posts, which started to blare out classical music. If it was meant to calm us down, it did not succeed.

Our lorry was in a convoy of eight. I reckoned there were about fifty people in each truck, so that was four hundred of us. I spotted my uncle in another transport group.

The old man in front of me complained at our treatment, and his protests earned him a baton strike. He fell backwards to the ground, dazed.

"*Aufstehen*," barked the Stormtrooper.

"I… I don't understand…" he whimpered. "I don't speak Germ—"

"*Aufstehen.*"

I moved over and held out my hand to the man on the floor. "He's saying stand up. Come on."

The old man took my hand gratefully, and I hauled him up from the ground. The soldiers pushed us roughly towards a grey, windowless building.

"Don't wind them up," I whispered. "These bastards aren't regular SS; they're Death Heads. Look at their collars."

I did not know where we had been taken, but I could hear seagulls and smell the sea air. The camp layout was a bigger version of the one that my family and I were taken to three years ago, with scores of cattle sheds laid out in neat rows.

I soon learned that we were in Ramsgate Concentration Camp, the most brutal in Region 6. Hastings was a picnic in comparison. We stood in front of a sprawling prefab building housing the admin centre, cells and camp bakery. The complex was surrounded by razor wire and electric fences, with guard towers every hundred metres. More guards with vicious Alsatians patrolled the perimeter.

An open-topped army truck passed our queue, carrying canisters of Zyklon B-II pesticide. I assumed it was for use on local farms.

The Nazi obsession with bureaucracy always amazed me. We were registered on a computer database, photographed and fingerprinted. Lastly, I put my left hand, palm facing upwards, into a squat silver machine. It had the words *Tätowierung automatisch* printed on top. A guard held my arm firmly in place and pressed a button. A red LED illuminated, and I felt an unpleasant scratching sensation. Seconds later, the LED turned green, and the machine beeped. My wrist had been tattooed with my prisoner number, M700406019, and a barcode.

After processing, I was led to a cell, a tiny concrete room with a thin blue plastic mattress on the floor and a latrine in the corner, which stank. I shuddered at the bloodstains on the wall.

The guard slammed shut the steel door. The faint red glow from an LED on a ceiling camera was my only light source. I remained in the cell for days, and since I could not sleep properly, I completely lost track of time.

The only food provided was a bowl of watery soup and a bread roll, but it was random when you would get any. I knew that I could not survive for long on a diet like that.

I tried to ignore the screams that I could hear throughout the day and night. I feared for my own life, but I was more concerned about my uncle. He was not a well man, and would not survive long in here. Then there were the children. If they made it, would they be orphaned like I was?

Eventually, my turn for interrogation came. To weaken my resolve, I had not been fed or given water for two days, and every time I drifted into sleep, a guard would bang his truncheon on the cell door to wake me. I was a filthy wreck by the time I sat in front of a nameless Gestapo officer. These bastards were proper sadists, and it made me realise how lightly I had got off at Hastings.

Over the course of a fortnight, they tried to beat a confession out of me. The simple fact was that I knew nothing. I think they realised this, early on, but they took twisted pleasure in trying to break my spirit. I was always asked the same questions.

"All we want is a name. If you give us a name you can rest, enjoy a decent meal. You can see a doctor."

"I can't help you," I pleaded.

The room was windowless and dark, except for a desk lamp. The hot lightbulb created wispy convection patterns in the thick cigarette smoke.

"You should know," said the interrogating officer, "that I take a particular interest in history. Our German masters are great respecters of the culture of races that they feel are almost equal to themselves. Our medieval ancestors invented some wonderful instruments of torture, don't you agree?"

I ignored him.

"Well?"

"If you say so."

He stubbed out his cigarette in an overflowing crystal ashtray. "My French colleagues perform executions using the guillotine in deference to the French Revolution. In the olden days, in Britain, they used the rack to extract confessions. A marvellous invention, you have to agree. They have an original one in the Tower of London. Have you ever been?"

"No," I replied.

"They've moved on a lot since those days, of course," said the officer, apparently enjoying his history lecture. "We have the latest hydraulically operated model here at Ramsgate. It's all computer-controlled nowadays. I sometimes think that the technology takes away some of the enjoyment. It's not the same, you know, pressing a button on a keyboard as opposed to winding a pulley by hand. I think that you lose that intimacy with modern techniques."

I knew that the rack would leave me crippled for life. Being a cripple would mean that I could not work. This would condemn me to death by starvation, even if I got out of this hellhole.

He continued. "It's the popping noises that always fascinate me. You're never sure whether it's a bone breaking or just cartilage. Sometimes it's a tendon snapping." He chuckled. "I had one guy who passed out when we dislocated his shoulder. We had to administer adrenaline to keep him awake."

The threats were wasted on me. I could not tell them anything. They never used the rack, thank God, but what was to come was terrible enough.

The days dragged into weeks. At one point, I was close to death since they had not provided me with water or food for days. I wondered if they had forgotten about me. I remember the thirst and trying to quench it by lapping up my own piss from the cell floor. That was the point that I realised that I was going to die here. I took comfort that I would soon be reunited with my family.

Dehydration is not a pretty death, but strangely, towards the end, I felt at peace. It was as though I had accepted my fate. I would go quietly into the night and fade from this cruel world. I lay on my back on the cold concrete floor and closed my eyes. I could no longer hear the banging of metal batons or smell my own stench. When I closed my eyes, I heard the sea. I was making sandcastles on a beach that I had visited when I was a child. I smelled the salty sea air. My mum gave me an ice cream. I could taste the sweet vanilla flavour as it melted in my mouth. A freak wave washed over us.

I woke up, realising that a guard had chucked a glass of water over me. He gave me a second stein of water. I gulped it down. They gave me some stale bread, and an hour later, a doctor examined me, declaring me fit for more questioning.

This interrogation started in the same way as the others. I was handcuffed to a chair. A man sat at a desk, behind a blinding light. I squinted. The same questions came; I gave the same answers. Then I was raped with a broom handle. It was agony, but the physical pain was nothing compared to the feeling of being violated.

Afterwards, I was flung back into my cell, crying. My arse bled for days and taking a dump was agony. I was changed forever, but not in the way they wanted. All they achieved was to turn me from a resentful bystander into someone that would now actively fight the regime that had orphaned me.

✠

Two days after my rape, I was released and bundled back into a lorry with my uncle and twenty other people. We were all painfully thin, bruised, and in shock.

The same number of trucks returned us home, with less than half the people they had taken to Ramsgate. We had sitting room this time, but we were not grateful for the extra space. We sat there silently, wondering why we had been spared over our fellows.

I will never forget the sickly-sweet smell coming from the camp bakery. The same smell coming from the building in Hastings that I saw my family led into. Only, I knew what it really was this time. The ashes from the burning corpses fell from the sky like snow.

My uncle and I returned to a ransacked home. I cried when I saw that my father's treasured record player and LP collection had been trashed. Over the next few days, we cleared the mess and repaired the vandalism. The damage to our house was nothing compared to the anguish of the widows or mothers who returned home without their children or husbands. For the thirty people who lost their lives in London, ten times as many had been killed in revenge. There were probably no terrorists among them; it was just the Nazis' way of crushing hope.

I had always felt that I was meant for something more than a lifetime of toiling on a factory floor. I would harness my anger, in the same way I had done in the boxing ring. My heart hardened. Now, nothing was off limits where the Nazis were concerned. I would do as much damage to them as one man could, and if I died doing so, so be it.

8

Summer 1988

STEPHEN TALBOT

It was two years on from the bombing, and I had not completely recovered. I had a scar above my eyebrow. I considered it disfiguring, but friends told me it was barely noticeable. I think they were being kind. Phillip said it suited me. He said it made me look macho. My hearing would never completely return to normal. Finally, I suffered from panic attacks, so I was on anti-anxiety medication.

It could have been far worse. The bombing had changed my outlook on the world. It gave me more focus, a realisation of how precious life was, and how easily terrorists like the communists could destroy everything that our great party had achieved.

I watched the trials of the conspirators on television with my parents. The guilty verdicts gave us closure. As one of the victims, I was invited to witness their execution. Maybe I am squeamish, but I declined, though my parents attended. After the hangings, they had dinner provided, with the other survivors, at the five-star Mayfair Kaiserhof.

My mother had undergone some plastic surgery to reduce the visibility of her scars, and she wore a glass eye. This was almost imperceptible, though it did not move, making her look boss-eyed. She never complained about it.

After the bombing, I focused on my schoolwork, and gained good grades in my sixteen-plus exams. I had stayed on at school to take a baccalaureate, which I hoped would get me into university. I had done well in my mocks, and everyone had high expectations. I wanted more than anything to get into Cambridge University. I had a natural ability with numbers, so mathematics was my subject of choice. This, I hoped, would get me a job with a merchant bank.

Historically, Cambridge had been a notorious recruitment ground for communists and homosexuals, producing creatures such as Alan Turing and John Maynard Keynes. This changed during the social cleansing in 1944. Now it and its chief rival, Oxford, represented the pinnacle of ideological purity, providing a world-class education that even competed with the world's top university, Ludwig-Maximilians in Munich.

I spent the early summer revising in earnest, sacrificing my social life, with the notable exception of my weekly Hitler Youth meetings. These offered a respite from the intensity of my studies, and the outdoor activities helped to clear my head.

Otherwise, I was so engrossed in my textbooks that even my eighteenth birthday passed without any significant commemoration. My parents promised me that we would celebrate it properly after my exams.

I sat my exams over three weeks. It was tough, but waiting for the results was even worse. School finished on 17th July. It was the end of a happy era in my life. The results were due in mid August. I spent the intervening period hanging out with my friends. It felt as if we were in limbo. We enjoyed carefree days during a hot summer, playing football in the park or chasing girls.

Some evenings, we bought bottles of cider from the local off-licence and drank them in Verulamium Park in the spectacular backdrop of the floodlit cathedral ruins. We were a close-knit group, and those last few happy weeks together, before we went our separate ways, were tinged with a slight sadness, knowing that in two months, life would never entirely be the same.

Phillip and I had grown so close since the bombing. At the end of those boozy evenings, it was he who would half-carry me home. Sometimes, we would lie on the soft grass inside the nave of the cathedral ruins, gazing up at the starlit sky through the open roof, talking about everything and nothing.

My father was less keen on Phillip. It was snobbishness, no less, no more. Phillip had won a scholarship to our school due to his sporting prowess. His parents would not have been able to afford to send him there otherwise. It was unlikely that he would be able to attend university, given the high tuition fees that his caste had to pay. I was privileged in that the state would pay for my higher education, due to my family's position within the party.

On the morning of 14th August, I received the letter that I had been anxiously awaiting, along with thousands of other teenagers. I came downstairs to the kitchen in my pyjamas. My father was in uniform, about to leave for work. My mother handed me the envelope.

"Well, open it, I haven't got all day," said my father.

"I will... I just need..."

"Give him some space," said my mother. "Just take your time, dear."

"Can you stop looking at me like that?" I said.

"Like what?" said Father.

"I'm going upstairs," I said, clutching the envelope that contained the piece of paper which would decide my fate.

"It's always got to be a big drama with you," my father berated me.

"Leave him alone, Edward," said Mother. "You know how much this means to him."

I ran upstairs and sat on my bed. I opened the envelope and took out the thin slip of paper, my heart racing. My nervous anticipation turned into elation.

"I've done it!" I shouted, running back down the stairs. "I'm off to Cambridge."

"Come here," said Mother. "Give me a hug."

I embraced my mother warmly. She was smiling, but her good eye was welling up. I think it was a bittersweet moment for her, knowing that I would be leaving the family home, possibly for good.

My father extended his hand formally.

"Congratulations, son. Your mother and I have something special planned tonight as a belated birthday present, and now with these results, it's a double celebration."

"What's that?"

"Wait and see," he said, giving me a wink, then leaving.

I spent the rest of the morning telephoning my friends from the hallway phone.

"Will you get off that phone?" chided my mother from the kitchen. "I'm expecting a call."

"I'm off out now," I shouted from the hallway.

"Where are you going?"

"Bowling in Watford with the boys."

I went out the front door.

"Stephen," shouted my mother, opening the door.

"What?" I said, turning around.

"You've forgotten your ID card."

"Oh God, how stupid of me," I said, shuddering at the thought of what could have happened if I had been spot-checked.

I snatched the credit-card-sized document out of her hand and stuffed it into my wallet.

"You left it on the kitchen table, scatterbrain."

"Sorry, Mum. It's just that I'm excited."

"Don't I get a kiss, then? Or are you too old now?"

"You're so embarrassing."

She smiled and waved me off.

✠

I returned home late in the afternoon and headed straight upstairs to my bedroom.

"Would you come into the kitchen, please?" shouted Mother.

My father had finished work early and was sitting at the kitchen table with my mother, having a cup of tea and a slice of home-made fruit cake.

"Did you win at skittles?" asked Father.

"It's called bowling. Skittles is what you play when you're five."

"Whatever. Did you win?"

"No, I came second. Phillip managed to get four strikes in a row."

"Your mother and I are aware how hard you have worked over the summer. Since we did nothing for your birthday, we thought we would give you your present now."

I pulled up a chair.

"There you go," said Father, pushing a small box towards me, wrapped in silver paper.

I opened it excitedly.

"Wow," I gasped. "It's lovely. This must have cost a fortune."

"Well, it is your eighteenth," said Mother. "We wanted to get you something special. You can wear it tonight as we're going out."

I examined the round enamel swastika pin, with its elaborate leaf-patterned circumference finished in eighteen-carat gold. Heavier than its small size belied, it sparkled in the halogen kitchen lights.

"This is really smart. Thank you so much."

It came with a certificate of authenticity and a party membership card with a silver hologram of Adolf Hitler. It read: *Stephen Talbot, Member 96,359,234 of the National Socialist Party. Signed, Hans Eichmann, Region 6 Party Chairman.*

"I'm a full member of the party," I said, still taking it in. "It feels like I've come of age."

"It'll open so many doors for you," said Father. "Not to mention all the discounts you get."

"I'm just glad they accepted me."

"I knew they would," said Father. "You're too modest. You've a lot to offer."

"Well, I'm chuffed to bits. I can't wait to tell my friends."

"They'll be jealous, for sure," said Mother. "Not everyone gets approved at such a young age. Anybody can be an associate and pay the annual subscription, but you are a full member."

"What have you planned for tonight?"

"Dinner at Sopwell House," said Mother.

"Wow. Are you sure we can afford it?"

"You're only eighteen once," said Father. "Besides, it's good to be seen socialising at these kinds of places."

✠

Later on, we arrived at Sopwell House, a Georgian country house on the outskirts of St Albans that had been converted into a luxury spa hotel, popular with senior party members. Father's BMW was valet-parked by a Hungarian, and we were led through to the lounge bar, where I discovered my parents had organised a surprise party for me. Seven of my friends were there, including Phillip.

Father had spared no expense. The champagne flowed like water, served by Untermenschen wearing tuxedos, and we enjoyed a five-course gourmet dinner in the sophisticated surroundings.

I remember feeling that I had arrived. It was the best birthday ever. Everything in my life was going well. I had mostly recovered from the London bombing back in 1986. I had good friends. I had gained a place at Cambridge University. I was handsome and athletic, brimming with confidence and optimism, and I had a promising future.

9

1st September 1988

STEPHEN TALBOT

I answered the front door. Phillip stood there grinning. We went upstairs to my bedroom. Phillip sat on my desk chair, and I sat cross-legged on the bed. We gossiped for ten minutes before Mother came upstairs with a tray of tea and two slices of sponge cake. She sat on the side of the bed and tousled my mop of floppy blond hair.

"Just out of the Aga," she said.

"Thanks, Mum."

"I'm going to miss you," she said.

"Mum, please, not in front of Phillip."

Phillip was pulling a stupid face and sticking his fingers down his throat.

"Well, I *am* going to miss you."

"I'm only going to Cambridge. It's not even an hour on the autobahn. Besides, I'll come back during the holidays."

"I know. But it won't be the same."

I pretended to retch. Phillip laughed out loud.

"I'll leave you two to it," said Mother, walking out of the room, looking a little hurt. "Enjoy the cake."

"I think I'm going to vomit," said Phillip, starting to do a poor impression of my mother. "*Darling, I've loved you since you were a little egg in my womb*."

"Don't take the piss, mate. Your mother is exactly the same."

Phillip stood up and flopped onto the bed next to me. He looked me straight in the eyes.

"I know how she feels, though. I'm sure going to miss you." He put his arms around me and gave me a warm hug. "Life's going to be so boring without you. No late nights drinking in the park, carrying you back home after, 'cause you can't handle your ale."

"We'll still see each other during the holidays."

"I know."

I stroked his shoulder as he backed away from me.

"That cake looks tasty," he said.

"She's always baking something. I think she's trying to fatten me up before I leave home, in case I can't look after myself."

"It's lovely," he said with his mouth full of sponge. "I've been thinking. Before you head off to Cambridge to be a world leader, why don't you and I go out and celebrate? Just the two of us, in the park."

"Shall I meet you on the high street after supper – say around 20.00? We can get some cans and crisps."

"Sounds like a plan."

✠

I met Phillip at the off-licence on the high street, and we bought two six-packs of cheap lager and some crisps. A night out with Phillip was never a quiet one. We walked to the cathedral ruins and found a park bench in the remains of the nave. The views were stunning, overlooking the south-western edge of the town, the River Ver, and the acres of fields and hedgerows beyond. There was something magical about looking at this view framed by the ivy-covered stone arches, which would have once housed stained-glass windows.

Nature had reclaimed the inside of the building. The roof was open; soft, mossy grass grew underfoot; and aubrieta had germinated in cracks in the stone walls. There was a lovely smell of freshly cut grass from the park.

The sun was setting, casting a red glow on the horizon reflecting against the fluffy cumulus clouds. I was going to miss this. It had been a great summer, filled with happy memories.

Apart from a group of teenage lads playing football in the distance, the park and the ruins were deserted. Phillip opened a can of lager, which splattered him with froth, and handed it to me, before opening one for himself.

"Prost," he said, bumping his tin against mine and taking a long gulp. "Thanks for coming. The truth is, I needed to see you, and I'm glad that we're alone."

"Why's that?"

"I've gone over and over this conversation in my head for so long. I don't know where to start."

"You know I'm here for you, Phillip. I've never forgotten how you helped me get through the bombing."

Phillip downed his lager in one long gulp, then immediately opened another can. "I need some Dutch courage."

Not one to be outdone, I copied him, except that I could not quite manage a whole can in one go, and paused for breath a couple of times.

"Lightweight," said Phillip, handing me a fresh tin.

"Have you decided what you're going to do job-wise yet?" I asked, deliberately changing the subject.

"I've got a second interview at the Environment Ministry. It's just a clerk position, but there are good prospects," said Phillip, before glugging down the remainder of his second drink.

"Bloody hell, mate, you're really going for it. The world's not going to end in the next five minutes."

"Just finish your drink like a man."

Phillip had raided his father's drinks cabinet, and between lagers, we took turns to swig from a bottle of vodka. We spoke for a while about the things that teenage boys usually talk about – music, football and gossip. It was now dark, and the park was deserted. The cathedral ruins were floodlit with magenta lights. The stone altar looked ethereal, illuminated by a spotlight against the darkness of the building interior as though about to welcome angels descending from the heavens.

We became progressively drunk in the celestial surroundings, and our behaviour deteriorated. We began fighting. It started with mock punches, then Phillip began to demonstrate his judo moves. He managed to trip me over and pin me to the ground.

I looked up at his handsome face, and I could feel his athletic frame against mine. I gazed drunkenly into his eyes.

He backed off, laughing, and sat beside me. I hauled myself up.

"You're pissed," I said.

"So are you."

"You're a bad influence. My father's going to kill me when I get home."

"If I tell you something, you have to promise not to tell anybody, and I mean anyone in the whole world," he said earnestly. "Swear on your mother's life."

"Okay. I swear."

"Say it, then."

"I swear on my mother's life that I will not say anything about this to anyone."

"Do you promise you won't freak?"

I looked at him directly, "You can tell me anything."

"The thing is, it's tough…" stuttered Phillip. "I could be executed for telling you this."

He looked around furtively, to check that nobody was around.

"It's that serious?"

"I'm afraid it is."

"Well, the place is deserted, and there's no CCTV here. We should be safe."

He took a deep breath. "It's sort of like this… I think, I mean, I don't think… I kind of know—"

Spontaneously, I grabbed his neck and pulled him towards me. Our lips made contact. We kissed gently for a minute, and I ran my hand lightly through his blond hair.

"You were saying?" I said.

"I can't stop thinking about you," he said in floods of tears. "Every day, from the moment I wake up until I go to bed… I'm so confused… I'm sorry."

"It's okay. I feel the same."

"You do?"

"Yes, I think so. I think that I have done for some time, now."

"I don't know how it happened," he sobbed. When I'm with you, I just feel, you know, happy. I think if you'd died in the bomb blast in '86, I would have killed myself."

"Don't be silly."

"I'm not. I sat there watching you in the hospital two years ago, and I knew then how I felt."

"And you've kept this bottled up all this time?"

"What choice did I have?"

"I suppose."

"How are we going to get through this?" he said, looking around nervously again. "You know it can't be."

"Who says it can't?"

"I can't believe we just kissed in public."

"Relax. We're alone."

"Oh God," he cried. "What if there are hidden microphones? They'll send us to Ramsgate. Or worse. They think queers are as bad as Jews."

"There aren't any hidden microphones. You're being paranoid."

"How can you be so laid-back about it?"

"I'm hardly laid-back. I know full well that they'd execute us if we were discovered. But we're not exactly obvious, are we? Not like those creatures they warn us about on TV; the camp things that hang around toilets, preying on kids."

"No, we're not. But is that how we're going to turn out?"

"Don't be stupid. You and I... We're not like that. We're just... men... that, well, you know..."

"I have to keep seeing you, somehow."

"We'll make it work."

"You mean you want to... you know, date?"

"Yes. But we'll have to be mega discreet, I mean *really* secretive."

Phillip looked nauseous. "I think I'm going to be sick."

"I'm glad I have that effect on you. Was it my breath?"

"Don't be silly. I've drunk too much. And I'm shitting myself. I still can't believe we just kissed in public."

"We'll be fine."

"God, I hope so."

"You shouldn't have drunk so much."

"I had to get this pissed to pluck up the courage to tell you. I didn't know whether you'd have me arrested."

"I'd never do that to you, even if I didn't feel the same."

"I seemed to get signals from you. I felt that something was there, but I could never be certain."

"Well, you were right."

"It was eating me up from the inside. In the end, I think I was going mad. I thought, *What the hell, tell him and deal with the consequences.*"

"I'm glad you did tell me because I would never have said anything. Especially with my father's job."

"It's so unfair. We're loyal Nazis. Why do they persecute us like this? I just want to hold you, like any other couple. Is that so wrong?"

"This is life."

"Why was I made like this?"

"Why is anybody made like anybody? I know that I've always fancied other boys. When I've kissed girls, it's never felt right."

"Where do we fall in our Eternal Führer's plan? You're the party member. He made his views plain in *Mein Kampf*."

"I dunno. If I could take a pill that would make me normal, I would."

Phillip started sobbing.

"We'll get through this," I said. "I don't know how, but we will."

"We could defect?" said Phillip tearfully. "Maybe we could get a visa for a holiday in America and not come back. They tolerate people like us out there. We could claim asylum."

"I'm not going to that nuthouse. The kids walk around with guns, murdering their schoolmates."

"Do you believe that?"

"I've seen it on the news."

"Yes, but…"

"Half of them starve, while the other half waddle around like fattened-up turkeys, leeching off the poor."

"Have you ever wondered why none of them try to defect here, though?" asked Phillip. "I mean, I've never heard or seen an American ever, except on the news."

"My father says there are loads. They all live in Scotland where they can't corrupt us."

"If I could just go somewhere like New York. To see it for myself."

"You'd never get a visa to the USA unless you work for the government, and high up at that. Unless you're planning to stow away. Besides, there's no escape from the Gestapo. Remember the traitor Werner Heisenberg?"

"Yeah, course I do, everybody knows about him. Fucking traitor passed on all those secrets to the Yanks. He gave them the atomic bomb. The whole world could've been united under the Führer without him."

"They still managed to assassinate him soon after he defected. Even with all that security around him. We'd stand no chance."

"Bugger."

"I imagine he used stronger words than that when they put the garrotte around his neck."

"No, I don't mean that. It's almost midnight."

"Bloody hell, I need to get home. I promised my father I wouldn't be late."

Phillip looked around nervously. He pulled me in close. We kissed again. I felt a sense of contentment as he held me in his arms.

Our passion was interrupted by a cough. I separated quickly from Phillip and looked furtively in the direction of the sound. I could see a tall man in dark clothing, who seemed to have been hiding behind the font. He walked away hurriedly, disappearing into the darkness.

"Shit," said Phillip. "Do you think he saw us?"

"I don't know. It's fairly dark; he probably thought we were a married couple smooching or something."

"Oh my God. What if he reports us?"

"Stop worrying. I doubt he even saw us."

"Come on," said Phillip worriedly. "I'll call you tomorrow. Let's go home separately. You go first. I'll wait behind for ten minutes."

✠

Despite my bravado in front of Phillip, I felt tense and vulnerable as I headed home, and cursed my stupidity for being so openly affectionate. I was drunk, and I was not thinking straight.

I arrived home fifteen minutes later.

"You're late," said my father, who was sitting at the kitchen table, reading.

"Sorry, I got spot-checked by a constable," I lied. I walked into the kitchen and poured myself a glass of water.

My father snatched it from me. "How many times have I told you? We do not drink the tap water."

"Sorry. I forgot."

"There's bottled water in the fridge."

I opened the fridge and gulped down an entire litre bottle of water.

"You're drunk, young man. I can smell it on your breath."

"Sorry. It wasn't deliberate; things got out of hand."

"They always do with that Phillip."

I went upstairs, had a wee, then lay in bed, fantasising about Phillip. There was the roller-coaster euphoria of teenage love, but it was tinged with self-loathing; a realisation that we had to keep our relationship secret. Discovery would lead to arrest, imprisonment and, in all likelihood, death. It would bring shame to our respective families.

I had buried my attraction towards other boys all my life. I had lived a lie for so long that I had forgotten who I really was. I remember feeling ashamed and dirty as I looked at pictures of naked girls in a friend's pornographic magazine, desperately trying to be aroused in a vain attempt to change my sexuality. It was only a kiss with Phillip, but it felt so right. Perhaps it was just a phase. A result of too many hormones flowing around my adolescent body.

I looked up at the ceiling. The room started spinning, and I realised that I was much drunker than I had anticipated. Then the terror kicked in. Fear of a slow, lingering death at the hands of the state. I felt a tightness in my chest, a sickening, uncomfortable feeling. I had been exposed. Eventually, I fell into a restless sleep.

✠

Sometime later, I woke up. I still felt drunk. I was unsure of the time or how I got to this hellish place. I lay there on a hydraulic rack in a barren Gestapo torture chamber. My interrogator's face was hidden by a blank white mask. He taunted me, his voice muffled and full of loathing, yet vaguely familiar. He approached me, holding a black bin bag. He reached inside and took out Phillip's decapitated head, placing it on top of my chest. Phillip's eyes were shut fast; his skin had a bluish hue. Blood dripped from his severed neck, soaking my shirt. I screamed, unable to move.

My interrogator took off his mask.

"Father…" I pleaded.

Father smiled at me. He sat down and pressed a button on a computer keyboard. I heard the hissing of pneumatic pumps and felt my back being stretched.

"No," I pleaded.

My mother came into view. "The purity of the Aryan race must be maintained," she said unemotionally.

My doctrine teacher appeared beside her. "The eugenics programme is not optional."

My tormentors spoke in unison, a cacophony of discordant voices.

Phillip's eyes opened and blinked. They were cloudy as though he were blind. He looked straight at me.

"Why did you betray me?" he croaked. "I loved you."

I tried to reply, but no words came out.

"Betrayer," said Phillip, with maggots crawling out of his mouth.

"Poofter," said my teacher.

"Deviant," said Father.

"Traitor," said Mother.

A magistrate stood in front of me. "Guilty," he pronounced metallically.

Father pressed a red button on the computer keyboard. The hydraulic pumps whined. I screamed as my spine snapped.

I woke up in my bedroom, clutching sheets that were soaked in sweat. I gasped, sitting up. The relief was temporary. My twisted nightmares, worsened by the alcohol and my medication, continued relentlessly throughout the night.

10

2nd September 1988

THOMAS JORDAN

There was another curfew that summer on our side of the *zwischenwand*, because of a foiled attack by the commies. A Volkswagen Golf filled with fertiliser explosives was discovered outside the London Stock Exchange.

As a result, the SS were all over Ost-Bereich. The officers were drunk on their power. They strip-searched women they fancied, making plain their enjoyment. Anywhere else in the world, it would be called sexual harassment, but this was Nazi Britain. There was order on the streets, but no rule of law. The Gestapo and SS were a power unto themselves.

I had struggled with my feelings since Ramsgate. It was no longer enough for me to keep my head down, stay out of trouble and live with the drudgery of my crappy job.

One evening, I decided to approach Bill Watson, my boxing trainer, who I strongly suspected was involved in the resistance. I walked into his gym. He smiled at me, revealing a set of broken teeth, lost over decades of street brawls.

"You've got the whole gym to yourself," said Bill. "I was going to close up early."

"They're worried about the curfew."

"It doesn't kick in until nine; it's more that they're lazy fuckwits."

"Give me a spot on the bench press, will you?"

I stacked the barbell with weights, lay down and started lifting. Bill helped me push out a couple of extra reps as I began to fail, and guided the barbell back to the stand.

"You're in an aggressive mood tonight," he said. "Anything wrong?"

"Just the usual."

"What's that?"

"The fact that our country is run by a bunch of murdering bastards that have taken away our freedom and condemned us to a life of slavery."

"For fuck's sake, keep your voice down."

"Why? There's nobody here. Helmut Goebbels is a fat bastard. Himmler sucked cocks. Goering liked—"

"Do you want to get us both arrested?" interrupted Bill. "For all I know, this place is bugged."

"I know you're involved."

"What are you on about?"

"I know you're part of the resistance."

"When did you become a mind reader?"

"There are rumours about you. They've been around for years."

"What rumours?"

"That you have contacts in the resistance. You're up to your neck in it."

"This is a dangerous conversation."

"You have to trust me," I said earnestly. "I mean, come on, you've known me since I was a kid. You were there for me when I was orphaned. I hate everything that they stand for."

"I know you do."

"I've watched women and children being led to torture chambers or worse. I'm ready. I want to do my bit."

"Just calm down. I get what you mean."

"So that's all you have to say?"

"You have to understand that we have protocols, for your safety as well as ours. It's not just a case of getting you to fill out a form, then handing over a machine gun."

"So, I was right."

"I'm not saying that. Just be patient. And please don't say anything about this conversation to anyone, and I mean anyone, including your uncle."

"Okay."

"Just concentrate on your workout, and leave the rest to me."

11

2nd September 1988

STEPHEN TALBOT

I woke up quite late. After I had showered and dressed, the telephone rang.

"Stephen, it's Phillip on the phone," shouted my mother.

I ran downstairs and took the phone from her.

"Did you get back safely?" asked Phillip.

"Yeah, you?"

"Yes. Can you speak?"

"Not really."

"Okay. When can I see you again?"

"We've got a family lunch today. But I'm free tomorrow."

"Let's meet for a coffee at Tchibo's."

"Great; I'll call you tomorrow morning to sort out a time."

"I'll be thinking about you."

"Thanks. See you soon," I said cagily.

I walked into the kitchen and helped myself to some cereal. My parents were sitting at the table, dressed casually. My father was reading *The Sunday Times*, shaking his head.

"Food riots in New York again," he tutted.

"I've just made a pot of tea if you want some, darling," said Mother, ignoring him.

"Great," I said, getting a mug out of the cupboard. "Got any paracetamol?"

"You haven't got another hangover?" said Mother.

"Sorry. It was an insane night."

"There's some Voltaren in the medicine cabinet."

"Phillip on the phone," said Father. "Again?"

"What do you mean, *again*?"

"He's always calling you. Hasn't he got any other friends?"

"I know you don't like him. But he's my best mate."

"You two seem tied at the waist."

"Well, I think he's a very well-mannered and pleasant young man," said Mother.

"Mary, I just think the boy should mix with other people too. It's about time they both got girlfriends."

"It's not for want of trying," I joked nervously.

"Well, you won't find any nice girls by hanging around in a park getting drunk."

"What's the point of me getting into something serious anyway? I'll be at university in a few weeks."

I went upstairs to listen to some music. I heard the front doorbell, which my father answered. Before long, it was evident that my father was arguing with the visitor. I walked to the top of the stairs to listen in.

"...is this some kind of joke, Kriminaloberassistent Pearce? This is my son you're talking about."

"We have our orders, Kriminaldirektor. I'm aware of your rank, but I would respectfully ask you not to obstruct us from our duties."

"Stephen," shouted my father up the staircase. "Come down here. Now."

Terrified, I looked around frantically for an escape route. Short of jumping out of my bedroom window, there was none. Then where would I go? I knew in my heart why the Gestapo were here. I felt sick as I walked down the stairs.

I recognised the first officer as the one who had taken my

statement at the hospital. The other one was a thug – there to provide muscle if needed.

"Stephen," said Pearce. "We meet again. Do you know what this is about?"

"I'm not sure," I replied.

"Would it ring a bell if I mentioned your little indiscretion in the cathedral grounds last night?"

"Oh," I said worriedly.

"Stephen Talbot," said the officer, "I'm arresting you under Section 28 of the Sexual Deviancy Act. Namely, you have been accused of homosexual activity, aggravated by the fact it was in a public place and likely to cause distress to others. You are not obliged to say anything, but anything you do say may be taken down in evidence and used against you in the people's court. Do you have anything to say?"

"No," I replied.

"My son is not a homosexual," said Father. "I'll follow you down to the station, and we'll get to the bottom of this."

My mother stood in the hallway, sobbing, looking confused.

✠

Pearce handcuffed me and locked me in the rear of a black Mercedes. At the station, I was booked into custody. I never thought that anything like this could ever happen to me.

The thuggish officer flung me inside a claustrophobic cell, and muttered, "Dirty queer" under his breath, before slamming the door shut. There was a thin rubber mattress on the floor. I lay down. It was cold, and I started to shiver, or perhaps it was fear of what lay ahead.

There was little hope for me, given the policy of 'guilty until proven innocent'. I imagined that they would have arrested Phillip too. I cursed myself for my recklessness. The man by the font must have reported us. My only hope of salvation would be my father. He carried influence, but given the gravity of the crime, I did not know if it would be sufficient.

Eventually, I was led to an interview room. A cold, rectangular chamber, with white tiled walls, a desk and two chairs. I waited while being guarded by a disinterested junior officer, chewing gum.

My father walked in, looking anxious. He sat opposite me, holding some papers.

"Just tell me why?"

"I was drunk," I replied. "I'm sorry."

"Do you know how much trouble you're in?"

"I've got an idea."

"I've managed to do a deal. You've no idea how many strings I've had to pull, and how much money I've had to pay out in bribes."

"Sorry."

"Read and sign this statement."

"What?"

"Just do as I say."

I read the witness statement in astonishment.

"This is not how it happened. I was as much to blame as Phillip."

My supposed statement inferred that Phillip had plied me with alcohol, which he knew would react badly with my anti-anxiety medication, and had then taken the opportunity to seduce me. I had apparently described him as a *predatory homosexual*, and felt *disgusted and violated by him forcing himself upon me, while I was in a vulnerable state.*

"Here's a pen," said my father, handing me a biro.

"I can't sign this. There's not a gram of truth in it."

My father lowered his voice. "You have two choices. Sign this, and you'll go before a *Volksgerichtshof* tomorrow. They've promised me they'll show leniency. Or there's a D-11 form filled out with your name on it."

"What's a D-11 form?"

"A detainment order. You'll be sent to a correction facility."

"If I sign this, I condemn Phillip to death; it's practically accusing him of rape."

"Despite what you think, I like Phillip, trust me I do, he's a lovely lad, and he genuinely cares about you, but I know you. You're not like him. He's led you down a path that no parent would want for their child. If I could save him too, I would, but I can't. I can, however, save you. It's either one of you or neither. He'd understand."

I burst into tears.

"We don't have much time," he said. "You know what you have to do."

"I can't."

"If you want to live, you have to. Pull yourself together and pick up the pen."

I picked up the biro and hovered it over the line.

"Now, sign it."

Reluctantly, I signed my name. As soon as I lifted the pen from the page, my father snatched the papers and left the room.

After a few minutes, an officer collected me and brought me to the custody desk. I was charged with being drunk and lewd in a public place, with sentencing to be administered in the morning. I was led back to my cell.

✠

I did not sleep a wink, feeling an overwhelming sense of guilt at what I had done to Phillip. We had enjoyed a brief glimpse of what might have been. It was unfinished business, which I instinctively knew would never be resolved.

In the morning, I was given coffee and a slice of dry black bread. I was discharged from custody and taken outside, still under Gestapo jurisdiction. I squinted as my eyesight adjusted to the bright daylight. I was led across a car park to a black VW Transporter, and ushered into a cage in the back.

I looked out and saw a wretched figure being dragged along the tarmac towards another Transporter. It was barely recognisable as Phillip. His face was swollen and badly bruised. He looked at me with blank eyes, slits in a battered face that vaguely resembled the person whom I once knew.

"Phillip," I cried, shaking the cage doors.

He collapsed onto the ground before an officer hauled him up. I could see his lips move, but barely hear him over the sound of the van's engine.

"This is not your fault," he croaked, before being flung into his van.

My van doors were slammed shut, and we left the station. The windows were heavily tinted, but I could make out Phillip's Transporter behind us. I hoped that I would be able to speak to him when we reached court. Unfortunately, our vans headed in different directions. That was the last time that I ever saw him.

It was a ten-minute ride to the courthouse. I waited in a small room, flanked by two guards, before being called into the courtroom, an ornate chamber with mahogany panelling. A swastika was carved into the protruding panelling behind the podium, and there was a black marble bust of the Führer resting on a fluted column, staring directly at me.

I sat in the dock and awaited my fate. Three elderly judges entered the room, dressed in red robes, and took their places behind the bench. I stood up.

They barked, "Heil Hitler" and saluted, then sat. I remained standing, with my head lowered respectfully.

The court clerk read out the charges. "The accused stands before you today, Your Honours, that he, on 1st September 1988, in the vicinity of the cathedral in Verulamium Park, St Albans, drank excessive amounts of alcohol and engaged in disorderly and lewd conduct, unbecoming of a citizen of the Reich."

The head judge was distinguishable by a purple sash over his shoulders. He looked at me sternly.

"How do you plead?" he asked.

"Guilty, Your Honour."

"Do you have anything to say for yourself?"

"Only that I'm deeply sorry for my behaviour."

"I see your father has made a plea to the court for leniency. We will confer to discuss sentencing."

The three judges leant towards each other and spoke conspiratorially, looking through various papers. My fate was decided in less than five minutes.

The head judge spoke. "Before we pronounce sentence, I will make this very clear to you, young man. If I ever see you before this court again, I will not be so forgiving. Do you understand?"

"Yes, Your Honour."

"I can see from the reports that you joined the party as a full adult member a few weeks ago, shortly after your eighteenth birthday?"

"Correct, Your Honour."

"I can also see that before this episode, you had an exemplary record, with excellent academic and sporting achievements. I see that you were awarded a Golden Hitler Youth Badge with oak leaves, an outstanding accomplishment. I'm also aware that you were one of the victims of the 1986 terrorist attack."

"Yes, Your Honour."

"It may be difficult to believe, but I was young once. I can see that the pressure of sitting your exams was unequivocally stressful. You are no doubt suffering from a post-traumatic mental disorder caused by the bombing. I accept that this, combined with your medication, may have affected your judgement. You had a desire to escape from your troubles, using alcohol to achieve this, and were taken advantage of by an unscrupulous individual. You were in some ways a victim. However, that being said, it is necessary for discipline to be maintained in our society, lest we descend into American-style anarchy. Do you understand this?"

"Yes, Your Honour."

"I would also ask you to read pages 123 to 129 of your party handbook, which gives specific guidelines for codes of conduct and behaviour in public. Remember, a true National Socialist leads by example and is never divorced from his party, whatever the situation."

"I will, Your Honour."

"We have examined your medical records. Thus, it is the opinion of the *Volksgerichtshof* that you are guilty of a serious lapse in judgement brought about by ongoing psychological issues due to the 1986 bombing. You have admitted your guilt and shown remorse. My colleagues and I, therefore, conclude that it would be inappropriate to issue a custodial sentence in this instance and unfairly taint the future of an otherwise model citizen."

I felt a wave of relief.

"Instead, it is the sentence of this court that we fine you 2,500 Reichsmarks, to be paid within one calendar month from today. You will also have your party membership suspended for three months, with all associated privileges withdrawn. Does the defendant have anything to say?"

"No, Your Honour."

"You are a free man and may leave. All stand. Heil Hitler."

The judges saluted and walked out. I was led from the chamber back into the reception area of the courthouse, where my father was waiting for me.

"Well?" he said.

"They fined me 2,500 Reichsmarks. And I've got a three-month suspension from the party."

"You're very fortunate. Not many people get second chances."

"I know. And I'm grateful."

"You're my flesh and blood. But my influence has limits. I managed to protect you this time, but you must understand that nothing like this can ever happen again. I want your word."

"I promise."

"I mean it, Stephen. Your cards are marked now. They'll be keeping an eye on you."

My father pressed a button on the reception desk, and a frumpy-looking clerk came out. Father paid the fine, on the understanding that I would get a holiday job and pay him back. It was a lot of money to us, and it was on top of the bribes.

We left the court and walked back to the car. I slumped into the seat. Father drove us home, in awkward silence.

"How's Mother?" I asked, trying to relieve the tension.

"At home, worried sick. You have to stick to the story that it was Phillip who tried it on with you. I don't think she could take it if she thought you were..."

"What will happen to Phillip?"

"He was issued a D-11. They've taken him to a labour camp in North Wales. It's a ten-year tariff. He'll be twenty-eight when he gets out; he'll still have enough time to start his life over."

"If he survives."

"He's young and healthy. These places are about re-education. He'll receive counselling about his... tastes. There's every reason to hope that he can be cured and rejoin society a better man."

"I saw him in the car park. What's left of him, at least. Was that your work?"

"No, of course it wasn't. Stephen, none of us enjoy what we have to do. Maintaining order is necessary. Homosexuality is rife in countries like America; you have no idea of the problems it brings, the diseases. You've heard of AIDS, the gay plague?"

"Yes, of course. It's all over the newspapers."

"Millions of people in America are dying a slow, lingering death because they've allowed homosexuality to flourish unhindered. They're a cancer in society that have to be rooted out and eliminated, just like the Jews."

"But, Father, I don't think I fancy girls."

"Stephen, I don't want to hear this," said Father crossly. "You are not a homosexual. There are beautiful women out there; I know there's one for you."

"Is there?"

"I'm older and more experienced than you. You're still a teenager, full of hormones. I've known these queer types before. These creatures are insidious, they get under your skin, they try to convert people to follow their disgusting ways."

We parked outside our house. My mother was waiting for us. She hugged me tightly.

"Thank God," she said. "I've been frantic."

"It's okay. I've been fined, and I have to surrender my party membership for three months."

"Silly boy," she chided. "Your father always said there was something not quite right about that Phillip."

✠

Months later, I could not even accurately remember what Phillip looked like. His face disappeared from the football team photographs, all evidence of his existence was erased, and his family relocated. I dwelled on his last words: *This was not your fault*. If only that were true. All I had now were memories, the one thing the Gestapo could not take from me.

12

10th September 1988

THOMAS JORDAN

A week had passed since my chat with Bill. A couple of mates disappeared during the security crackdown. I hoped that I would see them again, but with every day that passed, it became less likely. At least the curfew had been lifted, finally.

That evening I trained at the gym with my buddy, Sam. In the changing rooms afterwards, I found a small piece of folded paper in my locker. I looked around. Sam was already in the shower. The note read, *Stepney allotments, 22.00 hours tonight. Come alone. Destroy these instructions.*

I chewed up the note. This was either a Gestapo trap or the resistance making contact.

I went home and cooked sausages and mash for my uncle and me, which we ate in front of the telly.

"I'm off to bed," I lied. The less my uncle knew, the better. I put on a dark hooded sweatshirt and crept out the front door.

I headed to the allotments behind Stepney Green Park, using unmonitored back streets. It was a mild, dry evening and the air was thick with smog that caught the back of your throat. I arrived and headed towards a potting shed, keeping warm by jogging on the spot and rubbing my hands. Two people appeared from behind the shed, wearing balaclavas and holding guns. I raised my hands.

"I'm Tom," I said nervously.

"We know who you are," said a burly man in front of me.

I felt a third person grab me from behind and put me in an armlock. He took me by surprise. I struggled as he put a handkerchief over my mouth, which smelled of pear drops. I felt dizzy. I clawed at the man's hand, but it was clamped to my face. I passed out.

✠

I woke up suddenly, as icy water was thrown over my face. I was gagged and tied to a chair. A man in a balaclava came into focus, his face centimetres from mine. He untied the gag and moved back. There were two others in the room, both dressed in dark tracksuits, their faces covered. One of them was female. I saw that we were in the ticket office of a disused Underground station.

"I need some water," I croaked.

"Here," said the man, retrieving a plastic bottle. He tipped it into my mouth, and I drank it gratefully.

"Thank you."

"You're Titan Tom," he said. "You're shorter than I imagined."

There was a dry laugh from the woman.

"Did you kidnap me just to hurl insults?" I said. "Fucking pathetic."

"There is some fight in you, then," he replied. "I was surprised how easy it was to overpower you."

"Are you Gestapo?" I said. "If you are, just get on with it."

"Are you stupid?" he said. "Do we look like Gestapo?"

"No," I said. "But you still look like a dick."

He raised his fist, but was restrained by another man.

"Come on, calm down," said the other man. "If we're going to sink to this, what are we fighting for?"

His voice sounded muffled but familiar. He took off his balaclava.

"Bill," I said, unsurprised. "I thought I recognised your voice."

"What are you doing?" said the first man. "This is not how we do things. He has to be interrogated properly. How do you know he's not an informer?"

"I'll put my neck on the line in this case," said Bill. "I've had enough of these childish games. I've known Tom since he was a kid. He's not an informer."

"How can you be sure?" said the first man.

"Because I *know* him," said Bill. "I knew his parents too before they were murdered. He was orphaned at fifteen and tortured in Ramsgate after the 14/6 attack. I think that's enough to warrant our trust."

"And what happened in Ramsgate, Bill?" said a male. "For all we know he underwent conversion therapy, and he's an agent."

"Conversion therapy?" said Bill. "What's that when it's at home?"

"I mean they could have radicalised him," said the male. "You don't know what they're capable of."

"Don't insult me," I said. "Or the people who died during that purge. I watched women and children being led off to a building with a chimney. They told us it was a bakery, that they would be warm there. They promised them paid work. I never saw them again."

"Still, they still let you out," said the male. "Do you know how many people get to come home after that?"

"Maybe they liked my face," I said sarcastically.

"What was the price of your freedom?" said the woman. "Did you agree to spy for them in return for your life?"

"I was starved and tortured for weeks, then raped for good measure. They let me out for one reason only: to be a warning to others. So that the battered, starving human wreck who turned up for his factory shift would let people know what happens if you step out of line."

"In two years, have I ever made a wrong choice in a recruit?" said Bill. "Tom's sound. I'd stake my life on it."

"How can you be so certain?" said the woman.

"I've known him since he was knee-high," said Bill. "He's no more a Nazi than Winston bloody Churchill… I've trained him in my gym, I've sat at his parents' dining table, got pissed with him down the local. And trust me on this – he's cleverer than he looks, no offence…"

"None taken," I said.

"…and as hard as nuts – we could really use a bloke like him."

"M700406019," I said.

"What?" said the first man.

"My prisoner number at Ramsgate," I said. "I know it by heart. Look at my left wrist."

The man glanced at my tattoo.

"Have you ever been in a concentration camp?" I asked.

"No," he admitted.

"Trust me," I said. "You'd be better off dead."

"All right," he said. "You've convinced me."

"We still have to vote on it," said the female. "Those are the rules."

"Tom, tell them why you want to join the resistance. Tell them what you said to me in the gym the other week," said Bill.

"Because I want to send the fucking murderous, racist Kraut bastards packing back to where they came from," I said venomously.

My anger seemed to convince them. The vote was unanimous to allow me to join the cell. The remaining members removed their balaclavas. One of them untied the knots and freed my arms and legs. I stretched my hands out in front of me. My limbs ached, having been held in an unnatural position.

"I called you a dick, didn't I?" I said to one of the men.

"You did."

"Well, I didn't mean it."

"I know you didn't. I'm Brad," he said, extending his hand.

I shook it. "Is that your real name, or is it a code?"

"We're not that sophisticated."

Brad was a tall, heavily built man in his early twenties, with a shaven head and a neatly trimmed black beard. He had sovereign rings on the fingers of both his hands, knuckledusters by another name. I was hardly soft, but I would not pick a fight with him. He was a rough diamond. As I got to know him over the coming months, I realised that you could not ask for a more loyal human being. Fiercely devoted to his young family, he was fighting for their future as much as his.

"Carla," said the female. "Bill speaks highly of you."

Carla was an athletic woman in her early thirties, of medium height. She was not wearing make-up, but had a natural beauty to her, with short brown hair and Mediterranean skin. She wore Medicare glasses, which magnified her brown eyes. Carla, I would learn, was secretive and very involved in army politics. Also, very smart, and obsessed with procedure.

Bill spoke. "Welcome to Adrestia."

"Adrestia?" I said.

"It's the name of our cell," said Brad.

"Adrestia was the Greek goddess of revolt," said Carla. "The restorer of equilibrium between good and evil."

"Blimey," I said. "Where did you learn all that?"

"She's the bright one," said Bill. "A qualified doctor. In a normal world, she'd be living a comfortable suburban life."

"What happened?" I asked.

"I applied for a consultant role in Charing Cross Hospital."

"And?"

"Their genealogy checks revealed my grandfather was a Jew. Even I didn't know. They stripped me of my qualification, and I ended up on this side of the *zwischenwand*, labouring in the Lehman Steel Mill."

"I'm sorry."

"Seven years of study down the pan."

"I'm Mark," said a gangly bloke with curly ginger hair and freckles. It took me a bit of time to understand him; he was a little odd, and a wind-up merchant with a dry sense of humour. For all his enthusiasm, though, he was not really a fighter.

"Is this HQ?" I asked.

"We don't have an HQ," said Bill. "We rotate where we meet, randomly. And we don't meet often. It's too risky."

"The Underground stations are ideal," said Brad. "There are miles of tunnels. The Nazis rarely venture down here. Since they've sealed the west side, they don't lead anywhere strategically important. Venture too far eastwards, and you hit the radioactive zone."

"You're a good fighter," said Bill to me. "Your father always hoped that you would follow in his footsteps."

"What do you mean, follow in his footsteps?" I said.

"Both your parents were active members of the resistance," said Bill.

"How come I didn't know?"

"You were too young," said Bill. "If you knew, you would have been put in danger. Their arrest wasn't just on a whim. They were betrayed."

"Who by?" I said.

"If only we knew that..." said Bill. "You should be very proud of them. They achieved so much for the cause."

"I knew they hated the regime," I said. "We all did, but I never suspected they were part of this set-up."

"Your father was a good man," said Bill. "And a valued friend. I wish he were still with us."

"I wish he was still here too."

"You may be a good fighter," said Bill. "But you've much to learn."

"And we're not a vigilante group," said Carla. "There's a chain of command. We take our orders from the British Liberation Army Council. They take theirs from the Americans."

"The Americans?" I said.

"They finance us," said Carla. "The Chinks fund the communist rebels. If... *when* we have the final push to throw out the Nazis, there'll be a power vacuum that the commies will want to fill. We're not here just to rid our country of Nazis, but to make sure we don't switch from one dictatorship to another. We're too low down to know the details, but there is a plan."

"A plan?" I said.

"Of course," said Brad. "We couldn't overthrow the Krauts without help."

"The international tensions have been building for a while," said Carla. "But most people don't know about it since the domestic news on RT is so biased."

"Do you have a short-wave radio?" said Mark.

"I made a crude one, but the SS smashed it up during the last purge," I said.

"Get a replacement," said Bill. "A lot has happened in the last few months."

"You'll learn the truth," said Brad. "The so-called thousand-year Reich is in terminal decline, and Goebbels knows it."

"They're losing territory," said Carla. "Millions of German soldiers have died in the African campaigns. Their policy of genocide has galvanised the world against them. Even the Chinese are colluding with the Americans, both arming the African rebels."

"They're holding their ground in Central Africa, and are starting to retake the north of the continent," said Brad. "The Nazis have already retreated from Sudan. Egypt is on the verge of being liberated. Now, they're trying to defend the oilfields in Libya."

"I thought the African campaigns were weeks from victory?" I said.

"Because you watch Reich Today," said Carla.

"Africa has catastrophically weakened them," said Brad. "The natives see it as a simple choice: fight and die a warrior's death, or die anyway as a coward."

"In their arrogance, they assumed it would be a case of marching their superior army across a primitive land of so-called 'subhumans'," said Mark.

"They've been bogged down in a guerrilla war," said Carla.

"Then they've had to divert resources to the Chinese border, where the Red Army is amassing," said Bill. "And, after years of neutrality, Japan has joined the Alliance of Free Nations, and is supporting US military efforts."

"Helmut Goebbels doesn't have the charisma of Hitler, nor the guile and cunning of his father," said Mark. "He's just a spoilt, fat bastard born to the right family."

"There's also the economy," said Carla. "Their 'economic miracle' was based on slave labour and stolen wealth. It's all coming crashing down around their heads."

"If it's this bad, how come they're still in power?"

"By maintaining absolute control of the media, and a drug called DHPA," said Carla.

"DHPA?" I said.

"The full name is dihydroxyphenyladenine," said Carla. "They've been adding it to the water supply for decades."

"It creates intense anxiety," said Mark. "A constant feeling of unease and paranoia. If there's any sign of rising discontent, they increase the dosage."

"Combine it with relentless government disinformation and the constant threat from the Gestapo," said Brad, "and you cow the population into total obedience."

"For any revolution to gain momentum, we have to remove the drug from the water," said Carla. "Boil your tap water for five minutes. You'll feel different in a couple of days."

"Now it's time to see the truth with your own eyes," said Bill.

"This won't be easy," warned Carla.

"It's time you learnt the fate of the Jews," said Bill.

"The Jews were resettled in the old Soviet Union," I said. "I remember seeing a documentary about it. The Germans built them cities in Siberia."

"That's the official story," said Carla. She handed me a thick envelope. "I know you're a volunteer, and you don't need persuasion, but you still need to know the truth."

I looked through the bundle of grainy black-and-white photographs in horror, leafing through picture after picture of starving human beings, their bones jutting out from their skin, clinging desperately to life.

"Literally tens of millions of people were exterminated like insects, using poisonous gas," said Carla. "A slow, painful death as they gasped for air, their screams silent as they suffocated."

"Others were starved, beaten and worked to death," said Brad. "The Nazis banned all photography in these places, for obvious reasons, but these got out."

"Those ones were taken near a Polish town the Germans called Auschwitz. It's very isolated, so they were able to hide their crimes," said Brad. "Jews, homosexuals, the handicapped, political undesirables – they were all sent there to their deaths."

"Whole towns were emptied across Europe under the Final Solution," said Mark.

"Helmut Goebbels shut it down permanently in 1976 and razed it to cover their crimes," said Brad. "These photographs are the only record we have."

"Those pictures are from Africa," said Carla. "They're more recent."

I looked through similar photos of skeletal human beings; the difference, this time, was that the individuals were African and the background scenery tropical, but the suffering was identical. These photographs were in colour, making them seem more real.

There were giant pits full of dead bodies, including those of children, being doused with petrol from jerrycans by Death Heads. The price of social cleansing. My eyes welled up. It was the first time that I had ever seen images like this.

"I know it's disturbing," said Bill. "The truth is hard to face sometimes. But we have to show you these so you never forget why we risk our lives for this cause, and why we have to win."

"They'll never stop," said Mark. "If they succeed in Africa and the Middle East, then they'll move on to Asia."

"The same pattern," said Carla. "The same murderous insanity, the same thugs, wearing the same uniforms under the banner of the swastika."

"Are you on board, mate?" asked Bill.

I bared my teeth. "You bet I am."

13

12th September 1988

STEPHEN TALBOT

My parents drove me to Cambridge, full of pride. Father took his car up to two hundred kilometres an hour on Autobahn 11, and there was barely a whisper from the engine, just a bit of wind and tyre noise.

"I reckon you'll get it to two fifty if you floor it," I urged.

"My reactions aren't what they used to be," he said. "Two hundred is fast enough."

We sped past Volkswagens and Austins chugging along in the slow lane. My mother switched on the radio, and my father and I sat in bored silence as she insisted that we listened to *Gardeners' Question Time* on Radio Four. Still, it was better than her Abba cassette.

We turned off at the Cambridge exit and queued at the turnpike. Our travel documents were swiftly examined while we sat in the car, and we were waved through the city checkpoint with minimal fuss.

I sat in the back of my father's BMW as we drove up the narrow, cobbled streets, seeing lecturers in gowns and mortar boards, and students cycling with piles of textbooks in their front baskets. I recalled the ringing of bicycle bells above the sound of the car tyres rumbling over the stone cobbles. The air smelled of freshly mown grass from the parks and university gardens. I remembered seeing the Gothic spires and arched windows of the various colleges. It was all so beautiful. An entire city dedicated to learning. I was treading in the footsteps of giants. I fidgeted nervously in the back seat of the car, wondering what the next three years held in store for me.

The excitement was dampened by the feelings that I still had for Phillip. The emotional scars ran deep. These would persist for many years, and I spent my first term at Cambridge battling depression at a time when I should not have had a care in the world. However, it would be hypocritical of me to portray myself exclusively as the grieving martyr who would never recover from his loss. I was young, and eventually I moved on.

I had been accepted into King's College, the jewel in the crown of the Cambridge colleges. An imposing sandstone building with its own chapel, a modest description of what could easily pass for a small cathedral. It backed onto the River Cam, where students, locals and tourists alike could hire punting boats in the summer. It was an idyllic, almost fairy-tale location. The cloisters, tiny leaded-light windows, and well-tended public parks gave a sense of stepping back in time.

Father parked his car at the drop-off point outside my hall of residence, the Joseph Goebbels Building, opened by its namesake in 1967, two years before he died, when the reins of power passed to his son, Helmut.

A swastika hung from a pole over the entrance, flapping gently in the light breeze. One of the porters, an amiable Polish Untermensch, came out of the building and carried my suitcases to my second-floor room.

The building was a 1960s concrete monstrosity, in contrast to the beauty of medieval King's College. How they could build it in such a picturesque city was beyond me.

My parents spent a little time with me before they headed home. As they left, my mother was trying not to cry.

My small bedroom was sparsely decorated. I had a single bed, a wardrobe, a chest of drawers, a desk and a vanity unit with a sink. The floor was tiled with dark green linoleum squares with a flecked marble pattern, which felt clammy barefoot. I had views over a small walled garden, through a steel casement window, partially obstructed by an ancient oak tree, which I would come to appreciate changing colours through the seasons. The walls were painted beige, and there was a pair of tatty curtains and a bare overhead bulb for light. It was basic but pleasant enough. The only decorative feature was a framed sepia photograph of Adolf Hitler at a rally in Nuremberg in 1952.

There was a communal bathroom at the end of the corridor and a basic kitchenette. On the ground floor near the head porter's office, there was a launderette and a common room with a television, pool table, and cheap sofas. There was also a payphone, a vending machine, and a *Space Invaders* console.

I unpacked my belongings and hung up my Blood and Humour poster on the wardrobe with Blu Tack. Then, I sat on my bed. This was my home for the next three years.

There was a knock on my door.

"It's unlocked," I shouted.

Two freshers walked in extending their hands.

"Heil Hitler," I said.

"Heil Hitler," replied the tall, dark-haired one. "I'm Mike."

"And I'm Klaus," said the shorter, blond-haired one in a German accent.

"Stephen," I said. "Good to meet you both."

"We came to tell you, everyone on the corridor is going to meet up at the Students' Union bar if you're interested?" said Klaus.

"Yeah, I'd love to," I said.

"I see you're into Blood and Humour," said Mike. "They're awesome. Have you ever seen them in concert?"

"No," I replied. "The dates never seem to work for me."

The conversation flowed effortlessly, and I had a feeling that we would become good friends.

We all met at the King's College Students' Union bar later. This was subsidised; a stein was only forty-five pfennigs. The drinks flowed, and I enjoyed the company.

That evening was the first of many good nights in that dingy bar in the bowels of the college building, and the first two people that I had met, Klaus and Mike, became my closest friends at university. During the summer holidays, I returned home to St Albans and worked as a barman in a local pub. It took me two full summers to pay back my father the money for the fine.

✠

I kept in touch with Mike and Klaus during the holidays; by phone with Mike and letter with Klaus, since international calls needed a permit, and were very expensive. Mike was an enthusiastic regime supporter; he had the same fervour that I used to have. Despite this, he was an all right guy, into sports and heavy drinking. Klaus was not a typical German. He had a great sense of humour, his timekeeping was atrocious, and he was so politically incorrect.

Having a German national as a friend also gave me the opportunity to visit the Fatherland. Klaus' family were based in the capital, Germania, and sponsored my visa application. During the Easter term reading week, I caught the 09.30 Pan-European Maglev from Waterloo International, arriving in Germania *Hauptbahnhof* at lunchtime. Klaus was waiting for me, with his family. They welcomed me into their home, a luxurious apartment situated near the Reichstag.

Like for most party members, visiting Welthauptstadt Germania was a pilgrimage for me. This was the centre of the empire and the birthplace of the Third Reich. My spiritual home.

The vast metropolis was even more spectacular in real life than in the pictures. The buildings were of an unimaginable scale. Every street seemed to offer a photo opportunity. As Rome was to their empire, this was a worthy centre of the Third Reich and a living testament to Hitler's grand vision.

I was blessed with fantastic weather. Klaus thought it too touristy to accompany me on an open-top bus tour, saying that he could not live it down if one of his friends spotted him, so I went alone.

I visited Hitler's mausoleum. This was an imposing Greek-style folly in red marble, resembling a miniature Acropolis, adjacent to the Great Hall on Großer Platz.

I queued for an hour to gain access. We were allowed inside in groups of twelve. I laid a single red rose upon his glass coffin, and kneeled, pledging my allegiance. His body was perfectly preserved. He wore his military uniform, which was decorated with medals. Even in death, his presence radiated throughout the room.

Outside of the reverential calm of the mausoleum, the city bustled with traffic and people. Unlike London, the air was clean, since most vehicles in Germany were electric, and they did not have London's heavy industry.

Most of the museums and art galleries were free to party members. I visited the Reich Museum of National Socialist Achievement, and the War Museum, both magnificent buildings on the edge of Großer Platz. Indeed, you could spend an entire day in each, and still not see everything.

Klaus met me later for a coffee at a nearby branch of Tchibo's, which had a terrace on the banks of the River Spree. I could not blame him for not wanting to tour the museums, as he had done it thousands of times. I guessed when you lived in Central Germania, you took it all for granted.

We did some window-shopping on the Prachtallee – the Avenue of Splendour. The shops were far too expensive for my budget, but Klaus bought some Hugo Boss jeans in Kaufhaus des Westens.

My visit was on 20th April, the bank holiday in celebration of the Eternal Führer's birthday. This meant that there were fireworks, military parades, and wild parties in the beer halls around the Prachtallee. Germans certainly knew how to celebrate in style. Klaus knew all the best beer halls to visit, and we partied until the early hours, but it was so expensive, especially the nightclubs, and I resorted to using my credit card.

✠

Back in Cambridge, I had rapidly assimilated myself into university life. In my first, Michaelmas term, I joined the rowing club and was chosen for the college's first boat. I also played rugby, usually as a fly half, for the college's second team.

Higher education was virtually an all-male preserve under National Socialism; females were expected to remain at home to cook, produce and raise children. For exceptionally academic women, Newnham College provided an all-female environment, the only college in the university to do so. However, these students were practically kept prisoner.

Conveniently for me, this segregation made it difficult to meet and socialise with girls. The only females we had in the college were the bedmakers, and while some were pretty, they were Untermenschen, so strictly off limits due to racial hygiene laws. Furthermore, the girls who lived locally were mostly married off in their late teens, which meant that there were a lot of sexually frustrated young men at university. For everybody except me, it seemed that this was the downside of being at Cambridge. I was spared the experience of dating females to maintain appearances.

I threw myself into my studies. I was not the cleverest in my class, but I muddled through, doing enough work to see myself through the course. I kept out of trouble, too. I became so adept at hiding my true inner nature, that lying became natural. Nobody really knew the real Stephen Talbot. I portrayed myself as a sports-loving, red-blooded heterosexual. Outwardly I was one of the lads, well liked, fashionable and dependable. The reality was that I was a frightened little boy. My father had told me that the right girl would come along one day. Instinctively, I knew that she would not, and I resigned myself to a life of celibacy.

Despite this confusion, my university years were mostly happy. In many ways they were uneventful. I enjoyed studying and the social life, and occasionally had furtive sexual experiences with random students. These encounters were emotionless, usually drunken, and though highly erotic, they were one-offs. The following morning would be awkward, but mutual fear of the consequences ensured it remained secret.

I accepted that by Cambridge standards, I was of average intelligence, so I threw myself into sport, and during my second-year Lent term, I rowed for the university in the Boat Race against Oxford. Achieving a rowing blue meant I was commended by the Nazi Party, who prized sporting ability. It also meant that I could drink in the Hawks' Club, where only blues could be members.

All students were required to attend a weekly one-hour political lecture. I feigned enthusiasm but still resented the system because of what happened to Phillip. I could never quite recapture my blind obedience.

To an outsider, I had an enviable lifestyle. I had access to an outstanding, free education, free dental and health care, world-class sports facilities and a decent grant. I polished the framed photograph of our Eternal Führer in my room every day and wore my party badge on my coat lapel. I greeted people with an enthusiastic "Heil Hitler" and a smile, but I knew I was living a daily lie.

Hiding such a significant part of myself from my peers proved to be stressful. Sometimes, I felt as though I would explode. I valued my friends, but I knew that if they had even the smallest suspicion about my sexuality, they would have nothing to do with me. It would be almost as bad as if I were a Jew.

I think this is why I took to binge drinking. I often had to bribe the bedmakers with a five-Reichsmark note, to clear up my sick or the spilt coffee on my bed. My alcohol consumption brought me to the attention of the proctors on more than one occasion. The student liaison officer also expressed his concern. I laughed it off but agreed to drink less, in part due to the threat of him writing a letter to my parents.

My drinking was negatively affecting my fitness, and cutting it out returned me to the top of my game in rowing, which had suffered in my final year.

I was expected to graduate with a respectable lower second. I knew that I wanted to pursue a career in finance. This would give me an opportunity to live and work in the city that I loved. London was reinventing itself as the financial centre of the Reich. The stock exchange had reopened and was booming. I wanted to be part of that dynamism and excitement.

14

Mid April 1990

THOMAS JORDAN

I could not believe that it was two years since my first resistance meeting at Mile End Tube Station. Time flies. I barely knew my comrades – this was not a social club. If our paths ever crossed, we deliberately ignored each other.

The exception was Bill, who was already a mate. I still trained at his gym, and we would meet for the odd stein at The Black Horse. I spent evenings at his home, another scruffy Victorian terrace like my uncle's. After his family had gone to bed, we sat at the kitchen table drinking whisky or vodka, while he showed me how to make home-made explosives and detonators out of alarm clocks. The Americans supplied us with some hardware, but our weapons hauls were always being discovered.

He gave me monthly lessons, giving me vital skills that I too could pass on. As a member of the Army Council, he was well briefed on developments. One spring night, I had dinner with his family, and after they had gone to bed, Bill and I sat up drinking vodka.

"This is good stuff," I said. "Not like that crap whisky you usually give me."

"It's Ukrainian," he replied, downing the contents of a shot glass. "So, when are you going to get a girlfriend?"

"It's not for want of trying," I joked.

"I heard a girl at the factory asked you on a date."

"Bloody hell, how did you hear about that?" I said.

"You know how gossip flies around this area," said Bill. "That and the fact that I know her mum. You're Ost-Bereich's most eligible bachelor. She's a good-looking girl; I wouldn't say no if I were twenty years younger."

"I don't want to date someone I see at work all day. Besides, she ain't my type."

"Fair enough," said Bill. "And you didn't like that girl in the pub last week?"

"Nah," I said. "She looked anorexic. What's all this interest in my love life all of a sudden?"

"No reason," said Bill. "I just want to see you happy. I think it's what your mum and dad would've wanted."

"Maybe I'm too fussy."

"Are you sure it's a girl you want?"

"What do you mean?"

"What do you think?"

"You accusing me of being a shit-stabber?"

Bill laughed. "Of course I'm not. You're as straight as they come."

"Thank God for that."

"But you know you can tell me anything."

"Yeah, well, you've no worries on that score."

"I'll mind my own business from now on."

"What's the news from the Army Council?" I asked.

"Nothing that I'm allowed to tell you," said Bill.

"We've spent months doing nothing."

"Maybe you and I can change that."

"How?"

"I know your dad would have been vocal about the lack of action."

"I can imagine."

"He was our chief liaison with our members on the other side of the *zwischenwand*," said Bill. "Being a bus conductor meant he could exchange coded messages with our contacts. You've no idea how useful that job was. It's so much more challenging communicating over there now he's gone."

"I bet."

"He was a massive loss to us. He could inspire people in a way that I never could or can."

"Don't put yourself down."

"Your father was twice the man I'll ever be."

"My last memory is him being led off to the bakery at Hastings – the gas chambers."

"Try not to think about the end of his life. Remember the good times."

"What was my dad like in the resistance?" I asked. "I never saw that side of his life."

"Where do I start with that one? He was brave, loyal and… foolhardy. I could have strangled him sometimes. But he was like a brother. If he had talked, I would not be here now."

"Why was it him that they singled out for arrest?"

"Come to any kind of mission, he'd volunteer straight away. He knew the Gestapo were onto him. I know if he were still here he'd be pushing to do something. Something big, to snap the ruling council out of their apathy."

"Maybe we should be thinking along the same lines?"

"It would certainly be a way of honouring his memory." Bill ran his hand along his shaven head. "Your father was a hero."

I poured myself and Bill another shot glass of vodka. I felt sullen.

"I miss him and Mum," I said, suddenly realising that I was in tears. "When I saw my mum murdered… If only I had had a chance to tell her… and Dad how much I loved them."

"They knew that," said Bill. "And they loved you as well. Your dad asked me to look after you if anything ever happened to him. I know I can't replace him, but you need to know that I love you like my own sons."

"And you mean the world to me, Bill."

Bill was as hard as nuts, with more tattoos than bare skin, yet he looked at me with tenderness in his eyes. I wanted to hug him, but that was for fairies.

Bill glanced at his watch. "You should go now, it's gone midnight."

15

3rd May 1991

STEPHEN TALBOT

It was my final term at Cambridge, just before the Hitler memorial bank holiday, the annual weekend when citizens across the Reich mourned the Führer. These three days of introspection were considered by many to be spiritually cleansing. A chance to renew oneself, to take the time to study National Socialist ideology, or read *Mein Kampf* in its entirety. The shops closed on Friday afternoon and remained so until Tuesday morning. Both television channels showed back-to-back documentaries about Hitler's struggle for justice and world peace.

There were no set guidelines as to how to mark the day. Some families chose to fast; others saw the anniversary of his death as a reason to celebrate his life, throwing lavish parties. The Hitler Youth used it as an opportunity to raise money for some of the charities he was a patron of, including the Animal Protection League and Help for Wounded Veterans.

I walked into town to stock up on groceries before the shops closed. The weather was overcast with intermittent drizzle. I had just reached Weltbild bookstore on Market Straβe when a man in a dark suit blocked my path. A black Mercedes with tinted windows pulled up beside me. The man flashed his Gestapo warrant card.

"Get in," he said, pointing at the car.

I got into the car, feeling terrified. Another suited man was sitting in the back. The first man sat on my other side and tapped the driver on the shoulder. The tyres screeched as we sped off.

Pedestrians walked past as if wearing blinkers, unwilling to become involved. I could not blame them; I would have done the same. Interference in state affairs was unwise.

I presumed I was under arrest, though no caution had been issued.

"Where are you taking me?" I asked several times.

All three men ignored me. The only response I received was when the man on my left swiped his forefinger in front of his mouth in a zipping motion, to tell me to shut up.

We passed through the city checkpoints without stopping and headed into the Cambridgeshire countryside, driving along single-track lanes, until we came to some wrought-iron gates with a swastika inset amongst the intricate pattern. An armed Stormtrooper came out of the coach house and approached the car. The driver opened the window and submitted his warrant card. The Stormtrooper glanced inside the vehicle, then opened the electric gates.

The car tyres crunched on the shingle driveway as we drove towards a beautiful Georgian mansion. The sandstone facade was covered with purple wisteria in full bloom. We parked in front of a stone portico, where four-metre-long swastika banners swayed between the pillars. A polished brass sign next to the door read *Heydrich House* in Gothic lettering.

A guard opened the car door, and we got out. I noticed a group of young males wearing shorts and green T-shirts, jogging as though part of a squadron. More worrying was the windowless single-storey building signposted *Correction and Re-Education Facility*. Was that my destination?

"Follow me," ordered the trooper.

My abductors headed in a different direction. I entered a large entrance hall with a magnificent staircase leading to a galleried landing. I was directed towards a desk at the foot of the stairs, where a stern-looking female adjutant sat. She wore an impeccably ironed SS uniform, and her blonde hair was tied into a neat bun.

"Sit," she barked. Her voice echoed around the room.

I sat on a green Chesterfield opposite her, admiring the oil portraits of senior Nazis hanging on the walls, while she rummaged through a filing cabinet, removing a ring binder. An ostentatious grandfather clock ticked loudly in the far corner of the room, but otherwise it was eerily silent, like a library. She put the file on the desk.

"Why am I here?" I asked.

"Everything will become clear to you shortly," she replied coldly. She picked up a phone. "Talbot is here."

I heard the faint sound of a male voice from the phone handset.

"Follow me," said the adjutant, standing up.

She moved very precisely, almost robotically. She led me upstairs, down a long, carpeted hallway, and rapped on a door.

I heard "Enter" from somebody inside.

"Go in," she ordered, opening the door.

I went inside. It was another impressively proportioned room, with tall sash windows commanding views of manicured gardens. I admired the oak panelling and marble fireplace. An overweight, bald man with a neatly trimmed moustache sat at a desk in front of a large canvas portrait of Chancellor Helmut Goebbels. He wore an ill-fitting uniform with several medals hanging from his tunic.

"Please, Mr Talbot, sit down."

I sank into a luxurious armchair. He stood up, reached over the desk and extended his palm, his underlying malevolence disguised by good manners. He was only about 150 centimetres or so in height. I edged forward and shook his hand.

"I'm Max Burgess," he said. "Please address me as Max. Helga, can we have some refreshments, please? You will take afternoon tea, I presume?"

"Yes please."

The adjutant turned around abruptly, clicked her heels, and left the office.

"May I call you Stephen?"

"Yes, of course."

"I prefer using first names. I've just been looking through your file."

"My file?"

"I see you have a strong academic record," he said, leafing through sheets of papers. "Top results in your baccalaureate from the Heinrich Himmler Academy. Only a predicted lower second in your degree from Cambridge, though. But you have a blue at rowing and are an excellent sportsman all round."

"Thank you."

"Have you thought much about what you want to do when you leave Cambridge?"

"I was hoping for a career in finance. Stockbroking or something similar."

"You have a gift for mathematics, certainly. And you have that competitive quality that might see you succeed in that field. There are fortunes to be made for the region's brightest, the well connected who are prepared to take risks."

"We have prospered under the benevolent and inspired leadership of Chancellor Goebbels, whose policies have created untold prosperity for all citizens in the Reich," I said, reeling off one of the many Ministry of Public Enlightenment sound bites that I knew by heart.

"I can see the appeal of stockbroking. It's certainly well paid. If you succeeded, you could afford to live in the capital. I know that it can be difficult to get through the recruitment process; it is very competitive, even for party members."

"What are you driving at?" I said. "Why am I here?"

"Do you know what this place is?"

"No. Aside from obviously being some sort of secret SS facility."

Max paused as Helga walked in with a tray of tea and biscuits, which she placed on the desk and left.

He continued. "This is where we recruit and train officers for the SS and Gestapo. And we're not talking Stormtroopers, like in Coventry, where your father attended. This is an elite training academy for the highest-achieving candidates who enrol on our fast-track programme. Our graduates achieve senior rankings in either sister organisation within five years. Most will rise to head a region or department within fifteen."

"Is this why you've brought me here?" I asked. "To recruit me?"

"Yes. We see that you have qualities that could be put to great use within our organisation. Tell me, your father's rank is *kriminaldirektor*, isn't it?"

"Yes."

"That means you have an idea of the commitment this kind of role would demand. The unwavering loyalty that we expect."

"Yes, but much as I respect my father and what he does, I just don't think that this is the career for me, Max."

Max poured tea from a silver teapot into two bone-china cups and tipped in some milk.

"It's such a shame that you're not more enthusiastic," he said, shaking his head. "There are so many that would jump at this opportunity."

"I respect what you do, but I don't believe I'm cut out for the Gestapo."

Max opened a drawer in his desk and retrieved a mauve wallet-folder. "I see you've had some involvement with us?"

I blushed, guessing what was coming next.

He opened up the folder and removed several pages of statements and photographs.

"Thank goodness your father has contacts high up," he said, shaking his head, looking at a witness statement from the man who had reported me on that night in St Albans. He turned my statement towards me.

"My witness statement—"

"Is a pack of lies," said Max. "There's more truth in the writings of Karl Marx. We know what actually happened. The person who reported you is a reliable informer. He observed your antics in the nave for an hour."

"So why am I here? Why would you want somebody like me in your organisation?"

"An excellent question," said Max, offering me a plate of Leibniz-Keks. "Our informers have been keeping watch on you. We note that you have had some… ahem… encounters at Cambridge."

I shuddered at his words, wondering who on earth the informers were. Lecturers, friends? Or both.

"I'm sure that you know full well National Socialist policy on this kind of sexual deviancy?"

"Yes, I do. I have attempted to remain celibate."

"Except that you haven't, have you?" said Max, taking out some photographs.

I cringed as I looked at photos of me kissing a fellow student, realising that the Gestapo had hidden cameras in my bedroom.

"I've always been discreet," I said.

"We know," said Max. "But you are acutely aware that this kind of behaviour is not tolerated."

"I'll submit myself for voluntary chemical castration. I promise to be celibate from now on."

"Fine words, Stephen, and I believe you'll try your best. But do you really think that you'll be able to abstain from sex for the rest of your life?"

"I've no choice."

"Chemical castration isn't a pleasant process. It's not a case of taking a pill and waking up in the morning. The treatment takes months. It's both physically and psychologically traumatic."

"I know."

"What if I said I could offer you a release from your frustration? A compromise that would allow you to... erm... explore this side of your character?"

"I don't understand?"

Max took a sip of his tea. "Let me explain. Homosexuals have specific skills that are very useful to us."

"Like what?"

"We realised some time ago that you make the perfect spies. Think about how you have been leading a secret life for all these years. Hiding your true self. It's become effortless. We could put you into an espionage situation, and you would blend in. We need to hone your skills, of course, but one can only be taught so much. What you have is a natural ability. You see, the rebellion against German rule is growing. We don't advertise it, but it is. The Americans are financing groups across Region 6. The slit-eyes are pouring resources into the communist resistance. Every county has at least one terrorist cell; London has dozens."

"Seriously?"

"It's true. We have to protect our way of life. The Nazi Party has brought unity to a continent in chaos. I know that you believe that."

"I have done since childhood. The commie bastards nearly killed me, and my parents. My mother was disfigured for life."

"There is another incentive for you. I mentioned allowing you to explore your sexuality. How can I put this delicately? I can guarantee that we would turn a blind eye to your exotic sexual activities. In fact, there are known homosexuals in the resistance movement. Your sodomy may even be actively encouraged in certain circumstances. Consider it a fringe benefit."

"Do I have a choice?"

Max leant forward over his desk and looked me in the eyes. "Everybody has a choice, Stephen. I suspect that your attempts to work for a merchant bank or a stockbroker may not be successful. These photographs are very incriminating. It's unlikely that your father could bribe you out of this a second time. Ten years in a re-education camp would take its toll on your health. But then you may get a judge with a more hard-line approach. He may insist on the death penalty, given it's your second offence."

"Is that a threat?"

"It's a prediction," said Max. "I'm good at reading the future. It's a gift. Besides, there are so many advantages to working for us."

"Such as?"

"You get to live here during your eight-month training period. The accommodation and food are five-star. The salary is competitive. We have a generous pension scheme, a company car package, subsidised housing and private healthcare. There are sports and social clubs. The work is fascinating too. No two days are ever the same."

"You know, thinking about it, maybe the Gestapo might be the ideal career choice for me after all."

Max sat back in his chair, smiling.

"I took the liberty of having a contract drawn up. I had this feeling that you were going to say yes."

He picked up the phone on his desk and dialled reception.

"Helga, please bring up Mr Talbot's recruitment papers."

I sipped my tea. Helga came in with an employment contract. I read and signed it, aware that my signature was committing my future and my soul to the regime. Helga took the papers and marched out of the office, with a brief salute.

Max leant forward again and shook my hand. "You start in September. Concentrate on your university finals, have a break and come to us refreshed. We'll be in contact to give you instructions on the next step. Remember that this meeting is highly confidential; you are contractually bound not to tell anyone about it, including your father, until you finish at Cambridge. Do you have any questions?"

"Yes. Do you know how Phillip is doing? The guy that I kissed in the park."

Max closed my folder and shook his head.

"I was afraid that you were going to ask."

I felt butterflies in my stomach, but I kept my reserve. "Just tell me, please."

"There was a typhoid outbreak in the camp that he was sent to. It was only a couple of months after he arrived."

"And?"

"I can assure you that he received the best medical treatment possible. Some of our finest doctors work at the labour camps. Despite their efforts, he didn't respond to the medication. He died peacefully in the camp infirmary, surrounded by his family."

"Oh," I said sadly.

"Are you all right?"

"Yes," I lied. "I had just hoped that he was okay. He would have been a third of the way through his sentence by now."

"If there's nothing else, you're free to go. My driver will drop you back in Cambridge. Heil Hitler."

I left the office and walked down the staircase, where my abductors were waiting for me.

"Congratulations," said the driver, who had suddenly become very personable. "You're going to love this place."

Another man patted me on the back and ushered me gently into the car. We headed back to Cambridge, where I was dropped off, exactly where I had been picked up. I continued my walk into town, bought my groceries as I had planned, and went back to my halls of residence as though nothing had happened. Except that I had finally discovered what had become of Phillip.

I lay face down on my bed and thought about him suffering. It was hard to try to see a bright side, but I took a crumb of comfort in the fact that he only endured the harsh camp conditions for a couple of months. At last, I had some closure.

16

14th June 1991

STEPHEN TALBOT

My last exam was on Friday 14th June. By the time I had finished, if I had ever had to solve a quadratic equation again, I think I would have screamed.

Klaus was flying back to Germany in two weeks. He was excited about starting a new job on the accelerated graduate scheme at BMW's headquarters in Munich. I was jealous of Mike, who had secured a trainee investment banker role with Commerzbank at their City of London office. My dream career. Necessarily, I remained cagey about my new job – I just told them I was working for the government. How I would have loved to swap with either of them.

I celebrated eight weeks of abstinence from alcohol in the run-up to my finals, with a session in the union bar that started at 14.00. Most of my friends had given up by 18.00, but I stayed until midnight, imparting my wisdom and considerable wit to various disinterested groups across the room. As the evening progressed, I became increasingly morose. Eventually, there were complaints, and the bar manager told me to leave and threatened to call the proctors. I stumbled back to my room, wondering if I was still being monitored. I had a sinking feeling that this was the conclusion of a happy era, where I had been cocooned from the harsh world outside.

I attended the King's May Ball, confusingly held in June, uncomfortable in the tight-fitting tuxedo I had hired from Hoffman Bekleidungsgeschäft. Despite having mixed with my fellow students for three years, I still felt an outsider. I hated small talk and found making conversation awkward with all but my closest friends.

There was a large marquee on the lawn bordering the River Cam, with the magnificent stone edifice of the college and chapel behind. The organisers had provided a gourmet dinner, live music, fireworks and a mini fairground. It was spectacular, but then it should have been with tickets costing 220 Reichsmarks.

I observed my peers having fun on the merry-go-round, chatting and flirting with the elegantly dressed girls invited from Newnham College. Later, they slow-danced on the lawn, serenaded by a string quartet. The girls were chaperoned, but there were well-practised ways to sneak away.

I remember standing alone on the bank of the river that evening, holding a flute of champagne. A warm breeze ruffled my hair, carrying the scent of freshly cut grass and honeysuckle. I saw a raft of ducks paddling downstream. I could hear music from the marquee, mingled with laughter and clapping.

It was a feeling of isolation, as though I was a perpetual outsider, an alien deposited on this blue planet, trying desperately to understand the enigma of humanity.

Klaus walked over to me, linked to a girl in a black dress, and interrupted my thoughts.

"Aren't you going to join the party?" he said.

"I will. I'm just thinking about stuff."

"I'm going to miss this place too."

"I know. I wish it could have gone on forever."

"This is Miranda," he said, introducing the girl.

"Pleased to meet you," she giggled, extending her hand.

"Come on, misery guts," said Klaus. "Join us at the bar. You need your drink topping up."

"Give me a moment. I'll come and find you."

He strolled back to the marquee with Miranda.

I needed a few more minutes of solitude, to build up the courage to rejoin the party. I felt jealous as I watched an amorous couple being punted along the river by a Czechoslovakian. The woman had her hand dangled in the water, creating small ripples which spread and merged with the gentle wake of the boat. They kissed openly. I wished more than anything that I could be normal.

I took a deep breath. It was time to be sociable. I shrugged off my negative emotions and made a personal decision that I was going to enjoy myself. I rejoined Klaus and my other friends inside the marquee, and we danced, laughed and drank.

I chatted with a girl called Monika. She was cute and intelligent, and undoubtedly into me. I flirted with her, and we shared a drunken kiss, or at least, I was drunk. I closed my eyes and imagined she was Phillip. Klaus gave me an approving wink as if to say, *Well done, mate*.

As much as I wanted to enjoy the intimacy, it felt wrong. She was a beautiful girl with a bubbly personality and much to offer, but I could not give her what she wanted. She suggested we take a walk along the banks of the Cam. I declined, but gave her my telephone number in St Albans, secretly praying that she would not call.

At midnight, the girls from Newnham College were escorted back to their residence by their chaperones. The waiters put out large wheels of *rauchkäse* on the tables, with thick slices of black bread. It was just what we needed to soak up the alcohol. We took off our jackets, undid our bow ties, and sat drinking schnapps, smoking cigars and stuffing our faces with cheese.

We talked nostalgically until the early hours, when apparently Klaus and Mike carried me back to my room. Our group ambition to achieve our place in the college hall of fame as May Ball 'survivors' had fallen flat at about 03.00.

A couple of days later, my parents arrived to take me back home to St Albans. I looked wistfully around my cramped bedroom, wondering if the Gestapo were filming me. The discovery of the surveillance and my subsequent entrapment had tainted life, but in no way had it ruined three years of happy memories. I would wholeheartedly miss Cambridge and my friends.

✠

Being back in St Albans was great, but different. Most of my school friends had responsible jobs. A few were working abroad on military service, and two of my ex-classmates were married with children, which meant that they had become insufferably dull. My parents were delighted when I told them about my forthcoming training. I do not think I had ever seen my father so happy. I could not help wondering if he had a hand in it, but surely that would be absurd. In the run-up to September, I prepared myself for life at the academy.

17

September 1991

STEPHEN TALBOT

The summer passed too quickly, and September was upon us. I caught a train to Cambridge, where a chauffeur was waiting to take me to Heydrich House. The accommodation block was a separate 1980s red-brick building behind the mansion. The bedroom was modern and comfortable with an en suite.

Another modern block housed the classrooms, canteen, and a well-equipped gym. The beautiful stone mansion where I had been interviewed was mainly used for administration, but there was an elegant lounge bar, with comfortable leather sofas arranged around a marble fireplace.

There were nineteen recruits on my intake, so we got to know each other well. Sadly, that was not a good thing. It was nothing like university, more akin to being thrown into a nest of vipers. I had to be constantly on guard.

I spent my time with people who were fanatical Nazis. I accepted Darwin's concept of natural selection and its implication that there are superior and inferior races just as there are higher and lower animals. However, I found the conversations in our free periods and evenings distasteful. I was no fan of the Slavs, especially Ukrainians, but still, I accepted they were human beings of a kind. Lesser breeds was the politically correct expression. I was disturbed by the thoughtlessness, callousness, and above all, by the sheer ignorance I heard around me. If I am honest, it was probably the vicious homophobia that stirred me most of all.

As each week passed, I found myself increasingly despising the organisation that I was part of. However, publicly I toed the party line, taking solace in my luxury surroundings.

I studied hard for my examinations. I must admit I found much of the work interesting. We had five hours of lessons per day, with two hours of physical education. It was necessary to study in the evenings too. Lessons included psychology, electronics and advanced computer studies as well as espionage, investigative procedure and law.

Module 12 of our curriculum trained us in interrogation techniques. This was not for the squeamish, and it included practice on unfortunate prisoners.

I look back with incredulity at my fellow students calmly making notes, while a victim slowly had his back stretched on a hydraulic rack, observing the process from behind a one-way mirror.

It was clear that some of them enjoyed the spectacle. Later, we lost the protection of the glass, which had provided us with anonymity and had somehow made the experience less real. It was when I had to look in the victim's eyes, smell the stench, and hear the screams for real, rather than through a loudspeaker, that my nightmares started.

The Nazis had developed an entire manufacturing industry devoted to creating instruments of torture, from precision-engineered computer-controlled racks to beautifully crafted stainless-steel tools designed to probe the human body while inflicting maximum pain. We studied thick textbooks full of information on the various methods used to extract confessions, all neatly indexed and cross-referenced.

The people that we tortured were barely human in appearance. They were usually donated by the concentration camps around the coastal areas. I remember retching at their malodour; their bodies were literally decaying.

What frightens me most, though, is how rapidly I became indifferent to it. The initial shock of these withered, skeletal creatures soon turned to dispassion. I almost resented them and the work that they caused me.

There was always so much paperwork. A pre-court evidential file for the simplest of political crimes would take many hours of preparation. The PRT/03 prisoner execution form alone was twenty-three pages long.

We were continually assessed during our training. Two of the most hate-filled recruits were selected for admission to the SS-Totenkopfverbände, or Death Head Division, after six weeks. They were issued subtly different uniforms, which included a badge depicting a skull and crossbones on their collars and caps. Perceived as the elite within an elite, they lorded over us throughout the rest of the course and formed a tight clique with a small group of teaching staff who themselves were retired Death Heads.

The five of us who were preselected for the Gestapo Division attended different seminars during the second half of the course. I never felt that I made friends, just uneasy allies. This was the environment in which I had to survive for the best part of a year.

As the course neared completion, I watched my fresh-faced colleagues change in appearance, stature and mentality. We all seemed to walk and talk differently, in a more militaristic fashion. I realised that I now emulated my father's mannerisms.

The months and seasons changed. I passed the final examinations with honours and received the first medal of my career, presented to me by the training camp commandant during a passing-out ceremony, held at a small on-site parade ground. It was official. I was now a Gestapo officer.

18

19th April 1992

STEPHEN TALBOT

My job came with perks, one of which was a furnished apartment in leafy Hampstead. It was on the top floor of a 1980s low-rise block. Although slightly dated inside, the communal gardens were well maintained, and the location fantastic, being just inside Zone Alpha. This gave me freedom of movement around the West End, the museum quarter, galleries and parks.

Job-wise, I was based at the SS/Gestapo head office close to Embankment Tube Station; convenient, as it was only eleven stops on the Northern Line. The Underground was reliable, and they had recently installed televisions in the carriages, showing Reich Today, making the journey pass quickly.

The head office, Himmler Tower, was built in 1988 to consolidate the multitude of smaller offices scattered across London. It was a glass skyscraper with seventy-four floors, nicknamed the Doodlebug, due to its passing resemblance to the World War II bomb. It was one of the tallest buildings in the capital, with spectacular views. Designed as a statement of SS power, it dominated the city skyline, reinforcing the omnipotence of the state. A twenty-metre-high sign was positioned on the roof, depicting the jagged SS insignia, leaving no doubt of this building's purpose, particularly at night when it was brightly lit and could be seen for miles around.

Timidly, I approached the building using the wide granite pathway leading from the Embankment. It was lined on either side with scores of swastika flags, which flapped vigorously in the wind blowing off the Thames. They produced a metallic ringing sound as the halyards thumped against the hollow aluminium poles.

As expected, security was tight. There were Alsatians, trained to detect explosives, and metal-detecting gates. Once inside, I was overawed by the colossal galleried entrance, with glass elevators running up the centre. An eighty-metre-high bronze statue of Adolf Hitler towered over the foyer desk, bathed in natural light streaming through the atrium.

The bulk of the Gestapo operations were housed on the thirty-fourth to forty-second floors, which is where I would be based when not on field duty. The mainstream SS and their subdivisions occupied most of the other levels. Himmler had remerged the two organisations at the end of the war, but while they were jointly commanded, they still remained distinct from each other.

The open-plan design of the building meant that the sound of ringing telephones, dot-matrix printers and chattering echoed around the immense space.

Senior-ranking officers occupied the top floors, where high-level management issues were dealt with. The interview rooms, secure cells, and torture chambers were in the lower basement, beneath the car park levels, with a separate entrance. The first four floors housed the archives and Department C, which was responsible for internal administration, accounting and personnel matters.

✠

My fellow trainees from Heydrich House and I completed a two-day induction, which included numerous health-and-safety presentations. We were each assigned a mentor, who would tutor us.

My work initially concentrated on investigative duties and covert information-gathering. Files were kept on millions of people and cross-referenced into a database on the central computer. I helped to update and collate this data. It was dull work. The Gestapo were fastidious regarding paperwork. There were forms about filling in forms.

My senior manager was Kriminalrat Francis Sutton. He was in his late fifties and a fervent Nazi. He was a tall, slim, elegant man, with a neat moustache, thinning silver-grey hair, and green eyes. He wore rimless bifocals. I would not have liked to cross him, but he was protective of his staff.

He headed a team of thirty within Department D4, which focused on political dissenters. Each subsection of this department concentrated on a defined geographical area. We policed an area of North London stretching from High Barnet to Finchley and along the Inner London Orbital as far as Harrow, or from Nord-Bereich 4 to 12.

My mentor was Hilfskriminalkommissar Frederick Stanning. He was an entirely different character to Sutton. He was in his early forties, a short man with thinning black hair brushed back to reveal a widow's peak, and glued down with Brilliantine. He had pasty skin, and was overweight, chain-smoked and spent most of the day eating junk food. He wore creased suits that had a cheap polyester sheen to them, and he reeked of Kouros. You could smell him from ten metres away.

Though physically unattractive, I warmed to Fred. He had a good sense of humour. His attitude towards our superiors was irreverent, to say the least, but despite his unorthodoxy, he got results. His investigative skills were second to none, and I learned a great deal from him.

I use the expression 'He was one of the nice guys' cautiously. The paradox of working for the Gestapo was that there were a surprisingly large number of decent people. Despite my experiences at the training college, where hunger and ambition were nurtured, there were a lot of old-timers here, who went about their jobs in an unassuming manner.

Over time, I became more forgiving of the government. Harsh though our system was, it had kept order and stability for decades. It was better than the alternative of American anarchy. I would never quite recapture the blind devotion that I possessed as a child, but over time, I accepted my part in society. National Socialism was the past, present and future.

Fred and I were part of a system which neither of us could change, but we would act with as much integrity as was possible. Over the months, I became close to him and regarded him as one of my few friends within the organisation. On occasion, he invited me to eat dinner at his home, with his wife and family.

He had a pleasant but untidy apartment close to Paddington Train Station. The first time I visited, aside from his children's toys scattered all over the lounge floor, I noticed a collection of medals in a glass cabinet, including an Iron Cross, first class, and a War Merit Cross with swords.

"Wow," I said, impressed.

"Oh, they're nothing really," said Fred. "They doled them out like Smarties in the '70s."

"My daddy got them in Cambodia," said Annie, his eight-year-old daughter.

"He's a hero," said Harry, his six-year-old.

"No, I'm not," said Fred.

"We're very proud of him," said his wife, Mary, a petite brunette with a mumsy warmth to her. "He's just modest."

"Why did you never mention you served in Cambodia?"

"It hardly seems worth boasting about it, given the outcome."

"The failure wasn't down to ordinary soldiers like you. The Chinese overwhelmed us. Nobody blames the troops."

"I know. But it's something I'd rather not think about. I'd have the medals locked away in a drawer; it's Mary who insists on putting them out on display."

"What he doesn't tell you," said Mary, "is how many soldiers' lives he saved, and how many times he risked his own life."

"I was only doing my job. They would have done the same for me. Now can we please change the subject?"

Mary gave me a large glass of Liebfraumilch, and I read some night-time stories to Annie and Harry, who were wonderful children and cuddled up to me on the sofa. Half an hour later, they were put to bed, and we sat down for dinner. That was the first of many fun evenings with Fred's charming wife and children.

When I passed my probation, at my request, I was partnered permanently with Fred. I was soon promoted to *kriminalassistent*, and the more stimulating work that I had hoped for started.

19

April 1993

THOMAS JORDAN

After I had joined the resistance, I was excited about the alliance making a big push into Europe, but it did not happen. Instead, in the early '90s, we stood still.

This was down to American politics. President Donald H. Williams had been kicked out in 1991 due to some sex scandal. A pity, as he was a strong leader and the Nazis hated him.

His affair had given the Nazis plenty of anti-American fodder. We hardly ever saw American TV, but the regime gloated in showing CNN news clips about stuff going on out there. The public could see first-hand how bent American democracy was. After the Vice President took over, America just bumbled along for a year.

Turnbull, a Democrat, won the 1992 election. The American public was sick of being the world's police force. Ammunition supplies dried up, as did our hope. We resorted to petty vandalism, like slashing tyres on SS vehicles. It was not why I had joined up, and I wondered what the point of it all was.

It was during these years of stagnation that I discovered that people listened to me. I never cast myself as a natural leader, but it seemed that I could inspire people, like my old man. I knew in my heart that we needed American backing to achieve anything significant, but we had to fight on without them for now, which meant manning up and taking a few risks. The arguments spun around my head for months before I spoke to Bill at his house.

"We have to do something," I said. "Vandalising police cars ain't going to win a war."

"You think like me. I've been trying to get that group of crusty old men to start acting like an army for years."

"What do you suggest?"

"I think we need to be more aggressive. It's time we started a bombing campaign, like the communists."

"Military targets? Like Hackney Barracks?"

"You won't even get close. There's a ring of steel around them."

"Surely you're not suggesting we stoop to the level of the communists?"

"I don't think we have a choice."

"You're condoning bombing civilians?"

"I'm not saying it would be my preferred course of action, but I think we need to make a statement. Plus, I'm talking about bombing on the west side of the wall, where the collaborators and the Germans are based."

"I still don't feel comfortable… We could lose a lot of support, and I don't know if I could live with myself, killing innocents."

"How innocent are those who can afford to live, work and shop on the west side? It's time to harden your heart. They're collaborators, who have grown fat and rich on the back of people like us."

"But still…"

"Ultimately, it's going to be a choice you'll have to make."

"Why me?"

"Because I've done my bit. I'm stepping down from being cell commander and from the Army Council."

"Stepping down? Who'll lead us?"

"I thought that was pretty obvious."

"No, I don't want to do it."

"Who else is there? No disrespect, but Mark's a ginger twat and as soft as shite, Brad's just not a leader, and Carla – well, she's a woman."

"I've not got the experience."

"Everyone has to start somewhere. And there's something else I want to say. I'm going to suggest that you replace me on the ruling council too. They could use someone like you – somebody with balls."

"Do you think I could do both those roles, then?"

"Yes, I do. It's not rocket science."

"Then I'll put myself forward, if you think I should."

"Absolutely, I do," he said. "And what about my idea of bombing a prominent target?"

"Did you have somewhere in mind?" I said uncomfortably.

"Yes. Wertheim."

"The big department store in Knightsbridge?"

"Exactly."

"Why Wertheim?"

"Because it disgusts me. I remember walking past it on my *zivildienst*. Maybachs parked outside, driven by fat men while in Ost-Bereich we practically starved. The women dressed in designer clothes and diamond necklaces, while my mother made us jumpers from scraps of cloth. The Stormtroopers spending their bribes on luxury hi-fis, while we shivered in our tiny house. That store is a symbol of their greed."

"True. But surely it's staffed by Untermenschen? They don't deserve to die. What about any children that might be caught up in the explosion?"

"Every war has casualties. I say that as a father myself. I think it is more of a crime to sit around and do nothing. Every day we wait, the slaughter continues in Africa, and it won't stop there. How many of our own people – including children – rot in labour camps? If we make a conscious decision to do nothing when we could have, we still have blood on our hands."

I nodded. "You do have a point."

"It could be your first act as cell commander. Think of the impression you'd make on the others, and with the Army Council. The hero you'd be."

"The Army Council would never approve it."

"Go over their heads."

"Are you serious? You and the others have consistently rammed it down my throat about respecting the chain of command."

"I have, but there comes a time with weak leadership when you have to act alone. You'd force the council to wake up and take notice."

"Do you know what you're suggesting?"

"Yes. Of course, I can't force you into this. It has to be your choice. But I know what your father would have done..."

✠

A week later, Adrestia met in the ticket office of Mile End Underground Station, sitting in a circle.

"I've been thinking about my position in the group for some time now," said Bill. "I've already resigned from my Army Council post, effective from next month. I need to put my family first. I want to quit as commander here too."

"You've been a good leader," said Mark.

"I'm proposing Tom to replace me."

After a brief discussion, the group unanimously voted me in as their new commander.

"I want to put something on the table," I said. "It's time we made a statement."

"What are you talking about?" said Brad.

"Are we the resistance or not?" I said.

"Of course we are," said Brad.

"Aren't we supposed to be *resisting*, then?" I asked.

"Obviously," said Carla.

"So why aren't we?" I said. "We've been sitting around for years, doing fuck all. It's time we did something as a unit, make the Krauts know we're still here."

"Take unilateral action?" said Carla.

"I must say," said Brad, "I do agree with Tom. I think it's time we acted."

"I'm in favour too," said Mark.

"Good, because if we carry on like this, we'll be drawing our pensions by the time Liberation Day comes," I said. "It's time to send the Nazis and the Americans a message. We're here, and we're not giving up."

"What do you have in mind?" said Carla.

"I have a plan. But I need to work out the finer details."

"Fair enough," said Carla.

"As your new commander," I said, "I order that we meet here one week from today, at 21.00."

"Get over yourself," said Brad, before adding hurriedly, "but I will be here."

"See you all then. Now fuck off, everyone, except you, Bill."

The others left.

"I hope we're doing the right thing," I said.

"You are," said Bill, putting his hand on my shoulder. "I'm proud of you. Your father would be too."

"Do you know what I've just committed us to? Bombing Wertheim. This could backfire on us spectacularly. I'm still not sure."

"Decisions like these take guts. Nobody said it would be easy."

"I know."

"The one thing Nazis don't do is negotiate. You have to come at them from a position of strength. That's why the war against them in Africa is being won."

"It's the reprisals that I'm worried about. And how I'm going to live with myself, knowing I've killed citizens. We have to remember what we're fighting for, or we become no better than the Nazis."

"I'm hardly ecstatic about doing something like this either, but I can't see that we have a choice."

"If only Dad was here. He'd know what to do."

"I know exactly what your father would be telling you to do. And so do you."

"Do I?"

"Yes, trust me. I knew him well."

"Supposing the cell agree to do this. How did the communists get the explosives across the *zwischenwand*? The checkpoint guards are thorough, there are manned towers every hundred metres. I know they can't get through the Underground tunnels as they've been sealed off."

"The same way that the black marketeers smuggle in their illicit goods."

"Do they bribe the guards?"

"There are some bent guards, yes. But none stupid enough to allow explosives through."

"Then how?"

"The sewers."

"You mean the Nazis haven't sealed them off?"

"Yes and no," said Bill. "The entire London sewer network was built in Victorian times. The whole thing is interconnected. If you brick off a section, you get raw sewage bubbling into the pristine streets in the West. So, they fitted sluice gates."

"Which can be cut through."

"Yes," answered Bill. "With specialised equipment. They use an exceptionally tough alloy, called uroferranium. We'll need heavy-duty welding equipment, and the alloy contains depleted uranium, so it's highly toxic."

"Surely the SS must inspect the sewers?"

"They do. But not often. It's an unpleasant job, as you can imagine. They typically send Untermenschen to do it, who aren't thorough."

"Who can blame them?"

"I can get hold of a map of the sewage network. It may be possible to sneak out from right under their noses."

"You could get a group of us outside Wertheim, in Knightsbridge?"

"I think so. But then you have to gain access to the store."

"Let me worry about that."

April 1993

THOMAS JORDAN

Bill and I met up at his house a few days before the cell was due to regroup. It was the usual routine of enjoying a home-cooked dinner with his hyperactive family, followed by resistance talk once they had all gone to bed.

He opened a drawer in a sideboard and took out a cardboard tube.

"Schematics of the sewers," he said. "Courtesy of the Army Council. I had to lie about why I wanted them. I told them we were going to submit a detailed proposal. They won't be happy when they discover the truth."

"You still think we should do this?"

"Absolutely. Though, it may cost you that place on the council."

Bill unravelled a curled-up map from the tube and spread it on the table. It showed a confusing maze of tunnels. He overlaid a second sheet of tracing paper on top, which displayed the streets above, with manhole covers marked in green. This was easier to understand.

"You have to bear in mind that this is an old map, so the street names are pre-war," said Bill. "Wertheim used to be called Harrods. It's on Brompton Road, which is now called

Josef Kramer Straβe. I've circled a manhole cover on a quiet road behind the store."

"Where we'll have less chance of being spotted."

"Exactly. I suggest we do a dry run tomorrow."

"Can you get us some suitable cutting equipment?"

"Yes, I've a contact in one of the Thames Estuary shipyards. I suggest that you and I clear a route to the side street near Wertheim. We'll do a recce at night."

"Agreed."

"That's everything for now, I think."

"Thanks for a lush dinner."

"It's amazing how far my wife can stretch a couple of pigeons."

"I thought it was chicken?"

"Chicken is for special occasions."

"If I have my way, we'll all be eating fresh meat every night."

✠

I made my way back home. There was a full moon that shone with an eerie green glow through the thick blanket of smog. I heard a vehicle approach, so I hid up an alleyway. It was a police car. Its V8 engine purred gently as it glided past me, accompanied by a high-pitched whine from a slipping fan belt. Once out of sight, I ran home.

21

April 1993

THOMAS JORDAN

Adrestia met a few days later in the ticket office at Mile End, and I discussed my plan at length.

"Bill and I will make sure our path to Wertheim is clear," I said. "He's had experience of the sewers."

"How are we going to gain access to the store?" said Brad.

"Through the front door," I said.

"You mean you're going to plant bombs in broad daylight surrounded by regime loyalists in the most heavily guarded city outside of Germania?" said Mark. "Have you lost your mind?"

"Think about it," I explained. "We'll be in Central London. Everybody will assume that we have gone through all the checkpoints coming in."

"We'll have false papers," said Bill. "We'll be wearing west-region clothing. We'll look like any other wealthy shopper."

"Where are you going to get all this from?" asked Brad.

"We have our contacts and funds," said Bill.

"We're going to look fantastic, soaking wet and stinking of turds," said Carla.

"The clothes will be in waterproof bags," I said. "We'll change at the other end."

"In one of the busiest and most heavily monitored cities in the world?" she said.

"Bill's got a map of the sewer system," I said. "He knows of an area close to Wertheim that was bombed during the war. It's just a mound of rubble that's been fenced off. It gives us all the privacy we need."

"And where are we going to hide the bombs?" said Carla. "You're going to need a lot of explosives to do any significant damage."

"We're not doing a demolition job," I said. "Our aim is to wreck a few floors and create panic."

"We'll use plastic explosives on a timer," said Bill.

"They're easily concealable," I said. "Then it's a case of just putting them somewhere discreetly."

"What about the store's CCTV?" said Brad.

"That is, unfortunately, the one flaw in the plan," I said. "We have to accept that this could well be a suicide mission."

"You're not asking much from us, then," said Mark sarcastically.

"I'm only going to proceed with this if I have a unanimous vote from the cell," I said. "I need all of you on board. But don't feel pressured. If you don't think this is a good idea, speak freely."

Mark and Brad agreed straight away. Carla was more cautious.

"I'm just thinking through the implications," she said gravely. "I don't like the idea of taking innocent lives."

"As far as I'm concerned," said Brad, "if they can afford to shop at Wertheim, they've profited from the regime, so they're a legitimate target."

"It's not just the shoppers," said Carla. "What about the Untermenschen? And the reprisals?"

"Yes," I said. "And I've lost a lot of sleep over this, but Bill's convinced me. I know that we can't just sit here like gutter rats waiting for them to come to us. And believe me, they will. It may not be tomorrow, it may not be for years, but they will come. I'd rather die knowing I've tried to do something."

"I have major reservations," said Carla. "But I'm going to take a leap of faith and go with the group."

"It's unanimous, then," I said. "There's no point in wasting time. We'll attack on Sunday."

✠

Bill and I met a couple of days later, in a lock-up under the arches of a disused train line, with cutting equipment, wellingtons and hard hats. The nearest manhole was two minutes' walk away. It was pissing down with rain. I clambered down, and Bill passed me the equipment.

I was shin-deep in filthy water, flowing eastwards with a powerful current. I switched on my helmet torch. It was an old Victorian brick-built sewer with just enough room to stand. Limescale stalactites hung from the ceiling, and the stench was indescribable.

"God," I said, retching. "I knew it wasn't going to be paradise down here, but bloody hell."

"Get used to it."

I drew chalk arrows at intervals on the walls so we could find our way back easier.

"If I've got my bearings correct," said Bill, "we're just about under the *zwischenwand* now. I expect there to be some kind of barrier soon."

He was right: our path was blocked by a sturdy metal gate. I examined it, gripping the bars, making a vain attempt to loosen it from the wall.

Bill ignited the acetylene torch. Sparks of white-hot metal shot over the tunnel. Fifteen minutes later, I kicked the gate away. The hot metal gave off a short burst of steam before sinking beneath the water.

"That seemed too easy," I said.

"There's bound to be more. If you're looking to get any sleep tonight, you can forget it."

We repeated the process twice and reached our exit point. I climbed up the ladder and raised the cast-iron cover a few inches above my head. I peered out onto a brick-strewn patch of wasteland, with sparse patches of weeds growing through the rubble. It was surrounded by a corrugated-iron fence to keep out pedestrians. It was ideal.

We climbed out, enjoying the fresh air.

"If I'm right, you should be able to glimpse Wertheim from over the fence," said Bill.

We walked over.

"Give me a bunk-up," I said.

I looked over the top of the fence. The thin iron cut into my palms, as I supported my weight on the top. I could just make out the side of Wertheim from the fairy lights that covered the building, sparkling like a Christmas tree.

"This is fantastic," I said. "You couldn't have asked for a better spot."

We climbed back down to the sewers and made our way back following the chalk arrows. Once back home, I got out messages to our cell members to meet at the lock-up under the viaduct at 04.00 on the following Sunday morning, 25th April.

22

25th April 1993

THOMAS JORDAN

At 04.00, Carla, Brad and Mark arrived, and I gave them the final briefing.

"Bill and I have cleared a route to the designated area," I said. "If we get separated, follow the chalk arrows on the wall. I trust you've all brought torches."

"We're not amateurs," said Brad, waving his Maglite.

"Aren't you?" I said, putting on my hard hat and switching on the lamp, giving the others a wink.

"You've always got to upstage me somehow," said Brad. "You look like a member of the Village People."

"Who?" I said.

"Some poofy American pop band I saw on Channel Two," said Brad. "They mince around in hard hats, bumming other men."

"Well, you'd know," I said sarcastically. "Bill's brought all of us clothing."

"They weren't cheap," he said, tossing Brad, Carla and me a sealed plastic bag.

"But we'll need to dump them when we've finished the job," I added. "Don't be tempted to keep them. They'll draw attention to you this side of the *zwischenwand*."

"Shame," said Mark. "I could do with a new suit. In fact, I could just do with a suit."

"You won't need one," I said.

"Why?"

"I'm coming to that bit. Carla and I will be planting the bombs somewhere discreet, out of sight of the CCTV."

Bill reached into a holdall and took out four brick-sized pieces of what looked like orange Plasticine.

"You should both know how to use these," he said.

He tossed a plastic explosive over to Carla, who caught it nervously.

"Fucking hell, Bill," she said, "do you have to throw that stuff around?"

"It's perfectly safe. It's completely stable without a detonator."

"I'd rather not take the risk."

"Talking of which. The detonators."

He retrieved some crude home-made detonators. "My own invention, primitive but they're effective," said Bill. "The alarm is set for 14.00; don't try to adjust the settings, it could cost you your life. When you've found a suitable place to plant the Semtex, all you need to do is stick these two prongs into the top about two centimetres apart."

"We should be way out of the area by the time they go off," I said.

I distributed some little two-way radios. "Obviously, try not to use these," I said. "They're not secure, and they have a crap range anyway. They should be set to Channel Seven."

Bill handed everyone an automatic pistol. "One magazine each. If it comes to it, save the last bullet for yourself."

"We will," said Carla.

"Mark," I said. "You've got the easiest job. I want you to stay in the sewer. If anything happens to us, you need to get back here and report. Bill's going to remain here in the lock-up. Carla, you're going to be my wife. Here's your ID card and cover story."

Carla examined them. "Mrs Tracey Smith? Classy."

"I'm Craig, your husband," I said. "We're buying you a new dress for my cousin Juliet's wedding in September."

Brad examined his identity card. "These are really professional. They've even got the eagle-swastika hologram."

"Be aware," said Bill. "If they try to run them through a portable scanner, they'll show as fake."

"That's handy," said Brad.

"You'll be dressed like wealthy collaborators," said Bill. "There's no reason they should spot-check you. Just behave confidently, and if you're asked to produce ID, keep calm."

I started handing out papers. "These are your cover stories. Sorry if you don't like them, but I'm a freedom fighter, not an author. Everybody is to read them now, memorise them, then we'll burn them here. The chances are we won't get stopped, but we need to be ready. Remember, informers are everywhere. A casual remark to a shop assistant, or forgetting your name, could get you arrested in minutes."

The team read my notes.

"I can't believe you've called me Calvin," said Brad. "Do I look like a Calvin?"

"Well, I'm called Rupert," said Mark. "Rupert of the sewer. For fuck's sake, Tom, were you pissed when you wrote these?"

"Nobody wrote a book on how to do this stuff," I said. "Quit your moaning, and let's get down to business. Brad is going to be a lookout. You need to find a table outside a restaurant called Café Richoux, opposite Wertheim, and have some breakfast. Radio us if there's any unusual activity."

"Unusual activity?" he enquired.

"If a van turns up with a squadron of Stormtroopers, you know they might be on to us. At least we might stand a chance of escaping if we get some warning."

"This is for you," said Bill, handing Mark a grenade. "If they track you down to the sewer, run, throw this behind you, and keep moving. It'll bring down that section on top of them."

"Lastly, I've got some money," I said. "This is all we've got, so no splurging. Ten Reichsmarks each."

"Wow," said Carla.

"It's expensive over there."

Bill collected up my notes, put them on the concrete floor and set fire to them with his Zippo.

I looked at my watch. "It's 04.40 now; sunrise is in about an hour. We need to get a move on."

"Good luck," said Bill. "I'll be waiting."

"You're not coming?" asked Carla.

"Do you think I'd pass as a Wertheim customer with these?" said Bill, pointing at the tattoos on his neck.

"Good point," she conceded.

"Let's do this," I said.

I led my team to the sewers. I climbed down first. Brad handed me down the clothes parcels, and the others followed.

"Fucking hell," said Brad. "It stinks."

"At least it's not raining, like it was when Bill and I went down a few days ago. It smelled even worse then."

"Vile," said Mark.

Carla shone her torch around. "Which way is it?"

"Follow me," I said. "I've put chalk marks every few metres."

We waded through the sewers for about an hour. While we complained about the smell and the dank conditions, we were all excited but terrified about what we were about to attempt.

Eventually, we reached our destination and climbed out of the tunnel. It was still dark, but the sun was beginning to rise above the horizon.

"Breakfast," I said, handing them a Ritter Sport bar each.

"Call me Mr Picky," said Mark sarcastically, "but the thought of eating hazelnuts in chocolate is not particularly appealing, given what I've just walked through down there."

We unwrapped our parcels and changed into our neatly folded clothes and shoes, brushing out the creases as best we could.

"Who the fuck chose this dress?" said Carla. "It's three sizes too big. Can somebody do me up?"

Brad and I put on the suits. I was careful to make sure that my Ramsgate tattoo was covered by my cuffs. I handed Carla two bricks of Semtex, which she put in her handbag. I hid the other two in my jacket pockets.

It was now light, and you could hear the hum of traffic over the fence as London sprang into life. I could feel the hazy sun on my face as it struggled to burn through the clouds. I stretched my arms and took a deep breath of London air. Even the diesel fumes smelled good compared to the sewers.

A Lufthansa Zeppelin passed overhead, briefly blocking out the sun. I waited for the drone of the electric engines to die down before I spoke again.

"It's nearly 07.00," I said. "Let's get on the other side of the fence before it gets too busy. Carla and I will wander around together, looking touristy. Brad, you need to go alone. Wertheim opens at 09.00 on Sunday, so we've got two hours to while away. Try to look casual."

I checked the coast was clear, and Mark gave us all a bunk-up over the fence, before going back down the sewer, the poor sod.

Brad walked ahead, and Carla and I followed a few metres behind, holding hands. In a few minutes, we were on Josef Kramer Straβe, admiring the window displays packed with goods that we would never be able to afford.

"Just promise me one thing," said Carla.

"What?"

"If it looks like we're going to be caught, put a bullet in my head. I don't think I've got the courage to do it myself."

"Don't worry, I'll take us both out."

I had been to the west side during my *zivildienst*, but it was a long time ago. I had forgotten how different it was. It dripped with money. The cars were new and gleaming, with loads of Mercedes, Porsches and BMWs. The roads were freshly tarmacked, unlike the potholed streets in our sector. Even though it was Sunday, by 08.00 the area was bustling with pedestrians.

We walked past Wertheim, an old red-brick building covered in fairy lights and decorative swastikas. The first window had a display of golf equipment and mannequins wearing Pringle jumpers; others were filled with expensive televisions or kitchen gadgets.

It was easy to get swept away in the glamour, but I reminded myself that this was a Nazi show capital; a facade to the West, so foreign journalists on strictly guided tours could be duped into believing London was a thriving city like New York or Sydney. Occupied, yes, but safe, with clean streets and reliable transport. An example to the free world.

It was all a lie. Behind the glittering boutiques and restaurants lurked a brutal police state. The people here had got wealthy at the expense of eighty per cent of the population, who, like me, worked like slaves in sweatshops. The pavements may have been spotless, but it was Untermenschen who scrubbed them clean. They looked half starved, yet they smiled, perhaps hoping for a tip, or maybe to avoid an SS beating.

There was a smell of baking bread and coffee from the street cafés. There were delicatessens and patisseries packed full of mouth-watering food, while in Ost-Bereich, we fought over cans of Spam.

We walked along the road. Nobody was paying us any attention, which was a good thing. The pavement cafés were busy serving breakfast, and I was tempted to spend some Reichsmarks on a fry-up, but I reminded myself that this was not a day out. The less contact I had with anyone on this side, the better.

"How much more walking do you intend to do… darling?" said Carla. "These heels are killing me."

"Sorry, love. Let's head back to Wertheim; it should be opening soon."

The great thing about this side of London was that nobody bothered you much. People were only concerned about themselves.

Bill said the Gestapo were lazy fuckers in the western sector. They would have assumed that we had passed through at least one checkpoint on our way into the centre. Our dress made us look like wealthy collaborators. We were all part of the same club, enjoying the fruits of the National Socialist utopia.

✠

By the time we got back to Wertheim, it was open. I could see Brad in the café opposite, drinking coffee. The ground floor of the department store was a perfumery. We caught a lift, operated by a Romanian Untermensch in a dark green uniform, to the second floor – ladies' clothing.

Carla was not girly, but I could tell she was enjoying looking at the dresses. It was not hard to play the bored husband. A snooty shop assistant with a pointy face and hair tied into a bun, wearing a navy suit, walked over to us.

"Can I help you?" she said sternly, looking at us as if we were something that she had trodden in.

"Yes," said Carla, pointing to a peach-coloured summer dress. "I like this dress here. Do you have it in a size nine?"

The shop assistant rummaged through the hangers and found a dress that was the right size. "Is it for a special occasion?" she asked.

"Yes," said Carla. "My cousin is getting married in September."

"Oh, really?" she said. "How lovely. Where's the wedding?"

"In the Hitchin civic hall in Bedfordshire."

"Bedfordshire?" enquired the assistant curiously.

"She means Hertfordshire," I interjected quickly. "Honestly, Tracey, your geography is truly awful."

The assistant handed Carla the hanger, which she held against her body and looked in the mirror.

"Would you like to try it on?" said the assistant. "Being Chanel, it's very expensive. We do have some cheaper dresses in the sale that might be more suitable for you."

"Can we afford it, Craig?" said Carla.

"Nothing is too much for you, my dear."

"Follow me," said the assistant, leading us to the changing rooms.

"May I go in too?" I asked.

"Yes," said the assistant. "I'll wait for you both here."

We walked into a corridor with compartments that had curtains that drew across for privacy. We chose the one at the end, against the back wall, and went inside. I shut the curtain and lowered my voice.

"Give me the explosives," I whispered.

Carla and I retrieved our Semtex.

"You change, while I sort these out."

I inserted the prongs into the soft orange plastic, while Carla put on the dress. I looked upwards at a floating polystyrene ceiling.

"Perfect." I stood on the bench in the corner of the compartment and said, "If I give you a lift, do you think you'll be able to prise off one of those ceiling tiles? We'll put the bombs up there."

"Easy."

I gave Carla a bunk-up. She tucked the two charges away in the ceiling and replaced the tile.

"You look beautiful," I said. "I'm not just saying that. You really do scrub up well."

Carla gave me a peck on the cheek.

"We shouldn't leave just yet. Let's keep up the act for a bit, just in case."

Carla followed me out of the changing room wearing the peach dress.

"What do you think?" she said to the shop assistant.

"You look stunning," she said, almost sounding sincere. "It really suits you."

"Doesn't it," I said.

"I simply must have it," said Carla, twirling in front of the mirror.

"How much is it?" I asked.

"Eight hundred and ninety-nine Reichsmarks," said the assistant.

I spluttered, "How much?"

"Oh, darling, I had no idea it was so expensive."

"As I mentioned earlier," said the assistant snidely, "we do have some more suitable stock at the other end of the store."

Carla looked crestfallen. "Never mind."

"Come on, dear. Take it off, and we'll see if we can find something more affordable. Thank you for your help."

"You're welcome," said the shop assistant, wallowing in her superiority.

I waited for Carla to change back, and we browsed for a few minutes, before leaving the floor, this time using the escalators. We left via the front entrance. I was shitting myself, paranoid that I had been spotted.

I nodded towards Brad in the café, who left some money on his table and started to walk in the same direction as us. I took a deep breath. We were almost out of danger; just a few more minutes.

Without warning, a Gestapo van screeched up a few metres in front of us. We froze on the spot. Six uniformed officers jumped out of the vehicles and ran towards us.

"Shit," I said.

"Remember what I asked you earlier?" said Carla.

The officers ran past, nearly colliding with Carla. I realised that they were not after us, and left my gun in place.

The officers ran across the main road, dodging the traffic.

"Keep your cool," I said. "They're not here for us. Just keep walking."

It turned out that the officers *were* after Brad, who started running. I reached for my pistol.

"No," warned Carla. "You'll blow the entire operation."

I saw Brad reach for his gun. He turned around and tried to fire at his pursuers. No sound came from the weapon. He reloaded the magazine and tried again. He pointed it at his head and pulled the trigger. Nothing. One of the officers fired a shot. Brad dropped the gun and collapsed onto the pavement, clutching his bleeding leg in agony. The Gestapo surrounded him.

"Don't look back," said Carla.

We turned right into the side street that led to our escape route and climbed over the fence. I snagged my trousers on the rusty iron, wincing as I grazed my ankle. Mark was waiting for us in the sewer.

"Where's Brad?" he asked.

"He didn't make it," I said. "He's been arrested."

"What happened?"

"I don't know. What I do know is that his pistol didn't work."

"Shit," said Mark. "If he talks, we're all fucked."

"Come on," I said. "We don't have time to discuss this."

I picked up the parcel with my own clothes inside and started walking back to the East.

"Wait a minute," said Carla. "I can't walk in these bloody heels."

She put on her wellingtons and tossed the shoes away.

"No," I said. "Pick them up. We can't leave any evidence."

"For fuck's sake," complained Carla, but she fished the shoes out of the foul water.

"What went wrong?" said Mark.

"I don't know," I said. "We did our bit – the bombs are planted."

"Let's hope they work better than Brad's pistol," said Carla.

✠

We worked our way back to our starting point. Bill was waiting for us in the lock-up.

"Where's Brad?" he asked.

"Captured," I said.

"What happened?"

"I don't know. Carla and I left Wertheim, and we were walking back to the rendezvous point when a bunch of Gestapo officers turned up."

"How would they know who he was?"

"I don't know."

"We have to get him out," said Carla.

"Out of where?" said Mark. "We don't know where they've taken him; he could be dead already for all we know."

"Mark's right," I said. "Brad knew the risks when he signed up. We all did."

"Surely we'll be able to get some intelligence that will help us locate him?" said Carla. "He's got a five-year-old son."

"I lost one good man today. I'm not about to lose any more."

"So, we just abandon him to the Gestapo," said Carla.

"I don't like it any more than you. But what's the alternative?"

"What do you think happened?" said Mark.

"You know what it's like," said Bill. "A casual comment, a seemingly innocent exchange. Someone's always watching you."

"We need to get rid of these clothes," I said, starting to undress.

"I'll take care of it," said Bill.

"Remember, we must have no contact for at least a month. Once that bomb goes off the whole of Ost-Bereich will be teeming with the SS and Gestapo. Keep your cool. If we've done our jobs properly, and Brad keeps his mouth shut, they won't have anything on us."

23

25th April 1993

STEPHEN TALBOT

I glanced at my watch. It was almost 14.00. It was a lovely spring afternoon, and I was enjoying a walk on Hampstead Heath. There was a sea of bluebells flowering underneath the tree canopy. The sunshine was weak, but there was a hint of summer in the air.

There were families and courting couples milling aimlessly around the ponds, off-duty soldiers and pensioners sat on benches, all enjoying the glorious day in this natural oasis in the heart of London.

I had made myself a simple packed lunch of ham sandwiches, banana and a can of *Apfelschorle*. I found a free bench in front of one of the ponds and sat munching on a sandwich while reading *The Sunday Times*.

I had been working for the Gestapo for eighteen months, including training at Heydrich House. I still harboured doubts about working for the organisation, especially as a homosexual man, but it was a large institution; it employed a broad range of people and offered varied career paths. There were plenty of power-hungry thugs, but I reconciled my conscience by steering my work towards counterterrorism, where I discovered that I was a naturally talented investigator. I was motivated by my first-hand experience of Piccadilly Circus.

I felt a vibration in my jeans pocket. I took out my pager. It displayed a message: *Call the office immediately.* I sighed, feeling resentful that work was intruding on my weekend.

Rather than use a phone box, I walked back briskly to my apartment, about fifteen minutes away. I was aware of an unusually large number of emergency vehicles speeding through the traffic with their sirens blaring.

Once in my flat, I called HQ. The lines were busy, and I held for five minutes before being connected to my departmental head.

"Kriminalrat Sutton," said the weary voice on the phone.

"Sir, it's Talbot. I'm responding to your pager message."

"You need to get here right away."

"What's happened?"

"You mean you don't know?"

"No, I've been on Hampstead Heath for most of the afternoon."

"For God's sake, Talbot. Get your head out of the clouds. I suggest that you watch the news, then get here as soon as you can. The Underground is not running, so use your car."

"Yes, sir."

I switched on the television and saw an earnest-faced reporter standing in front of Wertheim department store in Knightsbridge. The area had been cordoned off with police incident tape. There were fire engines and a myriad of ambulances and police vehicles outside, their blue lights strobing. Smoke billowed out of the first-floor windows, with firefighters hosing them down. I could see body bags being removed from the building. The headline scrolled across the bottom of the screen: *London suffers a major terrorist attack.*

A suited man began to speak into a camera at the scene.

"Currently, eleven bodies have been retrieved from the rubble, but several more people are reported missing. Many more have injuries, some serious. No warning was given, and so far, no terrorist

group has claimed responsibility. One man is currently helping the Gestapo with their enquiries. The scene here is of absolute devastation. The bomb exploded at 14.00 hours when the store was packed full of shoppers. We know from the fire brigade that the second floor has partially collapsed, making rescue operations difficult. This is Michael Cameron, reporting for Reich Today."

The picture changed back to the stony-faced newsreaders, John Jeffries and Maria Thorpe. Jeffries spoke.

"Thanks, Michael. A devastating picture there outside Wertheim. Just a minute... We're just going to leave the studio again as the Prime Minister is about to make a statement."

The picture changed to a lectern placed in front of 10 Downing Straβe, with dozens of reporters waiting patiently in the foreground.

The Prime Minister emerged and stood in front of the microphones.

"My fellow citizens. It is with a heavy heart that I stand before you, for the second time in my premiership, in the wake of a callous terrorist attack. Firstly, I express my heartfelt condolences to the families who have lost loved ones. My prayers are with them. I also pray for those who have suffered serious injuries. I assure you that they will have full access to the best medical treatment available.

"I can promise you that this cowardly act will not go unpunished. Our revenge will be absolute and without mercy."

Throughout the statement, cameras flashed.

One journalist came forward. *"Prime Minister, what action do you intend to take?"*

"My press secretary will answer your questions. As you will appreciate, the Cabinet and I have a tremendous amount to discuss."

As he spoke, a motorcade pulled into Downing Straβe. Four police bikes, with blue lights flashing, surrounded a black

Bugatti Atlantic. A swastika pennant, fixed at the end of the overly long bonnet, fluttered in the breeze. A senior adjutant opened the rear door and the Governor General, Hans Müller, climbed out, ignoring the camera flashes and questions shouted by journalists.

"Shit!" I exclaimed, switching the television off. I did not bother changing; I just grabbed my car keys and ran to my Beetle. The engine turned over three or four times as I twisted the key. I repeatedly pumped the accelerator in frustration and managed to flood the carburettor. Eventually, I coaxed it to start. The air-cooled engine spluttered into life, and I headed to work.

✠

In the ten minutes that I had spent in my apartment, London's landscape had changed drastically. The cafés, that a short while ago had been bustling with diners, were closed. The streets were eerily devoid of pedestrians. The roads were jammed with cars heading away from the city, but the inward roads were empty.

Upon entering Himmler Tower, it was evident that there was a crisis in full swing. The reception staff looked flustered as they attempted to deal with the massive volume of telephone calls, and the elevators were packed.

I sat at my desk and started rifling through a pile of briefing notes in my inbox. The phones were constantly ringing, and the usually muted calm in the office had been replaced by a sense of nervous urgency. Dot-matrix printers screeched, photocopiers worked overtime, and telex machines tapped out messages.

The forthcoming crackdown was called Operation Iron Hammer, due to begin in less than an hour. An executive decree from the Governor General granted us emergency powers for seventy-two hours, which in essence meant that we could do anything we wanted without jurisdiction or legal restraint, as long as our actions fell within the deliberately vague ministerial edict of bringing the perpetrators to justice.

Effectively, we had absolute power. Should I want to, I could murder, maim or rape without fear of prosecution or recourse. I thought about the two recruits that I had trained with, who were selected for the elite Death Head Division. I shuddered at the thought of what they would be doing over the next three days. I wanted revenge as much as anybody else in the organisation, but against those responsible, not by randomly killing as many people as possible to cow the population into obedience.

I started reading the briefing notes. There were endless pages of the usual dull Gestapo waffle, which I skim-read, circling anything pertinent with a highlighter pen.

A suspect had been arrested but, at this point, he had not given us any useful information. The only thing that had been established was that he was connected to the American-backed resistance, not the communists. Apparently, he was a lookout at a café opposite Wertheim. The restaurant manager was an informer and had become suspicious. The man's clothes were ill-fitting, his accent seemed fake, and he had insisted on a table overlooking Wertheim. The manager engaged him in conversation and apparently knew the suburb where he claimed to live. He dropped in a couple of fake landmarks, and the suspect did not spot glaringly obvious mistakes. Forensics had discovered blood and clothing fibres on a fence enclosing an old bomb site behind Wertheim, where the terrorists were believed to have escaped using the sewers.

My parents often shopped at Wertheim. I was acutely aware that they could have so easily been among the dead. The whole event brought back memories of my hospitalisation after the Piccadilly Circus bomb, my mother's disfigurement, and my impaired hearing.

I used to have a grudging respect for the American-funded rebels, but it seemed that they were now resorting to the same depraved tactics as the communists. There was just no excuse to indiscriminately kill and maim innocent citizens, whatever the cause.

Fred Stanning usually occupied the desk next to mine, but he was notably absent. I was sure that he would be in a meeting, and my instincts proved correct when he emerged from one of the boardrooms at the far end of the office

"How are you?" said Fred.

"I'm just trying to get my head around the briefing papers."

"'Brief' being the irony. This bunch wouldn't know how to write anything concisely."

"Thoroughness is not a bad trait. I see the Stormtroopers are set to go into Ost-Bereich in less than ten minutes."

"There're truckloads of them at the *zwischenwand*. It's like hitting a nut with a sledgehammer. All they'll do is terrorise the inhabitants, destroy valuable evidence, and summarily execute anyone they think is involved. They'll turn the population against us, including our informers. Then, mugs like us have to go in and try and sort out their mess, wondering why nobody wants to talk to us. I remember exactly the same bloody thing happened in the 1986 bombing. They never learn."

"I was caught up in that attack."

"I know. I guess you'll be wanting to get some payback after this?"

"Absolutely. My mother lost an eye because of them. I hate them."

"I'm not surprised. I just want them to realise that their efforts are futile and stop killing innocent bystanders."

"The trouble is, anybody in a uniform or associated with the party is a legitimate target in their eyes."

"Women and children should never be targets."

"I agree."

"I've come to take you to Floor 57. We have a meeting with Kriminalrat Sutton and Oberregierungs Weber."

"Weber? Why would someone like that want to see low-downs like us?"

"I'm as much in the black as you are. However, Sutton has promised me it's nothing to worry about."

"Thank God."

"Hurry up. Trust me when I say that patience is not one of Weber's virtues."

We caught an elevator to the fifty-seventh floor. The executive boardroom was an ultra-modern office with a long walnut table in the middle, surrounded by padded leather chairs. There were conference telephones in the centre of the table. Floor-to-ceiling windows offered panoramic views over the Thames, emphasising how uncharacteristically quiet London was. There were no planes or Zeppelins, and nearby Waterloo Bridge, usually gridlocked, was deserted. The only traffic consisted of police or military vehicles.

Sutton and Weber sat at the far end of the table and beckoned us to take a seat near them. Weber was in his thirties, a tall, Aryan type with neatly cut blond hair, a square jaw and piercing blue eyes set in his chiselled face, which could be described as handsome, were it not for his permanent severe expression. He wore an impeccably pressed black Gestapo uniform with a gold swastika badge on his left lapel, a Glashütte watch, and smelled of expensive aftershave. He was aloof and did not bother to make pleasantries.

"Heil Hitler," said Weber. "Please sit."

"Heil Hitler," we replied in unison, saluting and taking a seat.

"First of all," said Weber, "you should congratulate your sponsor, who we have just promoted to *kriminalinspektor*."

I looked at Fred, who smiled back. I shook his hand warmly.

Weber turned towards me. "We've been very impressed with your record, so far."

"Thank you, sir."

"Talbot has applied himself to his duties, and the quality of his work is akin to an officer with a far greater length of service," said Sutton.

"I respect agents who throw themselves into their work. I've been looking through your personnel file," said Weber. "We have an operation that requires certain – how can I put it? – skills that very few officers in this organisation have."

"Right," I said, confused.

"We would not usually throw an inexperienced cadet into such a critical role, but your two colleagues feel that you are an exceptionally talented recruit and that you would rise to the challenge."

"I would do anything asked of me to the best of my ability."

"An excellent attitude," said Weber. "We live in difficult times, Talbot. The New Order has created two generations of peace in Europe. These terrorist attacks undermine our way of life; everything that our Führer worked for could be destroyed under our noses if we allow this organisation to fester and grow. You are aware of the oath that you took when you joined our ranks?"

"Yes, I am. And I would do anything to protect our society and the legacy of our Führer. If you'll excuse my language, sir, I hate those bastards for what they did to my family and me."

"Good," said Weber. "Hatred is a powerful emotion, to be cherished. Hatred is what gave us the resolve to defeat the Jews and the communists. Sutton, pass Talbot the file."

Sutton handed me a ring binder, stuffed with pages of intelligence.

"You'll be required to read through that today," said Sutton. "It's highly classified, and not to leave your sight or the premises."

"What about the Ost-Bereich operation?" I said. "Will we not be needed for that?"

"No," said Sutton. "Leave the grunt work to the Stormtroopers. We have a much more important role for you to play."

"Really?" I said, intrigued. "Why am I being singled out?"

"If you can cast your memory back to an incident on your record dating from 1988," said Sutton. "Your… relationship with a certain Phillip Tyer, now deceased."

Hearing his name brought back floods of memories. I blinked and cleared my head.

"These tendencies are not tolerated," said Weber. "They undermine the mental health of the populace. It's a disease that we have virtually eliminated now. You have done well to suppress your desires."

"Thank you."

"Aside from Tyer and two isolated incidents at Cambridge, we are aware that you've had no sexual relationships with other males since," said Sutton.

"Correct."

"There are defined circumstances in which we can permit this deviant behaviour," said Weber. "When it is a matter of Reich security, which is why people like yourself are occasionally recruited."

I nodded.

"Open the file," he said. "There's a yellow divider. Turn to that page."

I opened up the ring binder as instructed. There were a series of pictures of varying quality. Most of them were grainy black-and-white photographs from spy cameras, or low-resolution colour images. They showed a muscular young man in his early twenties, with a shaven head and handsome but thuggish looks. The clearest picture showed him topless in a boxing ring, sweaty, wearing a mouth guard and covered in blood, lunging towards his opponent with a red-gloved fist.

"Answer the next question honestly and do not be embarrassed," said Sutton. "Do you find this man attractive?"

His question was direct, and I did feel embarrassed. I fiddled with my fingers under the table nervously and blushed. "Erm… Yes. He is a good-looking, athletic man."

"Good," said Sutton.

"Why are you asking?"

"The man in the pictures – Thomas Jordan – is responsible for the attack earlier today."

"Has he been arrested?"

"No," said Sutton.

"Presumably, he will be soon when the SS move across the *zwischenwand*?"

"That would be the obvious course of action," said Weber. "We can try him publicly, discredit him in any way we choose, then execute him."

"The problem with doing that," said Sutton, "is that we turn him into a martyr. And in any case, somebody will just come out of the woodwork to replace him. The resistance has been rudderless since President Williams left office. Thomas Jordan is a natural leader. He's putting them on the offensive. At the moment, he is only a commander of one small cell. But we have intelligence that he may soon be promoted to sit on the Army Council. The terrorist chatter we have monitored among the other cells shows that his actions are widely admired."

"Shouldn't we be taking him out?"

"As the saying goes, we can cut the head off the Hydra, but another will grow," said Sutton.

"What do you mean?"

"It's easier when you know your enemy, you understand his psyche, you know with whom you are fighting. Like a game of chess, you can predict your opponent's moves and outmanoeuvre him."

"We've had him under surveillance for some time," said Weber.

"Really? How come he got away with the attack on Wertheim?"

"Sometimes, Talbot," said Weber, "difficult choices have to be made."

"What do you mean?"

"If we prevented every single attack, how long before they would uncover our informers? Believe you me, we've stopped many more atrocities like these over the last forty years."

"You mean you could have stopped it?"

"They do themselves no favours when it comes to public opinion," said Weber. "It's a propaganda gift to us."

"At the risk of sounding impertinent, sir, what about the innocents that died in the attack?"

"When the Allies cracked the code for the Enigma machine during the war," said Weber, "they had to make choices over which attacks they would foil. If they anticipated every single one, we would have known that they had discovered the code and issued new machines. Lives have to be sacrificed for the higher purpose. The order came directly from Regierungs Schmidt."

"So where do I come in?"

"We want you to – how can I put this? – get to know this man," said Sutton.

"Erm..."

"Do I have to spell it out?" said Sutton. "We want you to get close to him. To infiltrate the cell he leads."

"You must form a relationship with him," said Weber.

"Are you implying that he is a homosexual?"

"We are fairly confident that he is," said Sutton.

"How confident? I wouldn't fancy my chances with him if you're wrong. I mean, look at the size of him – he's built like a tank."

"His PE teacher informed us that he had suspicions back in his school days," said Sutton. "He was put on a watch list for aversion therapy."

"Suspicions?"

"Teachers are trained to spot this disease, lest it becomes entrenched in society. We can offer these creatures a way out, the chance to have a normal life," said Sutton. "It transpired that Jordan was taken off the list, due to his healthy interest in sport."

"Are you sure it wasn't just a phase at school? Teenagers' hormones are all over the place."

"We don't think so," said Sutton, peering over the top of his rimless glasses, which had slipped down his nose.

"Has he had any kind of physical contact with men that we know of?"

"No," said Sutton. "He knows the risk, and besides, it would be difficult for him to meet other homosexuals in Ost-Bereich."

"We arranged to have various female agents proposition him over the months," said Weber. "They would have been able to get close to him. He has rejected all their advances, and believe me, they are attractive women."

"Perhaps they weren't his type?"

"There's more evidence," said Weber.

"He has been noticed… in the gym changing rooms," said Sutton, fidgeting.

"Noticed?"

"Put it this way: he has a wandering eye," said Sutton. "Our agents are trained to spot this kind of thing."

"That's all circumstantial. And even if he is queer, how do you know he'd be interested in me?"

"I think the easiest way to put it," said Sutton, "is that we believe you are his type. We want you to win his confidence. To seduce him, then pump him for information."

"Do I have a choice in accepting this assignment?"

"Refusal would not look good on your record," said Weber. "To put it mildly."

Sutton took a more positive tone. "Think of the hero you would be. As an agent, you can help us find their weapons stores, who their key commanders are. How they're smuggling arms into the area. You can help prevent another atrocity."

"We're not all about sticks," said Weber. "If you are successful, I can guarantee you a promotion to *kriminaloberassistent*. That means more money and a company car."

I thought about the material benefits that I would obtain from the mission; the esteem that success would bring within the organisation. I also thought about the thrill of being involved in the subterfuge; the excitement of living a double life. I also have to confess; the prospect of seducing Jordan was appealing. Lastly, it was my chance to get revenge on the scum who had maimed my mother and killed so many innocents. However, it was also terrifying. I was putting my life on the line, by associating with cold-blooded murderers. If they ever discovered who I was, the ending would not be pleasant.

"Forgive my caution," I said. "I was taken by surprise a little. I'd be honoured to carry out this mission."

"Excellent," said Weber. "I knew Sutton was right to recommend you."

"Thank you, sir."

"Please be aware that you report directly to me," said Weber. "I've provided you with my personal cell phone number.

If I'm unavailable, my phone will divert to Kriminalrat Sutton. Stanning will also be kept abreast of your progress. We're aware that you two are friends as well as colleagues. He's there to provide you with moral support. We've issued him with a cell phone – so you can contact him directly if necessary. These missions take their toll on us. I trust you will at least have some idea of what you are about to undertake."

"I have."

"Good, because the stakes are high," said Weber. "If you start making mistakes, it's your life that will be in danger. Read through the mission notes today. I'll meet you at 08.00 tomorrow morning."

"Yes, sir."

"The finer details will be in your notes," said Weber. "You will, of course, be moving to Ost-Bereich."

"I assumed I would be."

"It's only temporary," assured Sutton. "These roles have to be played out twenty-four hours a day. You will become the character you play."

"You'll be working alongside the primary target, Thomas Jordan, in the factory," said Weber. "You'll befriend him over a period of time, and we hope more."

"You mean…"

"I'm not going to draw a diagram," said Weber. "I suggest that you read your briefing notes thoroughly and return to this boardroom tomorrow. You're all dismissed."

Sutton, Fred and I left Weber in the boardroom and waited for an elevator.

"A word of advice," said Sutton quietly. "Don't fuck with Weber. Cross him, and he'll destroy you, literally. Prove useful to him and his career, and he'll reward you."

"He's a tosser," said Fred. "You know that and so do I."

I smiled.

"Don't encourage him, Stephen," said Sutton. "Mark my words, he's a dangerous man to get on the wrong side of."

"Thanks for the advice," I said.

The elevator arrived at our floor.

I went back to my desk and read through the mission briefing papers. They were extensive, but there were curious omissions. There was another agent in Adrestia cell, who was a lame duck, as apparently he or she was under suspicion. For reasons unbeknown to me, they did not identify him or her. This ignorance would be mutual. I struggled to comprehend the logic, but accepted that I was a pawn in a game played by powers far greater than me.

It was 20.00 hours before I finished studying the files, so I took dinner in the staff canteen. A television in the corner of the room showed coverage of the SS operation in Ost-Bereich on RT. It had started a few hours ago and was being conducted with ruthless efficiency. The office was much quieter as a result.

The news coverage focused on weapons hauls found during house searches, though often evidence was planted. The pictures of home-made bombs, machine guns and knives provided the regime with a powerful tool to steer public support away from the rebels. It was used to justify their harsh treatment.

The cover story for my mission was simple. I had been transferred to the Schwebke AG television factory from a state-run farm in Bedfordshire by the Sozialplanungsministerium, to replace workers detained or executed during the crackdown.

Thomas would be instructed to train me in soldering circuit boards on a production line. He was being paid an extra five Reichsmarks a shift to do this, a substantial sum of money in the East. It would be an excellent opportunity to mix with him.

My mission name was Stephen Jones. There were many fine details, such as my parents' background, my school, and other things, which I had to memorise.

I was allocated a bedsit in a Georgian town house in Ost-Bereich. I had not seen pictures, but I was not expecting the Berghof. I consoled myself that it would be temporary. Since my own clothing was too smart for a factory worker, I would receive a suitcase full of more suitable items.

I only had two weeks to prepare, but I was excited. I left the office at about 21.00 and enjoyed a rapid car journey home through the deserted streets. Thank goodness for auto number-plate recognition, which meant I could speed through the roadblocks.

✠

When I arrived home, I rang my mother. I let her know that I was not going to be able to speak to her or my father for a while, but not to worry about me. They knew not to ask questions.

I did not sleep well that night. My alarm sounded at 06.00, and I woke up tired. I showered and went to work. I met Oberregierungs Weber in the boardroom on the fifty-seventh floor. Our meeting lasted several hours. We discussed the subtler points of my mission objectives. Weber was very intense, and I was relieved when the meeting finally ended.

"You need to pack your bags tonight for a comprehensive training programme at Heydrich House starting tomorrow," he said. "A car will collect you at 07.00."

"I understand."

"Don't underestimate how tough your assignment will be," he said. "You need to be physically and mentally at your peak. I'll see you back here in two weeks."

24

25th April 1993

THOMAS JORDAN

A single chime from the bell tower of nearby St Dunstan's, indicated it was 16.30. I had watched the consequences of my actions on RT earlier that day. As a result of my decision, children were orphaned or killed. It did not give me pleasure. I knew that there would be reprisals. I deeply regretted that I had let Bill talk me into it. If I could turn the clock back and not plant those bombs, I would.

✠

Later that Sunday, tanks, lorries and Stormtroopers passed through the border checkpoints into Ost-Bereich, and into the cities of Northern England and Scotland. The usual pattern of multiple arrests, violence and random shootings occurred. People were loaded onto trucks, taken away for questioning or worse.

Houses were raided, sometimes torched. Women and children were shot without trial or mercy. There were rapes and beheadings as Nazi Death Heads marched through the East End, unrestrained by anything stupid like human rights.

The sound of gunfire, helicopters and screaming went on into the night. Powerful searchlights from helicopters shone through my thin curtains. The night sky was lit up by floodlights, shellfire and burning houses, accompanied by deafening supersonic booms from fighter jets. Alsatians barked, fire alarms rang, and Stormtroopers shouted at civilians. Tanks rumbled through our streets and bodies soon piled up on street corners.

Everybody was ordered to remain at home and keep their radios tuned to the emergency channel. I waited anxiously for our turn for a visit, but it never came. Stupidly, my uncle, desperate for booze, broke curfew. I begged him not to go. He never came home.

Three days after the purge started, the helicopters stopped flying overhead, and the tanks retreated, leaving devastation in their wake. The heavy police presence remained, and things were tense for a long time. Everybody knew somebody who was taken. Whether it be a missing teacher at school or a closed shop, there were constant reminders.

Five days after the attack, we were told to return to work. I was searched three times during my twenty-minute walk to the factory, which made me late. I felt sick every time I was stopped. The question always in my mind was whether I was being arrested. Had Brad or another cell member confessed? Or had they worked out who I was from the CCTV?

At one point, it even crossed my mind that Brad was a traitor. Perhaps, in reality, he was not stuck in a torture chamber at this very moment, but being debriefed by his superiors. Was he really shot? Or was it a rubber bullet and some good acting? That was how paranoid I felt.

After the attack, security was too tight to contact the other cell members. It would be at least a month before we could risk a meeting, assuming we were all still alive.

✠

When I finally arrived at work, I was bollocked for being late by the manager, Harry. It pissed me off as it was not my fault. Hilda was missing from the production line. We were told that she would be replaced. I toiled away with my soldering iron, full of worry.

There was an air of paranoia at work; people were glad to be alive but edgy, no doubt made worse by the DHPA. That evening, I walked home to my cold, empty house. I turned on the light and looked at the vacant armchair in the lounge. I sank down to my knees.

"What have I done?" I despaired. I looked up at the ceiling and did something that I had not done for many years. I started sobbing. Then the tears became uncontrollable. I clutched a cushion and buried my head in it, weeping.

25

27th April 1993

STEPHEN TALBOT

Any illusion that my stay at Heydrich House was a mini holiday before I was cast into Ost-Bereich was shattered at 05.00 by my personal trainer hollering in my ear. We went on a gruelling ten-mile cross-country run.

There were refresher courses in critical skill areas, including martial arts and target practice. I spent time in the classroom being tested on my identity change. Everything had been thought about. How I would react in certain situations. The names and birthdays of my fictional dead parents, their star signs, my star sign, where I was schooled, my father's occupation, my brother's favourite food. It all had to become second nature to me. They also gave me elocution lessons to tone down my plummy accent.

My cover story was that I was a farmhand on one of the sprawling state collectives in Bedfordshire. This and the adjacent three counties were known as the breadbasket of Europe, exporting wheat to the Lebensraum colonists in Russia. Mass relocation of workers after purges was commonplace and entirely plausible.

During the second week, I had my field equipment training with Kriminalsekretär Green. A jobsworth, to be sure (the session started with filling out a health-and-safety form), but he was thorough.

There was nothing exciting such as exploding pens or jetpacks like you would see in films, but nonetheless, some of the gadgets were pretty smart. I had a cell phone, which used a scrambled channel, hidden in a hollowed-out copy of *Mein Kampf*. An electric shaver doubled as a receiver for some pfennig-sized bugs. My gun – a Walther P73 – was concealed in a fake can of deodorant. They also gave me a key-fob camera. Lastly, I was issued with a silver St Christopher, which contained a cyanide capsule within the locket.

"Give the chain a sharp tug to remove the glass capsule from inside the pendant," said Green. "Bite on it hard to release the poison. It's instant, you'll feel no pain."

"Hopefully, I won't have to use it."

"One more thing," he said, handing me a brown bottle full of tablets. "Make sure you take one of these a day. Start them at least forty-eight hours before you cross over the *zwischenwand*."

"What are they?"

"An antidote to the DHPA we put in the water," he said. "They've just tripled the dosage."

✠

After completing the course, I returned to Hampstead and had a free day to get my affairs in order; mundane things, like making sure bills were paid. I packed a scruffy suitcase with old clothes, issued to me as part of my cover. Fred had warned me that it was only natural to feel anxious, and he was right. So much could go wrong. The resistance was ruthless. It was unlikely the SS could save me in time if I were discovered. That was the risk we all took. Like all servants of the government, from soldiers to postmen, I had sworn an oath to our Eternal Führer and promised to honour and protect the Third Reich with my life, and I would.

26

12th May 1993

STEPHEN TALBOT

The following morning, I met Sutton, Stanning and Kriminalsekretär Green in the fifty-seventh-floor boardroom. I signed out my field equipment and surrendered my warrant card. I had lunch in the staff canteen with Fred, which I expected to be my last decent meal for some time.

In the afternoon, Fred drove me across the capital, in his Passat, to a rendezvous point a kilometre from Checkpoint Delta at the *zwischenwand*. I took my suitcase out of the boot and shook Fred's hand.

"You'll be okay, Stephen," reassured Fred. "If you succeed, you'll help to smash up a terrorist organisation whose leaders think that killing children is a valid form of warfare."

"I'll try not to let you down."

"When you get back," he said, "I'll get us both seats in the Gestapo box at Chelsea."

"That's worth coming home for."

Fred patted me on the shoulder and got back into the car.

I walked to the end of the road. A rusty white minibus pulled up beside me, and I was instructed to sit on a vinyl bench in the back.

At the checkpoint, an SS border guard ordered me to step out with my paperwork. Two more guards had machine guns trained on me. I handed the trooper my documentation. He swiped my identity card through a reader, which displayed *VALID* on a small LCD screen.

"You're transferring from an agricultural complex in Bedfordshire," said the guard.

"I've been assigned a post at Schwebke television factory."

"Hand me your suitcase."

He took my luggage into a Portakabin. I could see him searching through my belongings. He rubber-stamped my papers, returned them, and I climbed back into the van.

"Welcome to Ost-Bereich. We hope that you'll have a most enjoyable life," said the guard sarcastically, before he waved the driver through the raised barrier.

A journey of a mere ten metres across no man's land transported me into an entirely alien environment. The potholed roads were so rough, my head banged against the roof of the vehicle as it bounced along the street. The west side of the wall was smooth grey concrete topped with razor wire. Flower beds had been planted to soften its visual impact, and there were advertising billboards mounted at intervals. By contrast, the east side was covered in anti-government graffiti. I was surprised that it was tolerated. Masses of stinging nettles and weeds ran along the perimeter of the wall in place of the western flower beds. The neatly manicured gardens and freshly painted houses in the West were replaced by scruffy prefabs, decaying Victorian terraces and forbidding tower blocks. The smart new BMW and Mercedes cars parked on the western streets were nowhere to be seen here. There was the odd rusty VW Beetle or the occasional pre-war Austin. It seemed that every lamp post had a collection of black bin bags around it, often split, with the contents strewn around by foxes.

The minibus drove me towards my new home, giving me a glimpse of the neighbourhood. I saw an old bricked-up London Underground station and what passed for a high street, if you call a collection of tatty shops and market stalls a shopping area.

We stopped on a road called Barnet Grove – a cobbled street of neglected Victorian terraced houses.

"Number 86," said the driver in a broad cockney accent. "Three Reichsmarks twenty."

I paid the driver, who unloaded my suitcase onto the pavement.

I looked around. I had never visited Ost-Bereich before, but I had seen pictures. They did not prepare me for the squalor and deprivation. The stench is what really gets you when you first arrive. Rotting food mixed with smelly drains and the ever-present smog, which seemed worse on the east side.

The property looked dire from the front. It overlooked a small park that was really just a piece of scrubland used as a fly-tipping area. I found it frustrating that these people lived like this. The government had spent millions of Reichsmarks trying to regenerate the area, but the people here just did not look after it. Even the new apartment blocks looked scruffy, with dirty net curtains and washing pegged out on clothes lines on the balconies. There was a threatening undercurrent, too, from the scrawny kids playing football in the streets to the thuggish adults drinking outside the pubs.

I rang the doorbell. A frail woman in her seventies answered. This was Ethel, my landlady. She wore a purple dressing gown and hair curlers. She was wrinkled and had thick Medicare spectacles.

"Hello, cock," she croaked, her voice ravaged by decades of smoking. "Mr Jones, I'm guessing?"

"Yes. I've brought my ID and papers."

"Do I look like I'm in the fucking Gestapo?"

I was taken aback by her language.

"The *Völker Wohnungsbaugesellschaft* should have written to you allocating me a bedsit in your house."

"Yes, they did," she said, lighting up a cigarette. "Your room is ready."

"Have they paid the deposit? They should have sent you a cheque."

She coughed into a handkerchief, bringing up phlegm. It was quite revolting to listen to.

"It's the bloody smog. Look at the colour of this."

I felt repulsed as she proffered me a handkerchief covered in dark green mucous.

"Nothing to do with your smoking," I said. I did not know how to take this woman. I had not met anybody like her before. She was just *so* common.

She cackled. "You've got to die somehow. The fags aren't the worst way to go."

She led me up a creaky staircase with a swirly patterned carpet, to a room on the first floor. The whole house stank of cigarettes and cabbages, partially masked by pine air freshener.

"Your room," she said, handing me a set of keys. "The large Yale key is for the front door – the smaller one is for your room."

"Thank you."

"The bathroom is at the end of the corridor. The five of you share it. If you want hot water, you need to put a twenty-pfennig coin in the gas meter in the airing cupboard. That's enough for a quick shower. And please don't leave skid marks in the bog; use the toilet brush."

I opened my bedroom door.

"If you need me, I'm in the flat on the ground floor."

I was at the front of the house, overlooking the park. The room was a 1950s nightmare. I had a small kitchenette in one corner with a sink, an under-counter refrigerator and a tabletop electric oven with some rudimentary utensils. There was a single bed, pre-war wardrobe and chest of drawers in sludgy brown walnut, and a foldaway table. The only luxury was an old Bush valve radio, which took an age to warm up. It was all a far cry from my home in Hampstead.

I started work the next day, so set my alarm clock for 06.00, which would allow enough time to walk to the factory. I busied myself unpacking my suitcase and called the office to let them know I was in place.

Once unpacked, I walked to a nearby corner shop and bought some staples. The shelves were almost bare. I bought the last tin of soup, a loaf of black bread and an English copy of *Der Stürmer*.

After dinner, I lay in bed reading the tabloid, which was full of mind-numbing rubbish, like horoscopes and gossip columns. I guess it provided a distraction for the masses, but at least there was a decent sports section.

I listened to the 21.00 news bulletin on Radio Four. Tensions in the world were building like a pressure cooker. Goebbels wanted to grab headlines to divert attention from the economy and the losses in Africa. The Luftwaffe were flying into American airspace, and the Kriegsmarine had anchored two aircraft carriers off the coast of North Carolina, just inside international waters. These were worrying times.

27

12th May 1993

THOMAS JORDAN

When I got home from work, I found my uncle's ashes left on the doorstep in a small black urn along with an invoice for his cremation. I scattered his remains in the Regent's Canal. He used to enjoy walks along the towpath. I walked back via St Dunstan's Church, lit a candle for him, then knelt in front of the altar and clasped my hands. I heard someone enter and turned around.

"Tom, it's been a while," said the vicar, a short, white-haired man wearing a black shirt with a dog collar. He had a wise face, wrinkled with soft, kind eyes.

"I'm sorry, Reverend. Since my parents died…"

"You don't need to explain. My congregation has been dwindling for years. What's troubling you?"

"It's nothing," I said, standing up. "I'm just leaving."

"It doesn't look like nothing. You've been crying."

"I got my uncle's ashes this morning. From the Gestapo. I've just scattered them along the canal."

"I'm sorry."

"They got the rest of my family. He was the last one. Now it's just me."

"Take a seat," he said, pointing at a pew.

"I'd rather just—"

"Please."

I sat down.

"I can't give him an official funeral – he's classified as a traitor. But maybe we could say a few prayers."

"You wouldn't mind?"

"Of course not. Your uncle was a very sick man. Your father was always worried about him."

"I knew the booze would kill him somehow. He went out to buy a bottle on the black market; he broke curfew. It's all my fault."

"How is it your fault?"

"I can't explain."

"You mustn't blame yourself."

"If only it were that easy. Do you ever wish sometimes that you could turn back the clock? Go back in time and talk to yourself, make yourself see reason?"

"Everybody makes mistakes. It's learning from them that makes us grow as individuals."

"It's the kind of individual I'm growing into that I'm worried about."

"Is there something you want to tell me? You know everything in here is confidential."

"I can't… You know, I never told my uncle how I felt about him. I really loved him."

"I'm sure he knew that."

"I mean – he was a rubbish guardian. He was always pissed, but then he never told me off, never made me clean my room. In a lot of ways, I was lucky."

"And he was fortunate to have you to look after him."

"God, I miss him," I said, welling up again.

"He's gone to a better place, Tom. Why don't we say those prayers?"

Reverend Ainsley picked up a prayer book from the shelf on the pew in front of us, and the two of us paid tribute to my uncle. That was the closest thing that he would get to a funeral.

✠

The following morning at work, I was summoned to see the manager. Harry was a small, rotund, bald man, who wore thick tortoiseshell glasses. He kept us all in line, reporting to the German board of directors. His office was like a broom cupboard. He sat at his desk, piled high with paperwork. A tall blond bloke in casual clothing sat in the other chair with his back to me.

"Ah, Jordan," Harry said, looking up from his computer screen. "Come in, close the door."

"You wanted to see me?"

"I want to introduce you to Jones, here," he replied, pointing at the blond guy.

"Stephen," he said, swinging around. "Call me Stephen, please." He was smiling. I noticed how white his teeth were. I shook his hand.

"Jones is our new trainee, to replace Hilda," said Harry. "The bosses want you to be his mentor."

"Me?"

"It wasn't my decision. The bosses were insistent."

"I can think of better people. What about McGuire?"

"Well, he would have been a more obvious choice. But orders are orders."

I sighed. I was not happy. It was hard enough trying to meet my own production targets without training some numpty at the same time.

"There is some good news," said Harry. "You're going to be paid an extra five Reichsmarks a shift."

"Well, whoopee shit."

"It's twenty-five Reichsmarks a week," said Harry. "That's enough to keep your uncle in whisky. Almost."

"My uncle's dead. I got his ashes yesterday from the Gestapo with a bill for 260 Reichsmarks. Fuck knows how I'm going to pay it."

"I'm sorry, I had no idea. I guess those extra marks will come in handy. You can usually pay the bill in instalments."

"With eighteen per cent interest," I said bitterly. "It'll take me years to clear the debt."

"What happened?"

"He broke curfew. To get some booze."

"I know he was a tortured soul. At least he's at peace now."

"That is some comfort."

"I would offer you some unpaid compassionate leave. But we're so behind with our production quota, I know I won't be able to get it signed off."

"I don't want special favours. Besides, work keeps my mind off it."

"I suggest you take Jones for a tour of the factory. Get him kitted up, then show him the ropes."

"Have you done this kind of work before?" I asked Stephen.

"Never."

"What did you do before this?"

"I was a farmhand. I used to work for the Millbrook Agrarian Collective."

"For fuck's sake. They send us a bloody peasant. You do know this is skilled work? Do you know anything about electronics?"

"We're not building rockets," said Harry. "My nine-year-old can use a soldering iron. Don't worry, Jones, you'll pick it up fine."

I sighed. "Come on then, Farmer Giles, follow me."

"Shut the door behind you," said Harry. "Oh, and Jordan. Try to have a positive attitude. Be thankful that you're fed and have regular work."

"Yes, Harry. What a great life I have."

"Heil Hitler," he replied dismissively, looking down at his computer screen.

✠

Stephen looked Aryan: tall with blond hair, blue eyes, and an athletic build. He was handsome in a toff-like way. I reckoned his grandparents were probably bourgeoisie. Now he was just a prole like the rest of us. I knew that he would go down well with the single women here. Most of that lot were desperate to get married off and start having babies. I did not have enough fingers to count the times I had been asked out.

"The khazi," I said, pointing towards the gents' toilets to the left of the shop floor. "Don't expect potpourri and scented soap. Oh, and don't use it for at least an hour after Mike over there has. I don't know what he eats, but I know the SS Chemical Weapons Division want a supply of his turds."

Stephen laughed.

I led him to a steel staircase at the rear of the factory floor.

"The third floor is where the bosses work," I said, pointing upwards at some windows overlooking the factory. "You hardly ever see them; believe you me, that's for the best. They're Germans, high up in the party. They don't bother us if we do what we're told – just don't piss them off. The second floor is admin. If you have any problems with your wages or anything else, they can usually help. Jackie is really friendly, she's been working here most of her life and knows everything about the company."

We walked up a flight of stairs to the first-floor gallery and looked across the factory floor at the workers in orange boiler suits busy assembling televisions. As always, there was a faint metallic smell, mingled with molten plastic from the injection moulding machines, and the clatter of machinery.

"Most of the stuff we make goes to Germany via the Docklands," I said. "Some of it goes across the *zwischenwand* for the rich. We're supposed to be leaders in the industry."

"I know, I knew somebody who had an eighty-centimetre Schwebke."

"Wow, they must have had money."

"It was our regional party boss," said Stephen hurriedly. "He was boasting about it on an inspection of the farm."

"That makes sense. They supply the party elite. They say Helmut Goebbels has a few in the Reich Chancellery."

"I know they're expensive."

"Well, we can't afford them on our wages," I said, opening the door to the first floor. "Left is the staff canteen. They make a nice lunch, and it's free. Try the goulash – it's got real meat in it and carrots. It's worth having because it ain't easy to get fresh food in the shops around here."

"I discovered that yesterday."

"The changing rooms are on the right. Has Harry given you a locker key?"

"Yeah."

"Good. You'll need to put on some overalls. There are clean ones on the rails. Dump them in the laundry chute at the end of the shift. I'll wait for you here."

After a few minutes, Stephen came out of the changing room wearing an orange boiler suit and a white baseball hat with the company logo on it.

"You're one of us now, mate," I said. I led him down to the production line "If you don't want to wear the hat, get your head shaved like me. There's a decent barber near to the old Bethnal Green Underground Station. He only charges two Reichsmarks."

"I'm not sure where you mean. I'm not used to living in a big city. Would you take me there next time you go?"

"Yeah, sure."

I suggested that he watch me work, while I explained what I was doing.

Stephen made a good first impression on me and most of our colleagues. He was amiable, easy to talk to, and the girls all fancied him, as I knew they would. He even laughed at my sad jokes.

I wish his work were as good as his personality, though. By the end of the day, he attempted to work on his own, following the diagrams. Unfortunately, he was shite, and we binned all of the boards that he worked on. He tried hard, though, and improved as the week went on. By Thursday, he was competent enough to work alone, which took the pressure off the rest of us.

✠

I took him to Mick the barber after work one night, and with a skinhead, he looked like a proper East Ender. I liked hanging out with him. He was new to the area and had no friends, so he latched on to me. I did not mind as I had lost a lot of my friends in the last purge and was glad of the company. He joined my local gym, and we became sparring partners. He had a powerful right hook, making him a tough opponent despite his smaller size. Definitely a wolf in sheep's clothing.

One evening, in the gym showers, I decided to start a towel fight.

"Ow, that bloody hurts," he said as I whipped him with the end of my towel.

"Fight back, then."

"I'm not twelve years old."

"Boring."

"God, it's not often I feel inadequate," he said, looking up and down my torso.

"A couple of years in the East End, and we'll soon turn you into a man," I said, enjoying the attention.

"Yeah, right."

"Exercise and diet."

"If *you* are what you eat, you'd be a giant can of Spam."

"Fancy a stein, once we've showered?" I laughed.

"Why not?"

After we had showered, I took him to The Black Horse.

"Let me introduce you to an old haunt of mine," I said. "You've not experienced class until you've tried this place."

"It's... erm..." He paused, looking at the faded, rusty sign swinging pathetically on its hinges, and the cracked windowpanes on the door.

"By class, I mean lower class. It's a shithole – but you'll learn to love it."

"It can't be any worse than my old local. That stank of manure."

"Remember, we are entering the world of the cockney pub. Some of their customs may seem strange, their mannerisms odd, their body scents offensive. Do not make prolonged eye contact. Only speak to people if you have to. Use the toilets at your peril."

"Dickhead."

"It's for your own safety."

I took him inside and walked over to the long mahogany bar. It was a quiet night with just a few punters.

"Meet Trev," I said. "He's a fat bastard with a BO problem, but his ales are the best in London. Or so he tells us."

"Charming as ever," said Trevor, running his hand through his greasy black hair. "Your usual?"

"Please."

"And what about your boyfriend?"

"I'm not his—" said Stephen.

"He's winding you up," I said.

"He's got to be a fairy with teeth like those," said Trevor.

"It takes one to know one," I said.

"Where did he pick up that accent?"

"Bedfordshire," said Stephen. "Can I have a strawberry daiquiri?"

"No, you fucking can't."

"He'll have a London Pride like me," I laughed. "What's a strawberry dack… whatever you said?"

"My attempt at humour."

"You are a very sad man. Very sad."

"Trev, make it a Bitburger, would you?" he said.

"You're a lager man, then?"

"My dad used to say two good things came from the Occupation – we get German lagers, and they lowered the drinking age."

"Nah, lager is shite," I said, taking a slurp of my beer.

"One Reichsmark ninety," said Trevor.

"Jesus Christ, Trev, that's gone up since Saturday."

"Don't you watch the news?" he said. "Does *Nationales Fitnessjahr* ring a bell?"

"Some bollocks about putting taxes up on unhealthy stuff to get us all fit," I said.

"It's wank," said Trevor. "Everything's going up. Food, petrol… everything except our bloody wages. Don't think I'm making any extra out of it."

"I'll pay," said Stephen.

"Nah, these are on me, mate," I said. "You get the next round in."

We sat at a private table near the dartboard.

Stephen downed half of his stein in one gulp.

"Steady on, mate. It's a school night."

"I was gasping for that."

"Fancy a game?" I said, pointing at the pool table.

"Sure – do you like losing?"

Stephen was brilliant at pool. It seemed he was bloody good at everything. Good-looking, intelligent, good at sports and exceptionally friendly. What a wanker. Except that he wasn't. I don't think I had ever met such a good bloke.

"They have a competition here every Thursday – it's fifty pfennigs to enter, and the top prize is ten Reichsmarks."

"I just play for fun," he said, potting the black and winning the third game in a row. "You're a pretty good player too. You just need more practice."

"Where d'you learn?"

"We had a staff games room at the Millbrook Collective. I've been playing since I was fourteen."

"Your round," I said.

"Do you like working at Schwebke?"

"Do I bollocks. It's a shithole. But it pays my bar tab. I just live for the weekends."

"The work's pretty dull."

"That's the understatement of the century."

"Have you copped off with any of the girls there?"

"Nah. The ones I fancy are either married or out of my league."

"I can't imagine anyone being out of your league."

"Yeah, right, I've just got so much to offer."

"What about Cathy? She's well fit. She's always flirting with you."

"You're welcome to her, mate."

"What's wrong with you? She's got tits the size of watermelons."

"She's also been through half the factory."

"Never!"

"It's true."

"How long have you been single?"

"Forever."

"You must have had a girlfriend some time. A good-looking bloke like you."

"I focus on my boxing so much, it's hard to find a girl that will put up with me training all the time."

"You've *never* had a girlfriend?"

"Well, there was one, once. She was a blonde. Gemma."

"And what happened?"

"We were six years old. We just grew apart."

He laughed. "Seriously, though, what would your ideal girl be?"

"I've not really thought about it," I said uncomfortably. "I never seem to have time for someone else in my life."

"There's always time for chicks."

"What's with all the questions? You're worse than Bill."

"I just don't get how someone as eligible as you doesn't have more of a history."

"Did you have anyone special back in Bedfordshire?"

"No," he replied. "I'm a bit like you. I like my independence. I'd much rather have a night out with the lads."

"Me too. Any significant exes?"

"There is one, but it's too complicated to explain."

"Try me."

"Another time. It's still a bit raw."

"Sounds a bit fairyish, but I'm so glad you were reassigned down here."

"Why's that?"

"'Cause you're an awesome bloke, and it's great getting to know you."

"Cheers for that," he said, raising his stein. "To friendship."

I clinked my glass stein against his. "To the best mate a bloke could get."

It was supposed to be a quiet night, a couple of midweek steins, but we stayed until closing. Sometimes, you have to live for the moment. Stephen was worried that I was a little too drunk, so he walked me home.

I put the key in my front door.

"See you tomorrow," he said.

"Yeah. Hope your hangover's not too bad."

He patted me affectionately on the back, which turned into a bear hug that went on for an unusually long time. I stumbled into my house.

28

August 1993

STEPHEN TALBOT

The first few months of my undercover mission progressed well. I worked shifts at the Schwebke AG television factory. The work was mind-numbingly dull, but the people were pleasant enough, though downtrodden – hardly surprising given the emergency DHPA levels. I reported to Weber daily. I also spoke to Fred regularly, who helped maintain my sanity.

I did not have access to my real bank account. Instead, I had to live off the factory wages, paid weekly in cash. Most of my income went on food, rent and booze. I also decided to rent a portable television from my landlady, who I did not trust. I knew that she had been snooping around my bedroom, as I could smell her cigarettes and cheap perfume. I was careful to keep my espionage equipment well hidden.

Tom was intriguing. Handsome in a rugged way, and very masculine, I found him attractive. I was still not sure if he was a homosexual, though. His body language gave nothing away. If anything, he seemed anti-homo.

The public enlightenment advertisements warned of effeminate creatures with an unhealthy interest in young boys, who lingered in public toilets. Tom was far removed from this

– a macho, sport-loving male, yet seemingly not interested in girls.

We spent much time together, and I knew that he valued my friendship. I forced myself to retain an emotional detachment. When I drank with him, I listened rather than spoke. It was not an overnight task to gain his trust. Above all, I had to remind myself what he was and what he had done. He was a cold-blooded murderer. The blood of dozens of innocent citizens stained his hands. It was due to people like him that my mother had lost an eye, and I had nearly died.

A large part of me hated him and what he stood for. Each morning, I shaved and looked at the scar above my eyebrow. The injury that was down to people like him. As physically attractive as he may have been, he was a terrorist. I tried to keep this at the forefront of my mind. I was working towards a time when he felt confident enough to talk about this hidden part of his life, but I knew that it required patience.

As expected, Tom was vehemently anti-Nazi. It was surprising how open the dissent was in Ost-Bereich. During these treasonable conversations with Tom, I drew upon some of my own disillusionment with the regime. I always kept in mind that I was part of the system, however imperfect, that had kept peace in Europe for over forty years as well as massively improving living standards for the majority. Objectors like Tom offered no real alternative, just anarchy.

Ignoring his darker side, I found him to be a surprisingly amiable guy, with a good sense of humour. He was uneducated but intelligent, loyal and effusive. If he had not been a terrorist, and the law on homosexuality had been different, I even think that I could have fallen for him.

Since it was likely that I would have to terminate him at some point, I put aside childish fantasies and focused on my mission. Oberregierungs Weber expected progress, and I was under tremendous pressure. My infiltration of the resistance had barely begun.

My mission was against a backdrop of ratcheting tensions between the world superpowers – the USA-backed AFN or Alliance of Free Nations, China and Nazi Europe. The current flaring point was Africa. Backed up by American air power and military equipment, the Saudis had successfully pushed the Nazis out of Egypt and were amassing an army on the border of Nazi-occupied Libya.

Libya was crucial to the Reich, both militarily and economically due to its oil reserves. The Mediterranean Sea had turned into a potential ignition point between the superpowers, with dozens of warships from both sides patrolling the coast of Africa.

There were frequent displays of brinkmanship with increasingly bellicose statements from Goebbels. This sabre-rattling continued, with Goebbels anchoring warships just inside international waters, but deliberately close to America's East Coast. There were regular intrusions by the Luftwaffe into American airspace. One mistake from a rogue pilot or a trigger-happy sailor could result in world war. America would only take so much provocation.

The international tension created an ideal distraction from the losses in Africa and buried other poor domestic news regarding the slumping economy in the Reich. Inflation was increasing in a continent where older people still remembered the hyperinflation that ravaged the Weimar Republic in the 1930s. The federal government's budget deficit was unsustainable, and unemployment was rising rapidly.

The Second World War had come to a grisly conclusion with Germany dropping five primitive atomic bombs on Moscow, Stalingrad and Leningrad. The fourth was dropped on another Russian city, Novosibirsk. It failed to detonate correctly, but poisoned the city with radioactive material. The fifth was destined for England – the industrial city of Birmingham – but the plane was shot down by the RAF near Dover. However, the pilot managed to detonate the bomb, wiping out a significant portion of the Kent countryside.

The Soviet Union surrendered to the Nazis within days. Britain held out for as long as they could against Operation Sea Lion, led by Field Marshal Walther von Brauchitsch, but catastrophically weakened from the nuclear attack, it proved futile. The royal family were evacuated to Canada, then later America, and Britain fell in a matter of weeks.

Now, five countries had nuclear weapons that were far more sophisticated and destructive. A third world war could mean the end of humanity. It was a worrying time.

The change in the American stance would in all likelihood mean a resumption in support for the BLA – the British Liberation Army, and a flow of weapons and equipment, which would ultimately mean more Wertheim-style attacks. Time was of the essence.

✠

In late August, on a Saturday night in what had now become my local, The Black Horse, I decided to make a move on Tom. I had plied him with beer to lower his guard.

The pub was packed. It was a typical London drinking establishment, an old Victorian building with high ceilings, a long bar, and little tables with four-legged stools. It stank of cigarette smoke and beer. It was rough but strangely charming, and I felt oddly at home.

We sat near the bar, and I lowered my voice conspiratorially. "Can I ask you something?"

"Where I get my good looks from?" slurred Tom.

I laughed nervously. "Well… I've often wondered," I joked, trying to gauge his reaction. "Seriously, though, I know that like me, you're a regime hater."

"Who isn't? I fucking hate Krauts. Hey, have you heard the song *Hitler Has Only Got One Ball*?"

"Shhhh," I warned, looking around furtively.

"It's my country. I'll say what I bloody want."

"There are soldiers over there," I said, pointing at a group of Germans from Hackney Barracks, talking to some local girls.

"Fuck 'em. I'm not scared. Oi, you German wankers, drink like Englishmen."

Fortunately, the officers did not speak good English, but they did not look impressed.

I put my arm protectively around Tom and whispered in his ear.

"Mate, you need to calm down, or you'll get us both in trouble – seriously."

Tom became more emotional and bashed his fist on the table. "They fucking killed my family."

Trevor, the landlord, moved in quickly, asking Tom to quieten down or leave.

"You shouldn't let the fuckers in," said Tom.

"Their money is what keeps this place going," said Trevor. "Any more language like that and you're barred."

"Dickhead," said Tom under his breath. "I mean, why do they come in this shithole when they've got all the lovely beer halls on the other side of the wall?"

"I guess, because it's cheap," I said.

"It's not like they don't get paid enough."

"I know how you feel, I lost my parents too, but they're regular soldiers, not SS."

"They're still Krauts."

"Tom…" I sighed wearily.

"I'm sorry. I can get a bit emotional when I get pissed."

He squeezed my hand before I withdrew it.

"I need to speak to you, about something delicate."

"What?"

"I'm taking a big risk in asking you this."

"Spit it out, then."

"Say… Just suppose that I wanted to get actively involved in the resistance. I think you might know who to speak to?"

"I don't know what you mean."

"Oh, come on, Tom. I've known you for months. I just need a name."

"Do you know what you're asking me?"

"This isn't a whim on a Saturday-night piss-up. I've thought very carefully about this for some time."

"We can't have this conversation in here," said Tom, who had changed from being rowdy and indiscreet to Mr Sensible. "Come home with me."

I helped him stumble back home. I knew where he lived, but had never been inside before. As expected, it was scruffy, and I did not think that Tom had heard of the word 'housework'.

"I need some water," said Tom, slumping onto a chintzy sofa.

"Where's the kitchen?"

"Over there." He pointed.

I filled up a glass with water from the tap.

"No," he said. "The tap water is… Just pour it away. There's water in the fridge."

I found a jug in the refrigerator and poured him a glass. He took it gratefully and glugged it down.

"Why don't you drink tap water?"

"Because of the chemicals in it."

"You mean the chlorine?"

"No. The bastards put a drug in it to keep us all pacified."

"Really?"

"Yeah, really. Try boiling your water before you drink it, you'll notice the difference very quickly."

"How did you find out?"

"I know things."

"Like how to join the resistance?"

"You aren't subtle, are you? Have you thought it through? Because once you're in, there's no turning back and the likelihood is you'll get caught and die in a Gestapo torture chamber. They get us all at some point."

"You said *us*. So, you do know something?"

"We're all aware of something. This is the East End."

I could see his eyelids drooping. I walked over to him and crouched down.

"You're so beautiful," he said sleepily.

"So are you."

My words were not empty. He looked stunning with his muscles bursting out of his tight T-shirt. God, I wanted him so badly. Daringly, I gave him a kiss on the cheek. He did not seem to mind, he even appeared to respond a little – but he was very drunk. Why did somebody so bloody attractive have to be a terrorist?

Tom shut his eyes and started snoring gently. I snapped myself back into work mode. For all his boasting, Tom was no match for me when it came to drinking. Three years at Cambridge had taught me how to handle alcohol like a professional. I knew I could function for hours longer if I needed to. If only I had not got Tom drunk to the point that he passed out, maybe I could have continued the seduction.

While he was sleeping, I took the opportunity to explore his house. I did not find anything directly connected to the resistance, but I did find a square biscuit tin of newspaper clippings and photographs under his bed, which gave me a glimpse into a life that could not have been more different to mine.

There were some grainy photos taken with a cheap camera. One was of his family enjoying a day out by the seaside. Tom was holding an ice cream. There was some writing on the back in red biro: *Southend, 20th June 1983*. He would have been ten years old in those pictures. He had a cheeky smile and bright eyes. It was hard to comprehend that an innocent little boy like that would turn out the way he did. It was apparently a special occasion as he had even kept the travel permit, like some kind of souvenir.

There were other pictures of him in the boxing ring, fighting or holding various trophies. He had kept press cuttings about the purges in Ost-Bereich in 1985 when he lost his family. Then there were articles from *Der Stürmer*, about the Wertheim bombing.

I put the box back under his bed. I rifled through his drawers. He had some pictures of football players and topless athletes torn out of magazines. There were several issues of *Boxing News* and *Muscle & Fitness*. I picked up one and leafed through the well-used pages, feeling aroused by the men with chiselled chests. I put it back embarrassedly. Was this evidence that Tom might be attracted to men, or just inspiration for his workouts?

I looked around the room, but there was nothing else particularly out of the ordinary. No guns or bomb-making equipment. I removed the duvet from Tom's bed and took it downstairs, where he lay on the sofa. I put it over him gently, and instinctively gave him a kiss on the forehead. Then I took the opportunity to plant a bug in the sitting room, concealed in a lampshade, which would be monitored by a crew in Hackney Barracks.

I took a long, lustful look at Tom, who had blacked out. Then I left, feeling a curious mixture of guilt and job satisfaction.

✠

When I arrived home, I made my report to the office. In theory, everything was proceeding according to the action plan laid out in my briefing notes. I had made my intentions clear, and with luck, Tom would invite me into the unit that he led. If I did my job correctly, he would be a valuable source of intelligence, notably, as it was likely he would join the Army Council.

Tom was affable, and his rough edges were endearing. There were many layers to him. Plainly, he had been radicalised at some point. However, I had to tread carefully and remind myself of his history. If he ever uncovered my real identity, I knew that he would kill me without hesitation.

29

29th August 1993

THOMAS JORDAN

I woke up, hung-over, on the settee with my duvet on top of me. I tried to remember the previous night. I recalled Stephen acting like a twat by asking me about the resistance in the middle of a busy pub full of Krauts. Then it came back to me that I was swearing at them. *Note to self: drink less in public.*

Stephen had proven himself to me, and I would put it to our group that we recruit him. We needed a replacement for Brad. Stephen was smart, a good fighter, and he hated the Nazis. Just what our cell needed.

On Monday evening, in the gym, Bill let me know that our entire cell had been summoned before the Army Council, to answer for the Wertheim operation. I was not looking forward to it. The best I could expect was a major bollocking; it was best not to think about the worst. The ruling Army Council did not look kindly on cells acting without their say-so. I had used their equipment, their maps, and operated in their name. I knew that I could not hide from them, and Bill had warned me not to even think about being absent.

The meeting was being held at the Bevis Marks Synagogue, close to the defunct Aldgate Tube Station, two blocks from the *zwischenwand* and close to the gleaming new financial district, which the Nazis boasted was proof of how well the economy was doing. A load of old shit that nobody with half a brain cell believed. Even if there was some food on the supermarket shelves, it was unaffordable these days.

In the shadows of the skyscrapers across the wall, lay a shattered piece of London laid to waste by the Luftwaffe, which had never been rebuilt. It was notorious for unexploded bombs, plus the rubble made the streets difficult for police cars to patrol, making it an ideal place to meet. The Nazis pretended it was a radioactive area to keep people out, but we knew this was bollocks.

It was a dry late-summer evening, with a thick smog. I made my way to the synagogue under cover of darkness, wondering whether I would come back with my legs attached. I climbed through a small gap in the wire fence, into the so-called radioactive zone, marked by ominous yellow-and-black signs.

This area had not been lived in for fifty years and had turned into a mini wilderness. Wildlife had blossomed. Trees had grown through the rubble. The ruined buildings were covered in ivy, where birds nested. To some, it was an apocalyptic scene, but to me, it was calm and beautiful.

Finding my way around with hardly any street names or landmarks was hard as I had never been here before. I had to use the Deutsche Commerzbank tower across the wall, with its bright orange sign on top, to get my bearings. *Just head towards it*, they'd told me. Needless to say, I got lost and was the last to arrive.

Bill, Carla and Mark were sat on a pew in front of two members of the Army Council, who looked intimidating, wearing balaclavas and holding machine guns. My friends looked unharmed but nervous.

"Thomas," said one of the masked men as I entered. He spoke with an upper-class accent. "The main culprit. Late. Take a seat."

I sat next to Carla on the pew, which was in surprisingly good nick given it was exposed to the elements. She squeezed my hand. I was grateful.

The synagogue had survived the German bombs, only to be desecrated by SS troops during the ground invasion. A few badly burnt wooden beams were suspended where the roof once was. The windows were smashed in, and the inside mostly stripped. The only clue to the building's past was the anti-Semitic graffiti.

I looked up at the dark, hazy sky through the top of the roofless structure. Was this a court martial conducted by a kangaroo court? Would they execute us as an example to the rest of the organisation? Why else would they bring machine guns?

A heavily built man in camouflage started speaking. "We don't use full names here. I'm Joe H. This meeting is far from ideal, but you've made it necessary." He raised his voice. "What the fuck were you all thinking?"

"It's not their fault," I said. "They followed me. I take responsibility."

"You acted as a unit," said Joe H. "You will all stand accountable."

"They followed my lead," I repeated.

"We'll face this together," said Carla insistently. "We're not sheep, we knew what we were doing."

"Are you going to kill us?" I asked.

"It's certainly crossed my mind," said Joe.

Bill spoke. "It was me who sowed the seed in Tom's mind. If anything, I should be the one facing punishment."

Another man stood up. He had the rank of general and referred to himself as Charles K. "We don't and won't tolerate vigilante attacks."

"Your actions have caused untold misery," said Joe. "Thousands have been murdered as a result."

"Don't you think I know that?" I said. "Don't you think it haunts my thoughts every day? Don't you think I lie in bed at night and wonder what became of Brad?"

"And you bloody should feel guilty," said Joe. "You've lost us a lot of popular support, not just in Region 6, but in America too. How do you think it makes us look? We're an army, and an army needs to have a chain of command."

"But think what we achieved," I said.

"And what, for fuck's sake, is that?" said Joe.

"We got the attention of the world."

"You don't win hearts and minds by having TV pictures of children dead on stretchers," said Joe. "You're seriously fucked up if you thought that would gain us public support."

"What are you going to do with me? With us?"

"Stand up and come here," said Joe.

I slowly rose from the pew and moved towards him. Joe took out a pistol.

"Kneel down with your hands on your head."

I looked at Joe's steely grey eyes through the hole in his balaclava. They were cold, emotionless, but full of conviction. Was I to be murdered by a fanatic whose face I had never seen? Slowly, I knelt down.

"Face the others," he ordered.

I shuffled around, terrified. The others looked on in disbelief.

Joe pointed the pistol at the base of my skull.

"You can't," shouted Carla. "This is murder."

"For pity's sake," said Bill. "Joe, you're better than this. This is not who we are."

I felt a sharp pain as Joe pistol-whipped me. I collapsed on the floor, clutching the back of my neck. He hauled me up and shoved me towards the others. Carla helped me sit down.

"God, that hurts." I winced.

"It was meant to," said Joe. "But it hurts less than a bullet through your knackers would have. Let me make this very clear. If you ever try anything like the Wertheim attack again, I'll execute you myself."

"All right, all right," I said.

"So that's it?" said Mark.

"For now," said Joe. "Unfortunately, we need you. We lost a lot of fighters in the last purge; we can't afford to lose you, particularly since you seem to be admired by so many among us."

"Really?"

"It may have been bloody stupid," said Joe, "and no doubt a self-induced testosterone-fuelled boost to your already overinflated ego, but it was brave."

"Thanks."

"It's the only compliment you'll ever get from me," said Joe. "Your own cell has been weakened, four others have been wiped out completely. However, some of our people seem to be in awe of what you did."

"I had to do something. We've been waiting around for years. What's the point of our organisation?"

"I've asked myself those questions too," said General K, frowning. "Perhaps we should be more proactive. Still, at least we have some positive news to share. There has been a development. This meeting is not just about giving you a bollocking."

"To put it succinctly," said Joe, "President Turnbull has approved a plan to liberate Britain."

"This is highly classified," said General K. "The plan is to attack in January next year. I realise that it's only months away, barely enough time to prepare adequately."

"We'll have the might of the American Navy, Air Force and ground troops on our side," said Joe. "The Nazis won't know what's hit them."

"We've waited long enough for help from them," said Bill.

"I know," said the general. "But we have to put ourselves in the position of the Americans. It's likely that they are going to spill a lot of their countrymen's blood to liberate a tiny island, thousands of miles away. Much of the plan remains confidential, but I can tell you that the operation is code-named Achaeans' Revenge, and the BLA will be playing a crucial role."

"Surely, you can tell us more than that," said Bill. "We need to train and equip ourselves."

"You'll be informed of your parts nearer the time on a need-to-know basis," said Joe. "For now, be patient, and that means you too, Tom."

"Keep up your physical fitness levels, and hone your fighting skills," said the general. "Re-familiarise yourselves with your firearms and focus on the task ahead. Remember, we're preparing for war. And stay alive. God save Princess Elizabeth."

"God save Princess Elizabeth," we all replied.

"May I ask something?" said Carla.

"Yes," said Joe.

"Is there any news on Brad?"

"None. If he's lucky, he'll be dead."

"Bill and Tom, I want you to stay," said the general. "Carla and Mark, it's time for you to go."

Carla and Mark stood up and left the building.

"There's something further that needs discussion," said Joe. "As you know, Bill is leaving the Army Council, meaning there is a vacancy."

"I don't like to admit it," said the general, "especially after what has just been discussed, but as immature as you are, I think that you might be right for the position."

"You mean, you'll be able to keep an eye on me," I said.

"That isn't our motive," said the general.

"Bill has been pushing you as his replacement," said Joe. "He speaks highly of you. It's not a responsibility to be taken lightly. But I do admit, we need someone with balls. Some fresh blood."

"And my lack of experience doesn't count against me?"

"We all have to start from somewhere," said the general. "Bill will sponsor you into the position."

"Don't underestimate the commitment," said Joe. "Or the risks."

"You'll make life-and-death decisions," said the general. "Every time you hear a knock on the door, you'll wonder if it's the Gestapo catching up with you."

"That's how it is now."

"But you'll become a much bigger fish," said the general. "Which means you'd be a more valuable prisoner. You'll have access to names, information and plans. You'll learn who our contacts are in the government. Any of the ruling council members have the knowledge to destroy this organisation from within."

"Bill has proposed you," said Joe. "I am prepared to second you. General?"

"Motion passed, subject to the approval of the rest of the committee, which I think will be a formality," said Joe. "Do you accept membership?"

"Yes, without hesitation."

"Congratulations," said Bill.

"And please don't think I was joking when I said I'd kill you if you repeat anything like Wertheim," said Joe.

"I've got the message. You won't regret this."

"I hope not," said Joe.

General Charles K handed me a two-way radio. "Switch it on at midnight every night. It's American made, highly advanced. The transmissions are scrambled."

"Time for you to head home," said Joe. "We'll be in contact with you over the next few weeks. You've a lot to learn."

30

Early September 1993

STEPHEN TALBOT

I sat at my workstation, next to Tom.

"Do you have plans this weekend?" I asked casually.

"I think I'm going to have a quiet one. I'm still recovering from last weekend's hangover."

"Fair enough."

"And I need to save money. I can barely make the rent this month. I'm lucky I've been allowed to stay in my uncle's house. If I'm late paying, they might put me in a bedsit like you."

"I guess I'll be having a quiet night too, since you're my only friend."

"Shall I get the violins out?"

I sighed. "I've got my portable telly for company."

"For God's sake. Come over for your tea on Saturday."

✠

On Saturday, I wore the smartest clothes that I owned on this side of the *zwischenwand* and doused myself with aftershave.

On the way to Tom's, I bought some beers and whisky from the off-licence. The whisky had gone up five marks in a week. I barely got change out of a twenty.

Tom opened his front door. He had made no effort to dress up or even shave.

"You look like you're off to the Ritz," he said.

I laughed. "I've brought some booze."

We sat on his tatty sofa, and I handed him a tin.

"What's for dinner?"

"My speciality – corned beef fritters."

Tom downed his can.

"Before you get too drunk," I said. "What I said to you last weekend..."

"It's all in hand, Farmer Giles."

"Stop calling me that."

"What are you going to do about it?" he teased. "You off to milk some cows, then? Careful you don't get the pox."

"I'll knock you out."

"Fancy your chances, do you?"

Tom started mock-punching me in the stomach. I blocked his fist.

"Come on, then. Fight back."

I stood up, and he rugby-tackled me to the ground. I struggled against his grip, feeling his muscular chest against mine. He pinned my arms back against the carpet, his face inches from me.

"Do you give up?"

Tom's confidence was misplaced, but I pretended to be submissive.

"Fuck off."

"Temper, temper. So, you're not the big girl everyone thinks you are."

"Who thinks I'm a big girl?"

"Half the factory."

"They're supposed to be my friends..."

"I'm joking. Fuck knows why, but you're quite popular."

I gave up pretending to try to free myself and let my arms go limp. He held me for a few seconds, looking at me with those hazel eyes. I glanced at his Ramsgate tattoo.

"Do you ever think about getting that removed?"

"No. It keeps me focused on the cause."

"'The cause,' he says to me. And of course – you're not in the resistance."

"Dickhead," he said. "I'm sure you're an Aryan. Not pure-blood, but there's German in you."

"That's what my parents used to say. Much good it ever did me."

"What happened to them?" he said, releasing his grip and rolling over onto his side.

I sat up with my back against the base of the sofa. "They were rounded up, one morning, along with half the farmworkers."

"How old were you?"

"Twelve."

"I was fifteen when they took mine."

"I knelt before the Führer's statue in our village square. I begged for his mercy. My parents toiled in the fields all day, never complaining. They weren't interested in politics. I never saw them again."

"I'm sorry."

"I want revenge."

"You'll get your chance."

"You *are* with the resistance?"

"Stop with all the bloody questions, will you?"

He ran his forefinger gently along the scar above my eyebrow.

"How did you get that?" he asked.

"An SS beating."

"What for?"

"Do they need a reason?"

Tom patted me gently on the head, then stood up. I sat back on the sofa.

"I'll get tea ready," he said, going into the kitchen.

I sighed. It was proving difficult to get an admission out of Tom.

"Put the television on if you want," he shouted. "I splashed out on a colour one from Granada Rentals."

I switched it on. It was an old model, so it took a few minutes for the valves to warm up. It was tuned to Channel Two.

"What's on?" shouted Tom over the sound of a sizzling pan.

"Bob Abbott's *Generation Game*."

"I hate that programme."

"It's that or the news."

Tom brought out two plates of red mush, which we ate from our laps, sitting on what Tom quaintly called the settee.

"What do you think?" he said, talking with his mouth full.

"Not bad at all."

"Nineteen seventy-five."

"What?"

"Bob asked them when the Treaty of Valencia was signed. When Spain became part of the Reich after General Franco died."

"Those poor fuckers never knew what hit them."

We had tinned fruit cocktail for dessert, and continued drinking in front of the television. *The Peelers* started, an urban police drama.

"Riga whisky," said Tom. He took a swig straight from the bottle, but cursed as he spilt it on his T-shirt.

"I'll get a tea towel."

"Don't bother. It needs a wash anyway. What a waste of good whisky."

He took off his T-shirt and flung it into a corner. I glanced lustfully at his incredible physique.

He stood up and turned off the television. "I can't cope with that acting. How about some music instead? Do you like classical?"

"Yes, I love it. Just not opera, I bloody hate opera."

He opened a box full of records. "Chopin?"

"Perfect."

The room filled with the sound of piano music.

"Nice stereo."

"It was my father's. He loved music. It got damaged in a house raid, but I managed to repair it. There's got to be some perks to working in electronics."

"*Waltz in C-Sharp Minor*?"

"You know your classical music, then?"

"My parents loved Chopin."

"My parents loved it too. The SS smashed up most of their LP collection."

"Bastards."

"Just because we're working class, it doesn't mean we can't do culture."

"You are full of surprises."

"I am, but so are you." He looked me straight in the eyes. "So much about you is a mystery. I always get this feeling that you're hiding something."

"What do you mean?" I said nervously.

"You turn up at the factory out of the blue, with some sob story about being orphaned at twelve, wanting to join the resistance. It don't add up. Are you a Gestapo agent?"

"What do you think?"

"You'd hardly admit it if you were."

"For God's sake," I said, feeling exposed. "I am *not* Gestapo. I hate them as much as you do."

"Prove it."

"How?"

"Why are you here tonight, with me, alone in this dump of a house watching shit television, eating crap food?"

"We're good mates, aren't we? I enjoy your company."

"There's something more than that."

"I'm lonely in a new neighbourhood that I know nothing about. I thought we got on."

"Why do you insist on spending so much time with me? I wanted to be alone this weekend."

"Maybe it's time for me to come clean."

"I knew something was going on."

"Tom, I promise I'm not Gestapo, but you are right – I do have an ulterior motive for being here. Can I be honest with you?"

"Yeah – of course."

"You have to be open-minded with what I'm about to tell you."

"I've got my own secrets, trust me on that one," said Tom, swigging some more whisky.

"When I was younger – God, where do I start with this? – I spent a lot of time with a lad called Phillip, who used to be in my school class. He was my best friend. We were close. Very close. He was my soulmate."

"God help me."

"Please, don't take the piss… It's hard for me to talk about this."

"All right, mate, I'm only messing."

"I spent a lot of time with Phillip. Shortly after my sixteenth birthday, we met in a… a field near the farm. We admitted we were falling in love." I took a deep breath. "We kissed. It was the most amazing and intimate moment of my life."

"Did I just hear right?" said Tom, standing up. He started pacing.

"Yes."

"Fucking hell, mate. I can't believe you've just sprung that on me."

"Sorry."

"What happened?"

"Somebody spotted us. We were reported. Phillip was arrested, but he never told them about me, or I wouldn't be here. He disappeared along with his family."

"I don't know what to say, mate."

"It was eight years ago, but I've never actually forgotten him," I said, half honestly. "You asked me why I'm here. It's because I really like you… a lot."

"What the fuck do you mean by that?"

"I've made you feel uncomfortable, haven't I?"

"Erm… in a word, yes," he said, staring out of the window with his back to me.

"I'm sorry. I can see I've badly misjudged the situation."

"Yes. You have."

"Please don't tell the Gestapo," I begged. "They'll kill me."

"I'm not going to tell the Gestapo."

"I should go. Please forgive me, I should never have said anything."

"I've never met a fairy. I would never have guessed."

"Are you disgusted?"

"I'm not sure, to be honest." Tom turned around. I could see he was uncomfortable. He was clenching his fists. I had no idea what he was going to do or say next. "It couldn't have been easy to tell me that. You must really trust me."

"I do."

"You've been a good friend to me," he said, taking another swig of whisky. "Honesty works both ways."

"Go on."

"Like you, this isn't easy."

"Tom, you can trust me..."

"I've never told anybody this," he said, gritting his teeth. "I'm not even sure myself. God, this is hard."

"What could be worse than what I've just told you?"

"Maybe I've led you on – created this situation."

"What do you mean?"

He started pacing again, avoiding eye contact. "I lead a double life... I put on this act seven days a week. The macho guy who boxes and drinks beer..." He paused to take another swig. "If only they all knew what I'm really thinking."

"What are you saying?"

"I've never fancied a girl in my life. I thought things would change as I got older, but they haven't."

"Do you find men attractive, then?"

Tom blushed. "I get these weird crushes on my mates," he replied uncomfortably. "I'd get my head kicked in if they ever found out. It makes me feel dirty."

"Why dirty?"

"Homosexuality is against nature. It's the one thing that my church, the regime and my friends agree on."

"Why is it so wrong?"

"Have you read the Bible? Leviticus is a good starting place."

"Do you really believe in God, then?"

"Don't you?"

"No," I said.

"I don't go to church much since my parents died, but I am a Christian."

"If there is a God, why is there so much suffering in the world? How come he didn't stop the Nazis coming to power, or the atomic bombs being dropped?"

"I can't answer that. I hang on to the thought that my parents are watching over me. That I may see them again."

"Tom, there's more I need to tell you."

"More?"

I gazed longingly at his handsome face and torso. "When I said I liked you—"

Tom turned away towards the window again. "I can't deal with this."

"Look at me. If you want me to leave, I'll go. I promise you, I'll never mention this again."

"I don't want you to go."

"Why?"

"Do you want me to spell it out?"

"Yes. I need to hear the words from your mouth."

He sat down beside me and took a deep breath. "I like you too."

"Really?"

"You must have suspected something."

"I wasn't sure."

"But I don't think I'm ready for this."

"Ready for what?"

"Starting something with you, or any man."

"Why not?"

"I don't like this feeling of being out of control."

"It scares me too."

"Please, this is wrong. I've changed my mind. I think you should go."

I ignored Tom and leant towards him. He obstructed me with his arm, but I pushed it out of the way. I could feel him shaking. Our lips met, and I felt a sort of electric current spark between us. I put my arms around Tom's muscular back and pulled him in close.

Tom gently moved his lips away from mine and gazed into my eyes.

"My God," he said. "I had no idea. What was that?"

"I think that was our first kiss."

"I never imagined..." he said, confused. He started sobbing.

"What have I done wrong? Am I that bad a kisser?"

"Why did you have to do that?" he said. "Do you know what you're doing to me?"

"It was beautiful."

"It was wrong, and you know it. A man cannot lie with a man the way he does with a woman."

"Stop quoting the bloody Bible."

"You came here tonight to seduce me," said Tom angrily. "You've deliberately got me drunk. I should bloody knock you out. You're a disgusting, dirty little queer."

"I know what you're going through. You're like I was. I hated myself once too."

He stood up and started shouting. "Everything was fine until you came along. Why did you have to pick me?"

He threw the whisky bottle at me. It missed and shattered against the wall.

"Calm down." I trembled.

"You chose me as your prey. I know how your type work. Befriend men, get under their skin, like scabies mites."

"What just happened to me – to us – just then, was magical."

"You're talking crap. I ain't bloody queer, it was just a weak moment."

"I don't accept that. We've found each other. I don't believe in coincidences. Maybe you're right and there *is* something up there. Me being reassigned to the Schwebke factory was fate. Somebody up there wanted us to meet."

Tom sat down again and buried his face in his cupped hands.

"You're doing my bloody head in," he said.

"Don't throw this away."

"Throw what away?"

"You're just going to pretend that kiss never happened, then?"

"It was just a drunken snog. It meant nothing."

"It meant something to me."

Tom started crying.

"Let me in," I said. "Please..."

"You don't understand," he said, quivering. "My family would be so ashamed..."

"You are so handsome. Sitting there topless with that bloody chest of yours."

Tom managed a weak smile.

"And you look even more handsome when you smile," I said.

He sniffed and wiped his eyes. "Just hold me," he said tearfully. "Please."

I held him tightly, and he wept uncontrollably. Years of self-denial had dissolved in a few short sentences.

"Sorry about throwing the bottle at you," he sobbed.

"It doesn't matter. Besides, you're a crap aim."

"I'm falling for you. I can't fight it any more."

"You don't have to be alone any longer."

I moved in to kiss him again. He relaxed a little more this time, and let me take the lead.

"You're not alone either, mate," he mumbled in my ear.

The tragedy was that I *was* alone. My god lay embalmed in a glass coffin in Germania.

31

5th September 1993

THOMAS JORDAN

The light streaming through the crack in the curtains woke me up. My back ached from sleeping on the settee. Stephen was asleep with his head resting on my chest.

I tried to adjust myself without waking him, but I couldn't get comfortable, so I decided to put up with it, and let him sleep for a bit longer.

He groaned and started to stretch. He sat up.

"Bloody hell," I said. "That was my knee."

"Sorry," he said, rubbing his eyes.

"Would you like some breakfast?"

"Please. God, I'm dying for a piss."

"Well, you know where the bog is. I didn't expect you to stay over, so it's only toast and jam."

I put the kettle on the hob and lit the grill.

"I've switched on the immersion if you want a shower."

"Your kitchen is filthy. Shall I do the washing-up?"

"I'll do it later."

I made two mugs of tea and brought through his breakfast.

"Aw, thanks, you've even spread my toast for me."

"All part of the five-star service at L'Hôtel de Thomas."

"I feel better already," he said, sipping the tea. "About last night…"

I looked away. "Yes?"

"It was pretty intense."

"That's an understatement."

"How do you feel about it?"

"I'm bricking myself."

"Do you want to leave it? I mean, nothing has happened yet, not really. We can carry on as before and still be friends."

"That would be the easiest thing to do."

"If we go down this path, it could earn us an express ticket to Ramsgate."

"I know."

"But I know in my heart that I can't give you up. I've waited my whole life for someone like you to come along."

"Me too," I admitted.

"We'll have to be discreet. I mean, not just a little bit careful; this has to be completely secret. Our lives are at stake. You can't even tell your closest friends, and that means Bill too."

"You don't have to state the obvious. And Bill's the last person I'd tell. He hates poofs. I reckon he'd deck me."

"For all anybody knows, we're just two lads hanging out together."

"Yeah. We're hardly screaming pansies."

"We'll take it as slow as you want. I'll give you as much space as you need."

"I appreciate that."

"Maybe we could get a travel permit to Wales," he said. "We could bribe a fisherman to take us across the Irish Sea, to Dublin. They give you automatic citizenship. Then we could save for a flight to America."

"Or die trying. Like the dozens that the coastguard execute every year when they're discovered. You'd be better off trying to swim across the Atlantic."

Stephen finished his toast and tea.

"I've left you a clean towel by the bath," I said.

He went upstairs. After he had finished showering, I also took one. I went into my bedroom to find him lying naked on my bed. I looked at his smooth, athletic body.

"Stephen..." I said embarrassedly as I became aroused. "I don't think I'm ready for this."

"There has to be a first time for both of us. Come and lay down. There's no pressure – we'll just see what happens."

I lay beside him, and we kissed. The kissing became more passionate, and we began to explore each other's bodies. I was nervous, but Stephen was gentle and seemed to know what he was doing. It was mind-blowing. I had never felt such intimacy with another human being, or such trust.

Afterwards, we lay there cuddled under the duvet, feeling content, like we had known each other for years instead of months. I toyed with his silver St Christopher, entwining the chain in my forefinger. "I thought you were an atheist?"

"I am."

"So, what's this?"

"It was my father's," he said, gently unwinding the chain from my finger. "It's the only thing the SS didn't steal when they searched the house. It's very precious to me."

"Was he religious?"

"Not really. I guess it's just tradition."

He nuzzled my neck, then rolled over and groaned, "I don't want to go."

"Then don't."

"Look at the time," he said, pointing at my alarm clock. "I have to get to the launderette before it closes."

I leant over and kissed him. "Stay for a bit longer," I pleaded, lying on top of him.

"Five minutes. Then I really have to go."

"Can you imagine? If we lived in America; say somewhere warm like California. They say that in San Francisco, two men can walk around openly holding hands."

"I wouldn't believe everything you hear."

"Do you ever think about defecting? Escaping this giant prison cell?"

"All the time. I also think about being shot trying."

He wriggled underneath me. "Tom, I really need to go. I'll see you at work tomorrow, yeah?"

"Sure," I said, rolling over onto my side.

He got out of bed and dressed. I lay there watching him. He came back over to the bed and gave me a kiss.

I followed him downstairs and let him out of the front door. It was an anticlimax watching him walk away. Suddenly, I had to deal with emotions that I had buried since puberty. I had always thought that a life without love was the only way to survive in Nazi Britain, but just maybe, we could somehow make this work for us.

32

5th September 1993

STEPHEN TALBOT

I felt euphoric when I left Tom's house. I knew that he would soon become a significant source of intelligence, given his recent promotion to the BLA council. He could possibly be our highest-level contact. I was looking forward to reporting to the office later.

While it was my job to seduce Tom, it was pointless to pretend that I could close off my emotions completely. I was not a robot. However, I was also aware that our relationship was founded on lies. Tom did not even know my actual name, or at least my surname.

Despite the fact that I hated everything that Tom stood for, something within me saw beyond this. Was I becoming radicalised? Had living in Ost-Bereich changed me somehow? I knew that I had to focus on my mission and remember that I was a Gestapo agent. My real life waited for me across the wall.

I spent the rest of the afternoon at the launderette, reading a copy of *Der Stürmer* that somebody had discarded. Dinner was tinned ham and potatoes, which had gone up in price since last week. Afterwards, I called Weber. I always shuddered when I heard his staccato voice.

"Heil Hitler," I said.

"Report," barked Weber.

"I had a breakthrough this weekend. My relationship with Tom has developed into a physical one, as you predicted."

"Yes, our monitoring crew stated that you gave a compelling performance. Your improvisation was outstanding. Well done."

"He trusts me. I know he'll start to confide in me."

"I cannot emphasise enough how critical your mission is. You have access to one of the key individuals who should shortly have knowledge of the American invasion plans. Our other contact is under suspicion, he's a lame duck at the moment, so the onus is on you."

"I'll do everything I can."

"I appreciate that I'm asking a lot of you, especially someone so young in the force, but your time's running out. My superiors have authorised the extension of this mission for one more month. If we have no solid results by then, you are to terminate Jordan and return here."

"Please, sir. I just need a little more time. I'm so close now."

"You have a month. Oh, and Talbot – lay off the drink. Your landlady informed us about the empty whisky bottles in the bin. It's a mission, and you're at work. Not on a four-month piss-up."

"My landlady is an informer?"

"Of course. You don't think we'd just put you up in some random house?"

He hung up.

I thought about my old life in the western sector, then about my intimacy with Tom. Those masculine but tender hands that had caressed me so gently were the hands of a murderer. The same hands that had planted explosives that blew up children.

I shuddered. There was a dark and frightening side to Tom's character. He was a terrorist, and he had to face justice. However, I made a pledge to myself. When the time came to kill him, I would make sure that it was swift and painless. I owed him that at least.

I went to bed, but was unable to sleep. I switched on my television and tuned it to Reich Today. I sat up suddenly and rubbed my eyes. The headline scrolled across the bottom of the screen. *Air Egypt plane disappears over the Red Sea. Eyewitnesses report seeing an explosion.*

The newsreader, John Jeffries, looked stony-faced as he read from the autocue.

"The Americans are claiming that the plane was downed by a missile fired from a German warship, an allegation fiercely denied by the Reich Chancellery. In a statement issued by the Reich Aviation Authority, it claims that it is investigating firm evidence that the missile was fired from Saudi Arabia, at the behest of the CIA in a crude attempt to discredit Nazi Germany and gain support from countries in the Middle East."

The camera switched to Maria Thorpe.

"Flight AE539 was travelling from Cairo to the Saudi capital, Riyadh, carrying 172 passengers. The plane gave no distress signal; it disappeared from the radar without warning."

The screen showed a map of Egypt and Saudi Arabia, with a red dot indicating where the last contact with the flight was.

"The plane's black box has not yet been recovered. Wreckage, including luggage and body parts, has been spotted close to the suspected crash site in the Red Sea. Joining us in the studio is aviation expert, Tony Hopkins. Tony, welcome to the studio…"

I switched off the television in disgust. There was a time when I would have believed without question anything that I saw on RT, but now I was more cynical.

We would probably never discover who was responsible for the shooting down of the plane. Americans claimed to respect life, but the Saudi Kingdom did not, and these two countries were uneasy allies at best. A CIA plot was not entirely implausible, but I knew that it was more likely to be a German warship in the Red Sea, looking to reassert influence in the area after the loss of Egypt and the precarious situation in Libya. This tragedy would escalate international tensions, and it would undoubtedly put further pressure on me.

33

6th September 1993

THOMAS JORDAN

The evening news was depressing. Yesterday, an Air Egypt plane was downed flying in international airspace. Most of the passengers were American, including diplomats and advisors to the provisional government in Cairo. The most shocking news was that Edward P. Lawson, the US Secretary of State, had been on board.

Predictably, Goebbels denied involvement, accusing the Americans of trying to create an incident as an excuse for war. I wondered how the newsreaders kept straight faces. It had to be the Krauts, but I doubt they realised Lawson was on board.

Goebbels had gone too far this time. The German Navy had been pestering fishermen in the Med for months and lobbing missiles towards the Suez to try and disrupt supply ships. A stray missile blew up a school in Adabiya, killing seventy-six children. Rather than apologise, the Krauts just issued denials. Up until now, the Americans had turned the other cheek. Now their citizens had been killed and important ones at that. This was serious. I listened to President Turnbull's speech from the Oval Office on my radio. He had promised a *robust response* before the signal was jammed.

The Army Council met in a new location, a disused garage under the arches of a railway bridge near Shoreditch. The workshop had been abandoned years ago, and it was like being in a museum. There was an old Austin Seven, covered in dust, and posters advertising things like Redline motor spirit and Dunlop tyres.

Two cell commanders, including myself, were present, but for some reason, Carla had also been invited. We sat on workbenches, while Joe H and General K briefed us.

Joe spoke first. "Everything I say is to remain completely confidential. I'm sure that you're all aware of the downing of the Air Egypt plane. In the shadow of this, I've spoken to senior members of the American military. The January date has been moved forward to two weeks from today."

"That's going to be a tough timetable," I said.

"Yes, but it's workable," said Joe. "Most of the background preparation has been in place for a while."

"There are several lines of attack," said General K. "Firstly, we remove the DHPA from the water supply. That should put some fight into the people who are regime haters and our natural allies."

"But they're not soldiers," said Ant, the leader of Veritas, a lanky male, barely in his twenties with spots and greasy black hair. "Sowing the seeds of rebellion won't help unarmed civilians fight the SS."

"Absolutely," said Joe. "Nevertheless, it's necessary."

"The water treatment plants are too well guarded," said Ant.

"Correct," said Joe. "We're not going to bother trying to disable them. They import the DHPA from Calais. It's stored in a Docklands facility."

"From there, it's transported by tanker to the water treatment plants," said General K.

"Then we blow up the Docklands facility?" I said.

"It would be pointless," said Joe. "Even if we succeeded, once the authorities knew that the supply had been disrupted, they would take measures."

"The Americans have developed a chemical that will neutralise the DHPA," said General K. "We've already infiltrated the storage facility. Once the antidote is deployed, people will lose their chemically induced fear."

"Then we have to convince them to rise up," said Joe. "If there's a general strike, the economy will grind to a halt. The stock markets will crash. We'll encourage public riots. We just need to convince people that there's help coming."

"The Nazis are so good at manipulating the media," said Ant. "Half the country wouldn't even know about a mass revolt."

"We're going to seize the Reich Today communications tower," said Joe. "Where the news programmes are recorded and broadcast."

"Once the tower is secure," said General K, "we can get our message out there."

"Taking the tower won't be easy," said Ant.

"Nobody implied that it would," said Joe. "But it isn't impossible with decent weapons and manpower. The entrance is well guarded, but get past that..."

"The Americans have given us a supply of undetectable plastic explosives," said General K. "Tom, you're going to deliver the bomb in a parcel."

"No problem," I said.

"We've acquired a courier van with false plates. It's hidden in a lock-up near Goodge Straβe. You'll deliver the explosives to the thirty-second floor, where the studio is located. The threat should get the production team's attention. You'll have photos of the concentration camps. They'll have a choice to continue being the mouthpiece of a regime that burns children alive, or join us."

"And if they don't?"

"Blow the place up," said Joe. "Tom, I'm putting you in command of Veritas cell as well as your own."

Ant saluted me.

"Thank you," I said.

"Your first-hand experience at navigating the sewers should help you find the pickup point at Goodge Straβe," said General K. "Do a dry run as soon as possible."

"Sewers," I said. "Great."

General K ignored my sarcasm. "If you succeed, if this plan succeeds, dead or alive, you'll all be heroes."

"How long do you think we can hold the building, once the SS arrive?"

"Ironically, the RT communications tower is terrorist-proof," said General K.

"What do you mean?"

"Once the security system has been activated, it's designed to be impenetrable. The building is automated and will go into lockdown. Uroferranium shutters will cover the external exits and windows. It has its own air, electricity and water supply."

"All controlled from a console on the third floor," said Joe. "You'll need to persuade a guard to activate it. It's coded to their palm prints."

"Remember," said General K. "If the guard is uncooperative – you only need his hand."

"You'll have five minutes at best before the SS arrive in force," said Joe. "You have to get the building secure within that time frame."

"What about the people trapped inside with us?"

"You'll need some of them to help operate the studio equipment," said Joe. "You can seal off each level from the console. James from Veritas cell will know how to use it."

He tossed me a folder full of maps, schematics and other information.

"Once you've secured the studio," he said, "you can broadcast live to the nation. There's a statement in the folder that has to be read out. Then, they can report on the battle as it unfolds."

"Battle?" said Ant.

"Operation Achaeans' Revenge," said Joe. "In deference to the Battle of Troy."

"Three thousand American marines are going to take London," said General K. "Obviously, the plan is classified. Tom, you'll get further information at a later stage, as a council member."

"The Nazis won't know what's hit them," said Joe.

General K spoke. "The Chinese are backing the resistance in Region 3, the former Soviet Union. It's been agreed that those territories will fall into their sphere of influence."

"You realise that this is the start of World War III?" I said.

"Yes," said General K, "I think that's a good analogy."

"It could end in Armageddon."

"I don't believe the Nazis will use nuclear weapons," said General K. "They know the Americans will retaliate."

"It's a gamble, though," said Ant.

"A considered one," said General K.

"We're all aware that there are enemy agents within our organisation," said Joe. "Therefore, we ask that you withhold information from your respective units until the very last minute."

"We'll brief the other cells individually on their tasks," said General K. "They'll be unaware of your mission, and vice versa."

"Finally, getting captured is not an option," said Joe. "If it comes to the worst, you know what you have to do."

"But if this operation succeeds," said General K, "Princess Elizabeth will be our Queen."

"God save Princess Elizabeth," we chanted.

At the end of the meeting, Joe asked Carla to remain behind. I wondered what they wanted her for. Of all the cell members, she was the most intelligent, but also the most secretive, and I was never entirely sure if I trusted her. She had been uncharacteristically silent throughout the meeting. I knew that something was going on.

34

13th September 1993

STEPHEN TALBOT

I bought a copy of Monday's *Der Stürmer* on the way to work. The front page was dominated by headlines about the ratcheting world tensions. There was this sinking feeling in the country that war was now inevitable.

Tom and I had been seeing each other for over a week. Despite Tom wanting to take it slowly, at his request, we had spent nearly every night together. He even bought me a toothbrush.

I retained an emotional distance, but I had to admit, the sex was great. We had both released many years of frustration. Afterwards, we always cuddled. This was when he was at his most vulnerable emotionally. The pillow talk started. He would offload his burdens. He trusted me entirely, talking freely about resistance matters while wrapped in my arms. In less than a week, I had uncovered a tremendous amount of information. He even radioed his contacts with me in earshot. My superiors were understandably delighted. I still only had a basic outline of the American invasion plans, though. Extracting this information was going to be the toughest part of my assignment.

In my locker at work, I found a note, instructing me to wait in the Stepney allotment gardens at 22.00.

I whispered to Tom excitedly, "I got the note."

"What note?"

Tom was distant, for reasons which I did not understand. He moved away from me in the canteen and barely said a word to me all day.

✠

I decided to go to the gym after dinner to kill time. It was also a place where I could enjoy a hot shower that did not cost me twenty pfennigs a minute, even though the communal facilities were grim.

"Where's Bill?" I said to one of the trainers.

"Not sure," he replied. "Nobody's seen him for days. I'm the mug that's expected to cover for him."

"Oh. I hope he's okay."

"Who knows? He's a loudmouth. In the scheme of things, he should've been carted away years ago."

My head was in the wrong place for hard exercise. Tom's abrupt change in attitude towards me worried me. Did he suspect something? I was concerned about the meeting tonight at the allotments. It had to be the resistance, but were they going to recruit me or kill me? I clasped my silver St Christopher. My insurance policy. I prayed that I would not have to use it.

After showering, I headed towards the rendezvous point under cover of darkness. I was early, so I waited around. It was chilly but dry. All I remember next was a handkerchief being clamped around my mouth, which smelled of pear drops.

✠

I woke with a thumping headache, realising I was tied to a chair. My vision gradually returned, and I could see three silhouettes in front of me, people in dark clothing and balaclavas. There was light from a bare bulb hanging from the ceiling in the middle of a windowless room. It smelled musty, and there were steel beer kegs stacked in one corner.

"Where am I?" I said woozily.

"Never mind," said a female voice.

"Have you ever heard of the expression, 'Curiosity killed the cat'?" said one of the males.

"You've been speaking to Tom," I said. "I've been pestering him for a while now to join you."

"Who are we?" said the female.

"The resistance, I assume."

"And why do you want to join us?" she asked.

"The same reason that you all joined, I imagine."

"How come, you suddenly turn up in Ost-Bereich out of nowhere?" said the male.

"I was reassigned from a state farm in Bedfordshire. To replace factory workers lost during the last purge."

"Which state farm?" asked the female.

"Millbrook. One of the largest in the Reich's breadbasket. They export to the Lebensraum colonists in Region 3 – the soil there is too radioactive to grow food."

"How many hectares?" she asked.

"I don't know. It's massive, but I can't reel off statistics like that. I was just a farmhand."

"Which part of the Gestapo do you work for?" said the first man.

"I hate the Gestapo. They murdered my parents when I was twelve."

"Anyone can make up a sob story."

"It happens to be true."

"You'll have to do better than that."

The second man took off his balaclava. "This is ridiculous," said Tom.

"Tom, thank God," I said.

"Untie him, Carla."

"We've not finished yet," protested the woman.

"Just untie him. Like Bill, I can't bear all these silly games."

"Shall we just let anybody join up, then?" said Carla sarcastically. "I could put an advert in the *Stepney Herald*."

"He's not a Nazi."

"How can you be so sure?"

"Because I've known him for months."

"I trust Tom's judgement," said the other man, taking off his balaclava.

"He's sound," said Tom. "We know more about him than we do about you, Carla."

"What do you mean by that?" said Carla defensively.

"We've only got your word that you were a doctor cast out here because of Jewish blood. We take your word for it, just like I'm prepared to believe he was a peasant up in Bedfordshire."

"If you've something to say?" said Carla.

"It can wait," said Tom. "Let me introduce you to Stephen, everyone."

The other male shook my hand.

"This is our resident ginger nut, Mark," said Tom.

Carla untied my hands. She was scowling at Tom. They obviously had some issues. "Isn't this all a bit melodramatic?" I said. "Like something out of *The Peelers*."

"Are you insulting my acting ability?" said Carla.

"No," I laughed nervously. "You were actually quite convincing. I thought I was going to get hurt."

"You still might."

"Where are we?" I asked.

"In the cellar of a derelict pub," she said. "A few streets away from the allotments."

"My head is killing me."

"It's the chloroform," said Tom. "Man up. It'll only last a couple of hours."

"I suppose it's better than knocking me unconscious."

"Carla," said Tom, "have you got the envelope?"

She handed Tom a Jiffy bag.

"They say the winning side writes the history books," said Tom. "Not even the German public know what went on during the war years. The atrocities, the mass extermination of nine million Jews and thirty million Russians."

"Come on now," I said. "Nobody hates the Nazis as much as me, but you couldn't get away with murder on that scale. The Jews were relocated to a land of their own in the East."

"They were slaughtered," said Carla. "In their millions, in death factories across Europe. They called it the Final Solution. Camps were built in remote areas and hidden from view. Everything was destroyed beyond recognition after they served their purpose."

"You can't just make millions of people disappear in a few years. Even the Nazis don't have the ability to do that."

"We have the proof here," said Carla. "See for yourself. And understand why we will die for our cause."

Tom handed me the envelope. I studied the pictures in horror. There were aerial shots of what looked like a vast concentration camp – I read the unfamiliar name: *Auschwitz*. I saw, with my own eyes, the emaciated bodies and mass graves. A train with carriages crammed full of bedraggled prisoners pulling into a station. I saw pictures of babies being tossed onto huge pyres.

"This is Vorkuta 1," said Carla. "Originally a gulag, but converted in 1947 to oversee the genocide of the Russian population, since mass starvation was taking too long."

I grimaced as I looked through the pictures.

"You can see how they evolved the killing process," she said. "It proved to be too labour-intensive and expensive, housing and feeding prisoners before their extermination. Vorkuta was far more automated and efficient. The containers of people were ferried in by train and hydraulically tipped straight into large macerators, killing hundreds of people in the cruellest way imaginable."

I looked at images of human beings struggling in vain to clamber out of an enormous stainless-steel funnel while being pushed back in by guards with shovels, onto the rotating blades at the bottom.

"It was SS guards who smuggled these photos out," said Carla. "Was it was done out of a reawakened conscience at the horror, or merely for posterity from people arrogant enough to think they would never have to face justice for their actions? What I do know is that we have indisputable testimony to back these photos up."

"The grinding machine was known affectionately as the Slav Mincer by the guards," said Mark. "It was dangerous work; often the operatives, themselves prisoners, would meet a grisly end if they weren't agile or quick enough."

"It just can't be true. People would have found out."

"Search your heart, Stephen," said Tom softly. "You know these aren't false. Look into the eyes of the terrified children. You can't fake that."

I looked away. I would play Tom's game, I had to, but I knew they were forgeries. Photographs created in sophisticated American studios by the notorious Black Propaganda Units of the CIA to discredit the Nazis. They had to be. I felt nauseous. I just had this lingering doubt in my mind. Could they be real? Could they? I thought of the SS Death Heads on my training course. Suddenly, I vomited.

"Sorry," I said, retching, before throwing up again.

"Nice," said Mark. "Why does sick always contain diced carrot?"

"Mark," said Carla. "There's a time and a place."

"Are you with us?" asked Tom.

"Yes," I said grimly, not knowing whether I actually was or not.

"Good," said Tom. "You've picked an interesting time to join. The battle of the century is a week away. The Nazis aren't going to know what's hit them."

"Am I allowed to know what the plan is?"

"We can give you an overview," said Carla. "We only know scant details ourselves, for obvious reasons."

"We're going to blow up all the water treatment plants in Ost-Bereich and the Northern Industrial Zone," said Tom. "It's a massive operation. The population will be drug-free. We'll spark a national revolution that the regime won't be expecting. How long before the army joins us? The young conscripts are not cold-blooded murderers. Would they open fire on their own?"

"We'll need to do more than that to defeat the Nazis."

"Absolutely," said Tom. "The Americans are going to launch a massive attack from Dublin into Liverpool. They have thousands of concealed troops and state-of-the-art military equipment flown in on passenger airlines. They'll bring tanks into the Liverpool docks on cargo ships, right under the noses of the German Army, backed up by massive air support."

"I thought the Irish were supposed to be neutral," I said.

"Officially they are," said Tom. "But they've been threatened with invasion for decades. They don't want to end up like Sweden did."

"Wow," I said. "The Americans are really serious about this."

"The attack should come as a complete surprise," said Tom.

"Welcome to the resistance," said Mark. "The only organisation where you don't need to worry about your pension."

"It's time for you to go," said Tom. "I'll see you at work tomorrow. Try and sleep off the chloroform."

"Where do I go?"

"Up the stairs, and out of the front door of the pub," he said. "Turn left. You'll soon get your bearings once you see the allotments."

I walked home, feeling bewildered. I knew the Nazis were not saints, I had witnessed their cruelty first-hand, but genocide on that scale was inconceivable.

I had looked up to the Third Reich all of my life. I had enjoyed a privileged childhood with wonderful holidays and an exemplary education. My parents had brought me up to believe in the purity of a doctrine that had brought peace and prosperity to a continent. What were the alternatives? The tyranny of communism, where a billion people languished in state-sanctioned poverty, or the greed and anarchy of capitalism. I thought about the USA, where children high on easily obtainable drugs opened fire on their classmates using automatic weapons that could be bought on any street corner.

My father always said that National Socialism was the biggest force for world order since the Roman Empire. Achieving the greater good and upholding the principles of our visionary Führer involved making sacrifices, often great ones, but I could not accept that the gassing of millions was justifiable. It just could not be true. The resistance were trying to brainwash me.

On a more positive note, I had gained some extraordinary intelligence tonight. Undoubtedly, with the American attack imminent, I would not be stationed here much longer. My old life waited for me on the other side of the *zwischenwand*. A comfortable and privileged existence. I could slip back into it so quickly and forget this ghastly place, and everyone in it.

✠

When I got home, I phoned headquarters. Kriminalrat Sutton answered. I told him that I had been recruited by the resistance cell known as Adrestia. I thought for a few seconds, then I spoke automatically as if not in control of my own words. Suddenly, I was a member of the Nazi Party again and back on the Gestapo payroll.

"I have vital information regarding an imminent American attack," I said.

I relayed the information that I had gathered from the meeting. This intelligence was a real bombshell and would give us a crucial advantage over the Americans. I could not quite believe that the cell members had been so open. Apparently, my relationship with Tom had earned his unconditional trust. How foolish he had proven to be. It suddenly dawned on me that I was good at my job.

"This is extraordinarily ambitious," said Sutton.

"I agree. But they seemed very confident."

"It correlates with the intelligence gained from the bug you planted. We have an enormous amount of additional detail on timings and locations that Jordan has been radioing. You've done well."

"Yes, I had my doubts about Sutton's choice for this mission," said Weber, who it transpired was listening in. "But you've exceeded my expectations. Their attack will fail."

"I hope so," I replied.

"As for the Micks," said Weber, "I've no doubt Chancellor Goebbels will find an extra-special punishment for them."

I shuddered at his words. The Republic of Ireland, reunited with the North and given independence by Hitler after centuries of British misrule, had a population of just four million. Its real neutrality had always been doubted. Goebbels often described it as 'a cancerous tumour on the arse of the Reich', and many believed it was only a matter of time before the Germans seized it. This would provide them with the excuse they needed.

"It's time for you to pack your things," said Sutton. "We're moving you out."

"Why? There's so much more I can achieve."

"We have enough," said Weber. "There's no more that you can do over there."

"Come home," said Sutton. "You've done your bit. You'll receive a promotion for your work."

"Thank you, sir."

"And you've been allocated a new company vehicle," said Sutton. "We know you share your father's love of fast cars."

"Your final orders are to eliminate Thomas Jordan," said Weber. "Then proceed to the main checkpoint at the *zwischenwand* at midnight tomorrow. Stanning will be waiting for you on the west side. Your exit has been authorised."

"Kill him? Would it not be better to bring him in for interrogation?"

"He's of no use to us now," said Weber. "We have all the information we need. He's long overdue termination."

"Yes, sir."

"Dispose of the body discreetly," said Sutton. "I want you to report to the office on Wednesday at 09.00 for debriefing."

I turned off the cellular phone and put it back in its hiding place in the hollowed-out *Mein Kampf*. I shut my eyes. All I could see were those ghastly images. Nothing could prepare you for them. Nobody living under Nazi rule, where the media was so tightly controlled, had seen anything like them. They had to be fake. They must be.

35

14th September 1993

THOMAS JORDAN

It was another dreary day at the factory. Stephen looked sad, like he was carrying a huge burden. The last week or so had been a headrush of emotions for both of us. We had to keep our relationship secret, so Stephen had been sneaking into my house via the back door so that the neighbours did not get suspicious.

In the ten days since we first kissed, I had seen him nearly every night. We were already close friends, but an even deeper bond was forming between us, which I treasured. When he cuddled up to me at night, with his arms around me, I felt a warm feeling in my chest, which I can only describe as contentment. I had never felt so close to another human being.

Now he was also in the resistance, I could talk to him more about my ideas, my fears and hopes. It was good to have his emotional support as it was a crucial time for the movement. However, the attack was now so close that the organisational work that I was involved in was taking up nearly all my free time. This meant that I had to push Stephen away. I think he was a little hurt. I had only ever had myself to worry about, as an adult – I was completely new to relationships, and I had a lot to learn.

While things were good with Stephen, other things in life were getting on top of me. I was desperately worried about Bill, who had gone missing; God only knows what had happened to him. His wife, Annette, was strong, but I could just imagine trying to console his kids. Annette had made enquiries with the Gestapo, but they refused to deny or confirm if he was in their custody. She said, every day she came home, she expected the dreaded black urn on her doorstep.

I was upset with Carla, who had been behaving like a bitch, refusing to tell me why the council had spoken to her privately. She was still alive, so it was doubtful that she was the traitor, but she was hiding something. I was the one that was supposed to be on the Army Council and the cell commander.

As I tried to concentrate on soldering, Stephen whispered to me.

"I need to see you," he said. "Tonight."

"Tonight is not good."

"Please. It's important."

"I just need a bit of space. You know how much pressure I'm under."

"I miss you. I need to spend time with you. I need to talk. We need to talk."

"It's only been a few days since you last stayed over. Stop being so insecure – everything's going well, isn't it?"

"Yes, but I've something important I need to tell you."

"Okay. You win. Do you want to come over to the house?"

"I fancy a walk. Can I meet you at the Mile End Lock? I thought we could stroll down the towpath on the Regent's Canal. It's quiet… discreet. Do you know it?"

"Yes, shall we say around 20.00?"

"Perfect," he said, lowering his voice. "I just want you to know that I love you."

I looked him in the eyes and whispered, "I'm sorry I've been a little distant, these last few days. It's just all this stuff going on."

A sense of relief swept over Stephen's face. My words certainly seemed to cheer him up. It would be good to spend time with him and forget about the BLA stuff going on, if only for a few hours.

✠

We met up as planned. It was an unseasonably chilly but dry night. We had both wrapped up well.

He leant forward to kiss me on the lips. I stepped back, feeling embarrassed.

"Sorry," he said.

"It's not that I don't want to kiss you. It's just not the right place. Anybody could be watching. Do you want to get us killed?"

"No, of course not."

"If you wanted a bit of nookie, you could've come to the house."

We started to walk along the muddy pathway alongside the canal. There was an abandoned London Tea Company narrowboat tied up close to a lock, which was listing badly. Apart from some old geezer walking a yappy Jack Russell, it was pretty deserted.

"I scattered my uncle's ashes around here. God rest his soul."

Stephen ignored my comment. "Do you love me?"

"What do you think?"

"I want to hear you say the words."

"It's difficult for me, you know that. They're just words."

"Please?"

"I know I've not been paying you much attention, but you know the reason why. We're about to go to war."

"I get that, and I want to support you, but I do have feelings as well."

I sighed awkwardly, "of course I love you. You shouldn't even need to ask."

"Thank you."

I noticed his eyes were moist.

"You're a bit morbid tonight. Are you drinking the tap water?"

We walked underneath a bridge, hidden from view.

"Yes, I've been drinking the tap water."

"Well, that explains the mood swings, then. I warned you."

"I drink it because I have an antidote to the DHPA. It's standard issue."

"What are you talking about?"

I saw him reach into his coat and take out a small pistol, which he pointed at me.

"Stand back."

"Is this some sort of sick joke?"

"You heard me. Move towards the bank and raise your hands where I can see them."

"You *are* a Gestapo agent," I said bitterly. "In the beginning, I always suspected you were. Then I began to believe in you... in us. I thought we had something special. Why didn't I listen to the others. What me and you shared together convinced me. My God, I have to give you credit, you're a brilliant actor."

"It has to be said, my work does have its perks."

"You little wanker," I spat. "I feel sick at the thought of you touching me... I gave you every part of myself, and you're just some... some Nazi stooge."

"Ouch."

"What do you care?"

"If only you knew."

"What was all that shit about before you pulled out the gun? Do you enjoy playing with my feelings?"

"It's not like that. It's complicated. I had to be sure."

"Sure of what?"

"Sure that you loved me."

"Why?"

"Because..." he looked at me sadly. "I'm sorry, I should have done it quickly and not subjected you to this. I wasn't being deliberately cruel, I just had to know."

"You're sick."

"Yes, perhaps I am, but not in the way you think."

"What happens next?"

"My orders are to kill you and dispose of your body. Then, I return to my old life on the west side of the *zwischenwand*. A lovely apartment, flashy car, decent food... Not like this shithole."

"You know, I always thought I could detect your plummy accent. There was always a hint of it, and when you got pissed, you'd let your guard slip. Carla saw right through you. We had a huge row about it. Fuck me, I'm stupid."

"I'm amazed how quickly you came to trust me. It was all too easy, really, but then, things just got—"

"What's your real name?" I interrupted.

"My real name *is* Stephen. They gave me a different surname. I'm Kriminalassistent Stephen Talbot, Gestapo service number 93047R6."

"Wow. What a mindfuck. Tell me something. Be honest with me, before you kill me. Was it all fake or did you ever feel anything?"

Stephen sighed sadly. "At sixteen years old, I nearly died in the Piccadilly Circus bombing. I woke up in hospital two weeks later. It took me years to recover. I still can't hear properly. My mother was disfigured for life. For fuck's sake, she lost a bloody eye – an eye. Do you know how it feels to see somebody you love be hurt like that? It's people like you who commit these atrocities. Men who think killing children and innocent bystanders is an acceptable form of warfare."

"And people like you who have sold out. People like you who turn a blind eye to genocide and torture, ignoring the conditions us workers suffer, so you can go on living a comfortable life on the other side of the *zwischenwand*. You even persecute queers when you're one yourself. Don't try to claim the moral high ground with me, it doesn't wash. *You're* the Nazi."

"A card-carrying party member," he said. "But that doesn't make me wish things could be different."

I looked at him with hatred. The creature that I had lost my virginity to. He had wormed his way into my life, pretending to be my friend. I would have trusted him with my life. I loved him, and here he was, the fraud, pointing a gun at me. I tried to get my head around the fact that the past few months had all been lies. His betrayal cut through me like a shard of ice. Had he not been armed, I would have strangled him there and then.

"I've been tortured at Hastings and Ramsgate. But that was nothing compared to how *you've* hurt me, Stephen. Congratulations. I hope you're pleased with yourself. You've done what those bastards never managed. You've broken me."

I saw a tear run down his cheek. "This is the hardest thing I've ever had to do in my life."

"Spare me the crap. I was just an assignment."

"No, it's far more complicated than that. You asked me if it was all fake, if I had ever felt anything towards you. The answer is yes. But you need to understand, you were the man who blew up Wertheim. A cold-blooded terrorist. I was a law enforcer doing my job. Standing up for innocents in the name of order and peace. Women and children died in that attack."

"Don't you think I regret that?"

"Yes, I believe you do. You have to know that my training didn't remotely prepare me for how I would come to feel about you."

"Bullshit."

"It happens to be true. Which is what makes this so difficult."

"Why are you playing these mind games? Just put a bullet in my head and be done with it."

"I can't," he said. His hand was trembling, and he lowered the gun.

"Coward. If you don't shoot me, your superiors will kill us both."

"I know that."

"How could I have been such an idiot, not seeing what was staring me in the face?"

"Oh God," he cried. "This is so hard... Tom... I... I can't..."

He collapsed to his knees, weeping. He slowly twisted the gun around as though his arm was being controlled by an unseen force, and pointed it towards his own head. He knelt there, three metres from me, looking distraught. I hated him, yet strangely, I pitied him too.

"You don't understand," he sobbed. He rested the barrel of the gun against his temple. I could see him tighten his grip on the trigger. Then he turned the gun back towards me, shaking. "I'm a National Socialist. I swore an oath of allegiance. I *must* obey my orders."

"Go ahead, then. You're a Nazi. Fulfil your oath. Prove your loyalty to the Reich."

He clenched his left fist and looked up to the sky as if pleading to a higher power. He screamed, a hollow, guttural cry. Then, his face hardened. He stood up robotically, like a puppet on strings. "Kneel down," he ordered.

I knelt on the damp grass on the canal bank. I knew that he had now made his choice.

I felt the cold mud soaking into my jeans. Soon, it would not matter. He stepped forward and pointed the gun a few inches from my head. I looked into his sad eyes. Somehow, despite everything, I could not hang on to my hatred. He was like a farmer shooting the lame family dog as it lay pathetically, knowing the end was near. An act of kindness, but not an easy thing to do. How fucked up is that, forgiving your executioner? Understanding that he has to do his duty, and it's not really his fault?

My intense loathing dissolved. I knelt there, praying for a painless end. I felt strangely peaceful, like I had done at Ramsgate. I was no longer afraid of death. I did not want my last sentence on this earth to be full of hatred. Maybe it was my way of pleading for my life, or perhaps I simply accepted what was going to happen. Either way, I just blurted out the words tearfully, looking into the eyes of the man that days ago I had made love to.

"Stephen, I want you to know that I love you. I hope you find someone, someday, who will love you as much as I do."

As I saw tears run down his face, I continued.

"Carry those words with you along your journey, mate… Don't let the Nazis drive out your humanity altogether, yeah? I know you're not one of them, not deep down."

I shut my eyes and waited for oblivion.

"Oh, Tom…" he sighed. "I'm so, so sorry…"

36

14th September 1993

THOMAS JORDAN

I heard a loud bang and a splash of water where the bullet entered the canal.

"…Sorry that you're stuck with me," he said, finishing his sentence. "If you forgive me and you still want me, that is."

"Fucking hell," I gasped, opening my eyes. "Was that necessary?"

"Someone will report the gunshot. It'll be registered on the police intelligence database. The powers will assume it was me shooting you, at… erm…" he glanced at his wristwatch, "exactly 20.23 hours, which will cross-reference with my statement."

"Right," I said, shaking. My left ear was ringing from the shot. "Have you any idea what you've just put me through? You could have bloody warned me."

"There's something you need to know," he said. He turned the gun around, held it by the barrel and handed it to me. "I wasn't entirely sure that I wasn't going to kill you tonight. But I've made my choice."

"And what is that?"

"Isn't it obvious? You're everything to me. When I saw you kneeling there, I knew I couldn't go through with it, any more than you could kill me."

"For fuck's sake, are you insane? Never do anything like that to me again." I stood up, still trembling from the shock, and not quite believing that I was still alive. "You're very trusting, giving me a loaded gun."

Stephen looked nervously at the gun pointing at him. I held it for a few seconds, looking him in the eyes. He was a Gestapo agent, and I could and probably should kill him. But I knew I could not. I tossed the gun into the canal.

Stephen burst into tears and put his arms around me. He sobbed. "What are we going to do?"

I held him tightly and kissed him on the forehead. "We'll figure it out. Fuck knows how, but we will."

The gravity of the situation that we were in, that I was in, that my friends in the resistance were in, hit me at once, and I started weeping too.

"Perhaps you shouldn't have thrown the gun away," said Stephen tearfully.

"What do you mean?"

"We could take the easy route out."

"You mean…"

"One bullet could do both of us."

"No way."

"Do you have any idea what's going to happen to us? When they catch us."

"Nothing bad is going to happen to us. I promise."

"You don't know what they're capable of."

"Trust me, I do." I separated from him gently and ran my hands down his cheeks, wiping away his tears with my thumbs.

"I used to believe in the swastika," he said. "I loved our Führer. I would have given my life for his glory."

"You felt *that* strongly?"

"I was swept up by the whole thing, like millions of us. It started as a kid in the Hitler Youth. The beauty of order, the national purpose… Then it all began to change in my late teens. I saw the regime for what it truly was. The story I told you about Phillip, the guy I kissed; it was true. I changed the location, but we did kiss that night, and we *were* reported. I saw what they did to him before he was driven off to a labour camp. Things were never the same from then on. Outwardly, I did everything expected of me, but inside, I was slowly going mad."

"But you still chose to join the Gestapo."

"I was blackmailed into joining."

"Blackmailed?"

"They used the file they held on me over the incident with Phillip. Then I discovered they'd spied on me at university. They had pictures of me…"

"Pictures?"

"Do I need to go on?" he said, looking sheepish.

"Oh. Those kinds of pictures."

"I don't want to lie to you any more, Tom. It was true, I was bullied into joining, but I came to terms with it. I even enjoyed parts of the job."

"You enjoyed it? Really?"

"The investigative work, yes. We're not all torturers. But I was always living a counterfeit existence. I hid who I was from myself as much as anyone else. Surely you must get that."

"How did you come to be placed over here?"

"Because I'm one of very few homosexuals in the organisation. We're despised, but I guess there are situations where we serve a useful purpose to the party. I was ordered to seduce you, win your trust… gain information."

"Well, you certainly did that."

"Apart from the fact I fell in love with you. Against all my training."

"How can you sleep at night, Stephen? You know what

the Nazis are capable of. You've seen the photographs of the extermination camps."

"I'd ask you the same question. Before I got to know you, I wondered how you could live with yourself. I wasn't lying earlier. I was taught to believe people like you were terrorists who wanted to destroy our way of life."

"And now?"

"I still can't condone killing innocents, but I know from what you've told me that you regret it."

"I allowed myself to be talked into it, against all my instincts. We should only ever attack military targets."

"Those pictures you showed me. I shut my eyes, and I see those children. I even hear their screams as they burn."

"And it's still going on. Here, in Europe and Africa. They'll never stop murdering – it's all they know. They have to be defeated, or the human race is doomed."

"They told us the Jews were resettled. At first, I just couldn't believe my eyes. I thought the photos had to be CIA fakes."

"Oh, they're real all right."

"I know."

"When you gave me the gun, how did you know I wouldn't kill you?"

"I know you feel the same way about me."

"There were times a few moments ago that I'd never hated anyone so much in my whole life."

"I'm not surprised."

"But you are right, I do love you, deeply."

Stephen leant forward, and we kissed. For those few dreamy seconds, I completely forgot about our predicament.

"Come on," I said urgently. "We need to get out of here."

"You can't go back to your house. They'll be watching it. You need to go underground, right now."

"Yeah, state the bloody obvious, why don't you?"

"Where are we going?"

"I've got somewhere in mind. Just trust me. It's not far."

We rushed back up the towpath, and onto the street. I knew a safe house off the Whitechapel Road, above an old greengrocer's shop. I knew there were some basic provisions and a radio. I just had to remember the way.

I took a couple of wrong turns, but eventually, I found the right place. The key was hidden behind a loose brick by the front door. We walked up the creaky staircase. There was just enough light from the street lamp outside to see. We were in a damp bedroom, with a stained mattress tossed in one corner, a cracked sink and a wardrobe.

"Well, I guess this is going to be home for a while," I said.

"We can't stay here."

"You're not going to."

"What do you mean?"

"As far as your superiors are concerned, you've completed your mission. They expect you to cross over the *zwischenwand* tonight. And that's precisely what you'll do."

"But what about you? What about us? I can't just leave you here."

"Don't worry about me. This won't be for long."

"You mean the attack?"

"Exactly. Here, help me shift this."

We moved the wardrobe a few feet from the wall, and I prised up a couple of floorboards with my penknife. Underneath there was a radio, a few bottles of water and some tins of corned beef. I took out the radio and switched it to frequency 3Y, knowing Carla would be monitoring.

37

14th September 1993

THOMAS JORDAN

After I had contacted Carla, I sat and talked with Stephen. To describe it as him filling in the gaps in his life was misleading as his whole life story was one big black hole. He talked me through his childhood. His actual childhood, not the bullshit about coming from a farming family.

It was odd, because he spoke in his real voice, instead of a fake working-class accent. He had never sounded like a cockney and always seemed a bit posh, especially when he was pissed, but it was like speaking to an entirely different person. How he kept that act up twenty-four-seven, I have no idea.

I soon realised that I hardly knew him. The real Stephen was a rich kid, privately educated, good university, all the trimmings. I was a bit jealous. He had skied, and used to have family holidays abroad in places like Crimea or Italy. Things I could only dream of. Yet even though I did not know him, I did. I knew his soul. I know that makes no sense.

We could not have had more different upbringings, yet neither of us gave a shit about that. This freaky, mad situation had brought us together somehow, and it did not matter about schooling, class or money.

He talked about the Piccadilly Circus bombing. It brought home to me that behind the news pictures of bodies on stretchers, there were real people. We argued about it. I had to remind him what happened to my family in Hastings, but I got it now, I understood what drove him, and he knew how much I regretted my involvement in the Wertheim bombing. In a couple of hours, I had got to know him better than over the many months since I met him.

At around 23.00, we heard someone coming upstairs.

"Hide," I whispered to Stephen, who crouched down behind the wardrobe. I stood behind the door.

The handle turned, and I raised my fist, ready to deal a sucker punch. I breathed a sigh of relief as Carla and Mark entered.

"God, am I glad to see you," I said, lowering my fist.

Carla gave me a hug.

"Nice place you've got here," said Mark sarcastically.

"Did you bring what I asked?" I said.

"Yes," said Carla. "Why are you in one of the safe houses, and what do you need the Semtex for?"

"It's a long story. I've got a plan; I've not got time to run it by the council, but I know they would approve it. Listen up—"

"No, you listen," said Carla urgently. "We don't have a lot of time. There's something I need to tell you; it's about a mission I was assigned to, why I've been so coy, and why the Army Council kept you in the dark about it. It's about Bill and…"

Stephen emerged from behind the wardrobe.

"You," spat Carla, retrieving her gun and pointing it at him. "Well, talk of the devil."

Stephen put his hands up.

"Carla, put your gun down," I said.

"You don't understand," she said. "He's an agent."

"I know."

Carla looked confused. "What do you mean, you know?"

Stephen started to lower his hands.

"I said keep your hands up," snarled Carla before turning back towards me. "Well?"

"He's a spy," I said. "Sent to seduce me and infiltrate the resistance."

"How did you find out?" said Carla, confused.

"Have I just missed something?" said Mark.

"Go on, Carla," I said. "Finish what you were about to say."

"Just before you signed up, I was transferred by the Army Council to Adrestia from another cell, to weed out a mole," she said. "We knew that information was leaking out to the Gestapo, and we had a suspicion of who was responsible."

"Who?"

"It was Bill," said Carla.

"Bill?" I said. "You've made a mistake, he's not a Nazi. He can't be."

"There's no doubt," said Carla. "He made a full confession before he died."

"Bill's dead?" I said. "I thought he'd been arrested."

"No," said Carla. "Joe did not want you to know about his suspicions. You were too close to Bill to be objective."

"Too right," I said.

"He's a pro," said Carla. "It's taken a long time to nail him."

"It crossed my mind that you were the spy," I said. "That's why I thought Joe had asked you to stay behind after the last meeting. Then, when you reappeared a few days later, I didn't know what to believe."

"Bill told us everything. We gave him an honourable way out to spare his family the shame. He put a bullet in his head last night."

I felt empty. "Do you have any idea how much that man meant to me? How do you grieve for somebody when they've spent their life lying to you?"

"He fooled us all," said Carla. "Don't waste your energy mourning him."

"If it were that easy…"

Stephen looked at me sadly, clearly not knowing what to say. He ran his hand gently along my arm.

Mark scratched his head. "I suppose that's why Brad's gun failed on the Wertheim mission. Bill insisted on fetching all the equipment from the lock-up."

"Yes," said Carla. "He sabotaged them."

"If the authorities knew about the mission," said Mark, "why let us go ahead?"

"Bill manipulated us into doing the bombing," said Carla. "It was all planned by the regime. It was in their interests."

"Of course," said Mark. "It was a propaganda gift to them. An excuse for a good old-fashioned mass cull."

"The clothes, the cutting equipment," said Carla. "All supplied by the Gestapo."

"When I think about it," said Mark, "it all seemed too easy."

"The attack badly damaged our reputation in America too," said Carla. "Which is what the Nazis wanted."

"Bill told me I was like a son to him. Why…?"

"I'll tell you why," said Carla. "Money. He was paid 950 Reichsmarks a month and promised a new life on the western side, once the resistance had been wiped out."

"Bastard," I said.

"He sold us all down the river," said Carla. "But the good news is we've suspected for a while. The council had been feeding him false information. That and the rubbish you've been disseminating on the radio in your bugged house should throw the SS off the scent."

I shook my head sadly, remembering the family dinners, the boxing lessons, Bill's stories about my father.

"So how do you know about this creature?" said Carla, pointing at Stephen.

"He told me," I said. "Down by the Regent's Canal. With a gun pointed at me."

"My orders were to kill him, then return across the *zwischenwand*," said Stephen.

"So why didn't you?" asked Carla.

"The truth? Because I've fallen in love with him," said Stephen.

"I don't know whether to cry or vomit," said Mark.

"It's true," said Stephen. "I couldn't go through with it. I'm one of you now."

"You'll never be one of us," said Mark. "You're a bloody Nazi."

"Did you know about Bill?" I asked.

"I swear I knew nothing," he said. "I was as much in the dark as you were."

"Are you sure?" I asked.

"I'm begging you," said Stephen. "You have to believe me."

"He's telling you the truth," said Carla. "Stephen was put into Ost-Bereich to take the pressure off Bill, their top agent. Think of all the information that Bill had access to. They were keen to divert suspicion from him. Ultimately, when Stephen's usefulness had run out, he would be ordered to kill Tom. He was to be discovered, then Bill would kill Stephen in revenge to regain his credibility with the council."

"Is that true?" said Stephen.

"You were totally expendable," said Carla. "A pawn in their sick game."

"I've been made a fool of," he said.

"They value your life about as much as ours," said Carla.

"Nice colleagues you have," I said.

"Yeah," said Stephen. "Makes me realise I've chosen the right side."

"Their whole plan went tits up when we got Bill's confession," said Carla. "He was an unrepentant Nazi to the end. His last words were 'Heil Hitler'."

"What a cunt," said Mark.

"We don't have a lot of time," I said. "Can I have the explosives?"

"Here you are," said Carla, digging out the Semtex from her coat pockets.

"You're just going to have to trust me about Stephen," I said.

Carla lowered her weapon. "How clear are you on this? All my instincts told me that he was dodgy, but you insisted we let him join the cell, despite my objections."

"This time it's different," I said. "I'd stake my life on it."

"And ours too," said Mark. "That's what it boils down to."

"I know that," I said. "Look, we have to get a move on; Stephen has to cross over by midnight tonight."

"And?" said Mark.

"Don't you see? We've got a man on the inside now."

"I'll do anything you want," said Stephen. "But I have to tell you something. You're not going to like this."

"What now?" said Carla.

"I told my superiors all the information about the American invasion that you gave me last night."

"Why did you do that, dickhead?" said Mark.

"Because at that point, I didn't know what I was going to do," replied Stephen.

"Nice one," said Mark. "That's fucked up the invasion before it's even started."

"Don't concern yourself too much about it," I said. "We can work around this."

"*We* can?" said Mark.

"I thought you'd be mad," said Stephen.

"All you have to do is cross over, pretend that you've killed me and that my body's in the canal," I said. "Carry on over there as normal."

"Right," he said.

"Except for one thing," I said. "How much do you know about explosives?"

38

14th September 1993

THOMAS JORDAN

Stephen had left the safe house just before 23.00, with the plastic explosives and my instructions. I knew that I had taken a risk, but my gut instinct told me that he would come good. Carla and Mark still did not trust him, though. I couldn't blame them.

When he joined our cell, we wisely assumed the worst, deliberately giving him false and out-of-date information, which we now knew had been passed on to his superiors. This, combined with my radio communications and the bull they had been feeding Bill, should mean that the American plans would still work, assuming there were no other agents on the Army Council. Thank God that Carla had twisted my arm.

The situation regarding Stephen had poisoned the atmosphere. Carla and Mark felt that my judgement was clouded, and were understandably angry.

"You don't know him," argued Carla. "You know nothing about who he really is. He's been feeding you lies ever since he arrived in Ost-Bereich."

"That's true," I admitted. "But I know him, the true Stephen. Even if I don't know *all* the facts about him, I know who he really is, deep down."

"You didn't even know his proper name until a few hours ago," said Carla. "You nearly lost your life."

"He made the right choice in the end," I said. "And even if I'm wrong, even if he goes over and grasses us all up, he knows jack shit. We've not given him any info about the real American plans. We all agreed he needed to prove himself. If he switches allegiance, we're covered."

"That's something," said Carla.

"Thank God you're on our team," I said. "And that I listened to you."

"I just wish you'd listened sooner. You even defended him when you found the bug in your living room. You told us it could not be him. Well now, it's pretty obvious it was."

"I've been wrong about a lot of stuff," I admitted. "But this time, I'm confident that I'm right."

"I hope so," she said. "Because the next few days are crucial."

"The Krauts will be putting all their resources into defending the wrong targets," I said. "And if Stephen carries out my plans, we'll have an even bigger head start."

"I've got another question," said Mark.

"What?" I said.

"When did you turn into a fairy?"

"I'm not a bloody fairy," I snapped. "I hate that word."

"All right, calm down. I was just curious."

"I think I've always been this way. I've had to hide it for so long that pretending to be straight became second nature. Then Stephen came along... well... you know, I've never met another person like myself before. Things just... happened."

"You don't look like a homosexual," he said.

"Does Stephen?"

"I suppose not."

"Should I be wearing a carnation and singing Liberace songs?"

"Of course not."

"Is it a problem?"

"So long as you don't try it on with me."

"For fuck's sake," I said. "I'm not being funny, but I'd rather shag a marrow. At least the conversation would be better."

"Nice," he replied. "Nah, I'm not complaining, it's just more skirt for real men like me."

Carla scowled.

"Because you're such a catch, you ginger twat," I said.

Mark laughed. "Don't knock us gingers; ginger is the new blond."

"Yeah, right," I said. "What about you, Carla? Are you okay with me being… you know?"

"I was surprised," she said.

"Is it an issue?"

"Of course not," she said. "To be honest, it just makes me respect you even more. I just wish that you had trusted me enough to tell me about it sooner."

"How do you bring it into a conversation? I wasn't even sure myself."

"You can't help the way you were born," said Mark. "Like you can't help being an ugly fuck."

"That's coming from the ginger beanpole," I laughed.

"Joking aside," said Mark, "you've still not convinced me about Stephen. Love can make you blind."

"I think Stephen proved himself tonight, walking along the canal. I knew he couldn't kill me."

"I hope you're right," he said. "Because I remember you talking similarly about Bill. He was like your second father, you used to say."

"That's slightly unfair," said Carla. "That man took us all in."

"Mark makes a fair point," I said. "I've laid our lives on the line, and I'm sorry. But I feel it in my gut… it'll be okay."

"He's trained in deception," said Mark. "His purpose was to win your confidence. And he succeeded."

"I trust him," I replied.

"Have you heard of the fable of the scorpion and the bear?" asked Mark.

"No," I replied.

Mark spoke slowly. "The rains fell for weeks in the jungle, the water levels rose, and the river burst its banks. A bear and a scorpion were stranded on a small island in the midst of the torrent. The scorpion asked, 'Why don't you swim across to the dry land over there?'

"The bear replied, 'Because the water is too rough and I can't see the way.'

"The scorpion said, 'Let me sit on your back, and I'll guide us both across.'

"The bear replied, 'But you'll sting me.'

"The scorpion said, 'Why would I do that? Then we'd both drown.'

"The bear swam across the river, with the scorpion on his back, giving directions. When they got halfway across, the scorpion stung the bear. The bear said, 'Why did you do that? Now we'll both die.'

"The scorpion replied, 'I didn't want to, but I couldn't help it. It's in my nature.'"

"What are you saying?" I said.

"Whatever you think about him," said Mark, "he's still a Nazi."

"I get that," I said. "But I just know he's on our side."

"I hope you're right," said Mark. "I really do."

"I am."

"We should get going, Carla," said Mark.

"I don't envy you staying in this place," she said.

"I've stayed in worse," I said optimistically.

"Where?" said Mark. "Ramsgate?"

"Oh, I nearly forgot," said Carla, rummaging in her pockets. "I brought you some whisky. It'll help you sleep."

"Thanks, guys," I said. "You've been great."

"Aren't we always?" said Carla. "Come here, you."

She embraced me and gave me a kiss on the cheek.

"God, I love you," I said.

"I love you too, little brother," she replied affectionately. "You just concentrate on staying alive."

39

14th September 1993

STEPHEN TALBOT

I headed back to my bedsit from the safe house. I rang the office and told them that I had shot Tom and gave them an approximate location and time. As I had hoped, the time and place coincided with a police log of a reported gunshot. I packed up my clothes and field equipment. It was 23.30. I had less than half an hour before crossing the *zwischenwand*. Tom had given me some undetectable plastic explosives and detonators, which I wrapped in clothes and stuffed in my suitcase.

I headed off towards the Bishopsgate checkpoint on foot. Despite the deprivation, I had become attached to Ost-Bereich, and I was going to miss it. The people were real, with an unbreakable spirit. Also, I had fallen in love here. That changes the way you feel about a place.

Fred was waiting for me at the border post. My passage was pre-authorised with security priority status. I was not searched, the guards were polite, and my ID was only quickly scanned.

Fred put my luggage in the boot of his VW Passat, and I slumped into the velour passenger seat. I leant forward and put my head into my cupped hands.

"It's over," said Fred.

"Thank fuck for that," I sighed.

"Welcome back."

I took a deep breath. The car smelled reassuringly of stale tobacco smoke and Kouros.

"Stressed?" enquired Fred.

"You have no idea."

"You've become a bit of a legend, while you've been gone. Even Weber's happy with you."

"I couldn't believe how nice he was on the last phone call."

"Trust me. He's impressed."

He started the engine and pulled away.

"I'd almost forgotten what it's like over here. It's just so clean."

"It's good to have you back."

"I just don't know who I am any more."

"Espionage work is a bit like that," said Fred, putting a cigarette in his mouth. "You become totally immersed in it."

"The lies became so natural, I started believing them myself."

We stopped at some traffic lights at the Angel interchange. I glanced at the cars refuelling at the Aral garage.

"Bloody hell," I said, looking at the prices on the illuminated sign. "Am I reading that right? Ninety-seven pfennigs for a litre of unleaded?"

"They keep putting up the tax on it. Some bull about saving the environment."

"It was thirty-five pfennigs before I went over to Ost-Bereich."

"Everything's gone up. We've all had to tighten our belts. You may not want your new car, after all; I gather it's quite thirsty."

"Do you know what it is?"

"Wait and see. You'll love it."

Fred pulled onto the elevated Inner London Orbital, accelerating to 160 kilometres per hour in the unrestricted VIP lane.

"I just want to soak in a hot bath and sleep in my own bed," I said, opening the window to let out Fred's smoke, which was making me feel queasy. The wind buffeted the inside of the car.

"I wish I could say that you've got some leave coming up to recuperate. But what with the imminent attack from the Americans, it's unlikely."

"I appreciate that. We all need to do our duty."

"There'll be extensive debriefings tomorrow. Be prepared for a busy day."

✠

After five minutes, Fred decelerated and exited the slip road signposted for Hampstead. We drove along the high street, turned right after the Hofbräuhaus beer hall, and pulled up outside my block of flats.

"Thanks for coming personally," I said gratefully. "It's good to see a friendly face."

"No problem at all. I've missed you. They paired me up with Richardson while you were gone. He's a complete plonker."

I laughed. "I look forward to hearing about it."

He pressed a button in the driver's footwell.

"The boot's open. Don't forget to bring your gun and the espionage equipment with you to work tomorrow. You'll need to sign it all back in. I've reserved an underground parking space for you."

"No problem. Except that I tossed the gun into the canal."

"That'll go down well with Department C."

I got out of the car and took my suitcase out of the boot. I looked at Fred through the rear window. Had he known that Weber intended to sacrifice me for the sake of the other agent? I could not imagine it. Then, nothing was unimaginable in my world any longer.

I slammed the lid shut and went into my flat. I expected it to be cold and uninviting, but presumably, somebody from the office had a spare key and had turned on the heating and table lamps. It was cosy, warm and clean, and I was glad to be back.

In the lounge there was a bottle of Moët in an ice bucket with a short note, stating: *Well done, Stephen, enjoy your night*. I noticed that there were two crystal glasses, which did not belong to me.

"Good evening," said an unfamiliar voice from behind me.

I turned around, startled.

"Who are you?" I said. "How did you get in?"

"I'm a present from Oberregierungs Weber."

A tall, handsome man with spiky blond hair stood in my lounge doorway. He was wearing my towelling robe. He took it off provocatively, letting it slip down to the floor, revealing his smooth, muscular torso. He wore nothing other than a skimpy pair of white Hugo Boss briefs. He walked over towards me.

"I'm your reward for the great job you've done," he said.

He started nuzzling my neck.

"God, you really are handsome," I said, starting to feel aroused.

He smelled of expensive aftershave. His skin was taut and smooth, with a chiselled chest and a six-pack. It was only hours ago that I had been talking to Tom about my feelings. Now, here I was, canoodling with another man.

"You're handsome too," he replied. "How about we open that bottle of champagne… and get to know each other?"

"I'll pass, thanks." I pushed him away gently. "Sorry, I don't even know your name?"

"Matthew."

"Look, Matthew. You're very attractive, but I just don't want this."

He looked hurt. "You don't like me?"

He ran his hands down my chest to my groin. Once again, I became aroused, but I pulled away.

"I'm sorry. I'm sure that they'll pay you for tonight, but I'm just not into this. I've never been with a prostitute. It's not what I want."

"I'm not a prostitute, I'm an escort," he said indignantly. "A very expensive, high-class escort, serving only the party elite. I'm known for my complete discretion."

"Whatever or whoever you are, I just want to be on my own tonight. It's not personal."

"Fine. Your loss."

40

15th September 1993

STEPHEN TALBOT

Surprisingly, despite my stress, I slept well in my own bed, which had been made up for me with pristine sheets and crisply pressed pillowcases. I had only been out of the East for half a day, yet it seemed like weeks. It felt like a strange dream from which I had awoken. That life was eleven kilometres away, but it could have been on the other side of the world.

I went into the kitchen and was pleasantly surprised that my cupboards and refrigerator were stocked with fresh food, and there was not a single can of Spam to be seen. I enjoyed a light breakfast. Afterwards, I changed into my formal uniform. I reconnected the battery in my Beetle and drove to work.

I parked in the basement and met Sutton and Weber in the fifty-seventh-floor boardroom.

"Heil Hitler," I said, saluting and standing to attention.

"At ease," said Weber.

"Welcome back," said Sutton.

He reached over the table and shook my hand vigorously.

"To put it succinctly – your intelligence will save thousands of lives," said Weber.

"How do you feel?" asked Sutton.

"Honestly? Emotionally drained and in need of rest."

"I wish I could offer you some leave," said Sutton. "But this is obviously a critical time."

"I understand."

"I'll authorise some, once the Americans have been defeated," he said.

"Thank you, sir."

"You might want to take a vacation somewhere warm," said Weber, sounding uncharacteristically sympathetic. "We can fast-track a travel permit for you. I understand that Libya is beautiful in autumn. Tripoli has some stunning beachfront hotels."

"Or there's the Prora Resort in Rügen?" said Sutton. "As Gestapo officers, we automatically get a thirty per cent discount."

"With respect, I can't even think about holidays at the moment, sir."

"You look like you've lost ten kilos," said Sutton.

"The food is terrible in Ost-Bereich. I've been living off tinned meat for months."

"You'll have a full medical this morning, before debriefing," said Weber. "You've no doubt been lacking nutrition. We'll get you back to full health in no time."

"Thank you," I said, remembering bitterly that Weber had planned to have me killed.

"I see that you did not appreciate my gift last night?" said Weber.

"Sir, it just came at the wrong time."

"You have a lot of paperwork to get through," said Sutton.

"I expected that."

"On a lighter note," said Sutton, "the fleet manager is based in Section 5 of Department C, on the third floor. We mentioned a new company car. You are going to love it."

"I look forward to seeing it later, sir."

"You earned it," said Weber. "Largely thanks to you, we're fully prepared for the American attack."

"Is there anything else, sir?"

"Report to Dr Waring on the fourth floor," said Weber curtly. "And once again, Talbot, congratulations. You're a credit to the force."

✠

I took lunch with Fred, who informed me that I would be reassigned with him next week, then set about the mammoth task of sorting through my overflowing in tray.

It felt surreal being back in the smoky office, surrounded by familiar faces. I had never considered myself fully part of the organisation, but today, I felt even more of an outsider. I took comfort in knowing that it would not be for much longer. Whichever way events transpired, I would not be here in a week. I would either be dead or living in a war zone.

I finished work late. Department C had given me some new car keys, but I did not know what it was yet. I took the service elevator to the basement and clicked a button on the key ring. A black Golf GTI sounded a short bleep and flashed its indicators.

"Wow," I said, walking around my new vehicle in the near-empty car park. It was the sixteen-valve model, with the full body kit. It only had fifty kilometres on the clock, and they had put a full tank of petrol in it. I drove home with a broad smile on my face, living in the moment, briefly forgetting about the task ahead.

The GTI felt like a racing car in comparison to my wheezy Beetle, and I made it from door to door in less than twenty minutes, enjoying the handling on the Inner London Orbital.

It was a bittersweet experience, though. I knew that I could no longer live at the expense of the other half of the population; those who had to choose between keeping warm or eating. In just a few days, that could all change.

41

20th September 1993

THOMAS JORDAN

I woke at 03.30. The day was finally here. I would be leading a team that would hopefully seize Television Tower. I was grateful to be out of that shithole of a safe house, where the damp and cold had made me feel ill.

It was a critical mission – stopping the flow of government lies was essential to our chances of success. We hoped that showing people pictures of the extermination camps would bolster our support.

The whole country's water supply had been free of drugs for a few days now. Expecting attacks on the treatment plants, the Nazis had upped security, further wasting their resources.

The official news had reported that there were war-game exercises in the Liverpool metropolitan area, with a large number of navy vessels stationed in the Irish Sea and the Mersey. The government had to provide some reason why there had been such a massive build-up of troops in this region. It seemed that they had bought into Stephen's reports and the bogus information that I had been putting out on the radio in my bugged living room.

The concentration of their military resources in this area left the rest of the country relatively undefended. The real invasion would come from the east of London. If the Americans provided the scale of support that was promised, it was hoped the capital could be secured in a few days.

Gestapo infiltration had forced us to abandon all of our old meeting places, which we felt sure were being monitored. We met in the vestry of a seventeenth-century church close to Bethnal Green.

Most of the fourteen people present had so far only been given a basic outline of our mission. I gave more details, using maps of London's sewers. Carla and Mark had conducted a dummy run of the route, marked it out with chalk, and cut through a sluice gate blocking the way.

The enlarged group did not have time to bond over a few steins at the local, but I gave our merged cell a name – First Strike Squadron. I appreciate this was a cliché, but it helped make us feel like a team. Most of us had never met before today, but it was entirely possible that we would die together.

Ant's team were a disciplined but scruffy bunch, a bit like him. The two cells had integrated well, bound by a common purpose and shared beliefs. A key individual was James. He was a slightly built seventeen-year-old but looked younger, with greasy brown hair parted into curtains and severe acne. He looked so innocent, and too young to be fighting alongside us. It was his brains that we needed. He was a computer programmer who worked for Deutsche Bank across the *zwischenwand*. Ant claimed he was a genius and would be able to hack the building's security software. He was certainly a geek, and I doubted he would last five minutes against a Stormtrooper, but scratch the surface of his introverted personality and he had a passionate hatred of the Nazis, who had murdered his family. We would find out later whether he was worth dragging along with us today.

Carla, Mark and I distributed weapons, grenades and chocolate bars. A few of us were lucky to have American-issued bulletproof vests, but there were not enough to go around. I allocated James one as his role was critical, not that I considered anybody expendable. I am not going to lie and pretend that we were not shitting ourselves, but the overall feeling was positive.

I looked around the circle of men and women. These were people who had been orphaned by the Nazis or tortured themselves. We all knew that this could well be a suicide mission. If the American attack failed, the Nazis' revenge would be absolute. There would be no mercy or forgiveness. Death would be the easiest, most painless option.

I thought about making some kind of inspiring speech, but I was not a great public speaker, so I kept it simple. "Let's do this, not for us, but for our children, and our children's children. So that they can have a better future. Let's put our egos aside and work together. And I'll buy us all a stein when we're done."

We split into smaller groups and headed to the manhole a few streets away, which led us to the main sewer, connecting to the west side.

Once in the sewer, we made our way slowly but steadily to the other side of the *zwischenwand* and then across a tunnel intersection, dodging the rats and the turds. This led us underneath a quiet road, close to Goodge Straβe Underground Station.

Carla and Mark led the way. We were all bitching about the stench, but were in good spirits, though I could sense that everyone was nervous. I crawled out of the manhole at the other end, checked the coast was clear and helped the others climb out. The garage was a few metres away. I undid the padlock and opened up the door.

The bright yellow DHL van was there, with the keys left in the ignition and a street map on the dashboard. I opened the rear doors to the loading area and ushered everyone in. It was a tight space for fourteen people, but we did not have far to go. Two employee uniforms had been left for us on the front seats, yellow boiler suits with the red DHL logo on the back, along with a parcel containing the bomb, photographs of the Holocaust, and a clipboard.

I could not drive, but Ant was a truck driver. I sat in the passenger seat and opened the map. Someone had helpfully marked out the route in red felt-tip.

Ant turned over the engine, which groaned pathetically. A red battery light illuminated on the dashboard, dimming as the van struggled to start.

"Not promising," said Ant, pumping the accelerator.

Eventually, the engine fired up.

I breathed a sigh of relief.

"Thank fuck for that," said Ant, running his hands through his greasy black hair.

The engine sputtered and seemed about to stall, so he revved it hard, which helped. It settled into a clattery idle.

"Will it be okay to get us to Television Tower?" I asked.

"It's knackered, and we're carrying a lot of weight, but hopefully we'll be okay. Where did they source this pile of crap from?"

"A scrapyard, apparently," I said, opening up the map.

"That I can believe."

The van kangarooed forward under acceleration, and Ant struggled with the gears.

"Could you not drive a bit more smoothly?"

"It's not my fault. The clutch is on its last legs."

We went over a speed hump, which shook the cabin.

"And the suspension."

"All right, let's just get there and try not to kill any of our passengers. Take the next right."

We turned onto an A-road. Ant managed to coax the van up to fifty kilometres per hour.

"Straight on here," I said.

"Shit," said Ant.

"What?"

"Pigs," he said, pointing at his side mirror.

I saw an Audi Quattro with its blue lights flashing and siren wailing.

"Now what?" he said.

"Just stay calm."

The car grew larger in the mirror, then overtook us at high speed.

I breathed a sigh of relief.

"Bloody hell," said Ant.

"They've got more important things to worry about."

"How much further?"

I looked at the map. "It's a couple of streets away. Take the next left."

A few minutes later, we were at Television Tower. One of the tallest skyscrapers in London, it was a futuristic cylindrical building, crowned with what resembled a flying saucer, making it look top-heavy. A jungle of satellite dishes and aerials were attached the walls of the circular section. It looked a bit like a giant air traffic control tower.

There was a temporary roadblock, with two SS guards armed with machine guns either side of a rising arm barrier.

"Keep calm," I said. "I expected this. London will be on high alert with the attack imminent."

The first Stormtrooper approached the van.

"ID cards," he barked.

Ant and I handed him our false cards. He examined them, then handed them back to us.

"What's your reason for being here?" he asked curtly.

"Parcel delivery for Television Tower," said Ant.

He walked around the vehicle suspiciously, hitting the metal panels with his fist. I watched him in the mirror as he came back towards the cabin.

"Open the rear for inspection," he ordered.

"Give us a break," I said. "We're on a tight deadline."

"I said, open the back."

"Okay, okay," I said, climbing out of the cabin.

I walked over to the rear door, aware that I was out of sight of the second guard, who waited at his post.

"It's only parcels and boxes. Feel free to look. It's not locked."

The soldier opened the rear door, revealing our squadron. Before he had a chance to shout, I placed him in a headlock, with my knife against his jugular.

"Make one sound, and I'll slice your fucking head off," I said.

Carla and several of the others jumped down from the van and disarmed him.

"Call your friend over," I ordered.

"Fuck you," he said.

I slid the knife gently across his neck, drawing blood. "Last chance."

"Schutze Fensome," he shouted. "Come here."

The other SS soldier came to the rear of the vehicle and was overpowered. I sank my knife into the first soldier's jugular, then immediately plunged it into the second trooper's heart. They fell lifeless to the ground.

"Get them in the back of the van," I said.

Several men lifted them into the back. Blood spewed out profusely from the first soldier's neck, forming a puddle on the van floor. I could see James was shaking. I hoped that he would not crack; we needed him.

"Was it necessary to kill them?" said Carla.

"They're wearing SS uniforms, and this is war."

"Even so. That one's got a wedding ring on. He might have a family."

"You might too. And I doubt he would have had a second thought about killing you. You two, Greg and Matthew, put on their uniforms. You'll man the blockade for now."

"This wasn't in the plan," said Greg.

"Neither was having the van searched. It's called improvisation. Come on, we're wasting time."

Greg and Matthew hurriedly put on the uniforms, which were too small. Neither man had shaved and Matthew had long, greasy hair, not to mention the bloodstains on the tunics. They looked about as convincing as Chancellor Goebbels' human rights charter, but with any luck, they would not be in place for long.

"Let us through the barrier," I said. "Then we'll radio when you're needed."

I shut the rest of the squadron in the back of the van and jumped into the cabin.

"Drive," I said to Ant.

We drove the van up to the entrance to Television Tower, where there was another manned barrier. An unarmed RT employee waved us through without any fuss. We parked under the canopy, in front of the glass entrance. I went in, carrying the package and clipboard, while Ant and the squad waited in the van.

Inside, there were armed security guards. Since it was assumed the guards at the raising barrier would have searched me, I was buzzed through a turnstile leading to the centre of the reception area, where the elevators were.

I took the lift to the thirty-second floor, where the news studios were located. It was nerve-racking. I knew that I had to secure this level while the others took the lower levels and control of the building's security systems. The elevator sounded a chime, and the doors opened onto a small reception area manned by a young woman sat behind a desk, wearing bright red lipstick, Gucci glasses, and a red suit.

"Delivery," I chirped.

She looked at me condescendingly. "We're not expecting anything."

"I'm just the messenger," I said, shrugging my shoulders.

I handed her the parcel and pointed my gun at her. "Put your hands where I can see them," I ordered.

"Please," she begged. "I've got a baby boy."

She started moving her hand under the desk.

"Don't even think about it. Move away from there."

She complied. I waved the gun towards the door leading to the central office, where journalists were busy on computers.

"Do exactly what I say, and nobody will get hurt. Pick up the parcel and head into the office. Slowly."

We walked through a pair of fire doors into the office. At the far end, there was a soundproofed room with a glass viewing window, where the director and producer sat. They had their backs to us and were not aware of what was happening.

I shot my gun at the CCTV camera, blowing it off the wall, then I took out the remote activator for the bomb.

"Everyone stay exactly where they are," I shouted. "This remote control activates a bomb inside that parcel. Move, and I'll blow us all up."

There was screaming, and some people stood up and started edging away from me. I shot into the air, blowing a large hole in the polystyrene ceiling. Wires dangled out of the cavity.

"Sit down, everyone."

I took out my radio and contacted Ant. "Phase one underway, over."

"Understood."

Through the radio's tiny speaker, I heard Ant rev the engine and the sound of smashing glass as he reversed the van into the reception area. I knew that we did not have much time. The fire alarm sounded, and the sprinklers sprayed out foamy water, soaking us. Missile-proof uroferranium shutters automatically drew across the windows.

The office became dark as the lights flickered, then failed. The emergency lighting kicked in, bathing the room in a dull amber glow. A klaxon sounded, competing with the fire alarm.

I shot at the fire alarm bell, which went quiet, and I ripped the klaxon from the wall. The sprinklers cut out, and I could hear myself speak again.

A pre-recorded news programme was playing on the monitor, but the director and his team behind the soundproof glass could see what was going on and were telephoning for help. I ignored them for the time being.

I reached into my pocket and handed an envelope to the receptionist.

"Open that envelope," I said. "Inside, you'll find photographs. Look at them, then pass them around. Do it. Now."

Her hands shook as she opened the envelope and took out the photographs of the concentration camps, which so few of us had seen. She started leafing through them in disbelief. I saw the horror on her face, followed by denial.

She shook her head and handed them back to me. "No," she said. "You're trying to trick us. These aren't real.

"It's obscene," said one journalist. "These are obviously fake."

"No, they're real," I insisted.

One of the production staff, who sat on a chair with *EDITOR* written on the back, put on a pair of spectacles and scrutinised the photographs. He passed them to his assistant.

"We doctor photographs all the time," he said, taking off his glasses. "Either the CIA have invented some kind of miracle technology that we don't know about, or these are genuine."

His assistant also started to examine the pictures. "I can't find any evidence of fakery," he said. "The angle of the shadows in relation to the sun, the background. In my view, even with the most elaborate techniques, you could not pull this kind of thing off."

"You're saying these are authentic?" said the receptionist, her face starting to crack.

The assistant editor nodded his head slowly. "I don't want to believe it either, but I'd say they are. In fact, I'd bet my life on it."

The receptionist started sobbing.

"You're a mother," I said to her. "Look at those desperate children."

A male employee put his face into his palms and started crying.

The lift in the reception area opened with a chime, and four of my comrades, including Mark, came out, armed with machine guns.

"Well?" I asked.

"The building is on lockdown," said Luke, a short man with spiky blond hair and a poorly corrected cleft palate. "One of the guards was compliant and gave us access to the security terminal. James says we're impenetrable from the outside, and we have control of the elevators, air supply, heating and telephones. All the floors are sealed. People are trapped there until *we* allow them to leave. We're just mopping up a few guards."

I pointed to the glass booth. "Get them out of there. We need these people to operate the equipment."

"I'm sure we can persuade them," said Luke, patting his gun like a faithful dog.

"I'd like them to volunteer," I said. "We're freedom fighters, not thugs."

Luke rounded up the directors, cameramen and newsreaders at gunpoint, bringing them through to the central office. We showed them the photographs and reeled off statistics of how many Jews, Russians, Africans, homosexuals, disabled and Gypsies the Nazis had murdered. Their shocked faces betrayed their feelings.

In the corner of my eye, I saw a fat, balding bloke pick up a telephone and start to dial out. I fired a warning shot, which ricocheted off the bulletproof outer glass. People ducked and covered their heads with their hands. "Put it down," I snarled.

Luke and the other three circled the office with their guns trained on the workers.

"What do you want with us?" said the fat man. "We're just reporters doing our job."

"Reporters? Don't make me laugh," I said. "This whole operation is just an extension of the Ministry of Public Enlightenment. But now you've got a chance to be real journalists."

"What are you suggesting?" said a young, freckly man in a short-sleeved shirt.

"You've seen what the Nazis did in Europe and what's happening now in Africa. This is the real face of National Socialism. Genocide, torture and mass starvation."

"So you say," he said.

"The pictures are real."

The editor spoke up. "I'm not saying I agree with this man's actions, but the photographs *are* genuine, of that I'm sure."

"I believe it," said the receptionist.

"Me too," said a blonde woman. "And I feel disgusted. How can they have kept this a secret for so long?"

"Because of people like us," said another worker. "I'm not stupid, I suspected something bad happened to the Jews. I knew the Nazis had fanatics among them, but mass murder on this scale..."

Many in the room nodded in approval, but there were also doubters.

I looked at the two people who would be most useful to the cause. I had seen them on television for most of my life. Newsreaders John Jeffries and Maria Thorpe. They were so familiar that I felt as though I knew them. They were the human faces of the regime, but they were also collaborators, peddling lies and propaganda. I had no idea which way this would go.

"You know how much influence you carry with the public," I said to them. "You could help us turn the battle around."

Maria studied me. "I've interviewed enough people in my career to know when someone is telling the truth or lying. I get the sense that you are telling the truth."

John Jeffries spoke. "I'm due to retire at the end of the year. I've done my service; I was looking forward to a good pension and spending my twilight years in my little cottage in Cornwall."

"How can we carry on, knowing what we now know?" said Maria. "I mean, look at those starving children. We're both parents. I can't undo this knowledge and pretend nothing has happened."

"I agree," said John quietly. "This is an outrage. We have to do what's right."

"We're with you," said Maria.

I raised my voice. "John and Maria are with us. I'm giving everyone here a choice. We can't operate the equipment on our own. We want you to join us. To spread the truth. To bring down this vile regime, and bring freedom to our great country."

"This won't be enough to bring them down," said a weaselly-looking man sat on a desk near me. "Even if you got thousands of people to join your cause, the SS wouldn't hesitate to fire on unarmed protesters. Then, when they regain control of this station – and trust me, they will, however many people they have to kill – they'll get Maria and John to tell the viewers that they said everything under duress, facing the barrel of a machine gun. I can even see the documentary now on how the photographs were faked in Hollywood studios. We do this kind of cover-up story all the time."

"But we're not alone," I said. "The Americans are attacking. Today. That's why you've been reporting about the military exercises in Liverpool."

The programme director, a tall man with neat black hair, pockmarked skin, a moustache and piggy eyes, bellowed, "Have you all lost your minds? You're listening to the words of a terrorist. This creature would bomb and kill our children in the cause of some lie."

"How can you say that, given what I've just shown you?"

"I don't care what my editor has said, those pictures are fake," said the director. "Don't believe him. All of us took an oath of allegiance to the party."

"A party responsible for genocide."

"How on earth can you try to claim the moral high ground when you're pointing a gun at me? You're a terrorist."

"'Terrorist' is the regime's choice of words. I call myself a freedom fighter. And why do I do this? Because I watched my mother being shot dead when I was fifteen years old. I saw the rest of my family led to gas chambers."

"Gas chambers. There's no such thing."

"Yes, there fucking is. Deny it all you want, but I've seen them. I've smelled the burning corpses at Ramsgate. The ash fell like snow. I'll never forget the stench."

"Bollocks. You're a criminal, no more, no less. And your attempts to dismantle our way of life will never succeed."

I raised my gun and pointed it at the director.

"Yeah, that's right. You've lost the argument, so you deal with it like any other mindless thug."

"Just shut the fuck up."

"Do as he says, Barry," said Maria sternly. "You've made your point."

"I want RT to start broadcasting the truth," I said. "We need to show the public the reality of the concentration camps and report impartially on the American attack. If you want to join us, move to the left. If you don't, move to the right – you'll be taken to another floor to sit this out. If the Nazis win, you'll be innocent."

"And what if the Americans win?" said the fat, balding man.

"Would you rather face American justice or a Nazi kangaroo court?" said Luke.

"I'm with you," said the woman near me.

"Me too," agreed another.

People stood up and took their positions. It was disappointing that the majority, about three quarters, had rejected us. On a positive note, that still left eleven people who had chosen to side with us, and including John and Maria.

"Heil Hitler," said one of the regime loyalists defiantly, giving a forward salute.

Luke radioed James. "Mate, can you open the fire exits to the rear staircase on this floor and the one below? Over."

"Give me a minute, I'm just getting used to this software. Over."

"You'll never get away with this," said the director, speaking to the defectors. "I *will* give evidence against you. Treason will earn you the most painful of deaths. You took an oath—"

"Be quiet," ordered Luke. "Or, unlike Tom, I *will* shoot you."

The fire door clicked as James unlocked it remotely from the security console. Luke ushered the regime loyalists down the fire escape to the floor below, where they were locked away safely. They had made their choice.

A substantial part of the back office, including the production staff, editor, assistant editor, and all the cameramen, had stayed. There was enough technical know-how to get us on the air. The next stage was even more critical. We had to start broadcasting to the people and call a general strike. Currently, the public would not know what was happening here since RT were transmitting a recorded programme, and the streets outside had been cordoned off. Soon, that would all change.

The receptionist came over to me. She looked different. Her mascara had run down her face. Her stern expression had gone. It was as though she had regained her humanity. She looked me in the eyes, nodded, then walked away silently.

I noticed a large man with a ponytail and a goatee, typing frantically on his word processor.

"Hey – what are you doing?" I asked suspiciously.

"Do you want your news programme to go out?" he said.

"What do you bloody think?"

"Stop interrupting me, then," he said. "I've got ten minutes to get a script written for the autocue, unless you know how to write the news?"

"No."

"Well then, piss off and wave your gun at someone else."

The office became a hive of activity. I wandered into the soundproofed area and found the studio. It felt surreal because it was such a familiar sight. The news desk in front of a red background with the RT logo that I had seen on the television every day was here in solid reality, except that you could see the cameras and overhead lighting rig that were normally out of sight. Soon John and Maria would be sitting down, as they did every morning during the week, but this time, the news would be from a somewhat different perspective.

42

20th September 1993

STEPHEN TALBOT

I had given up trying to sleep. I rummaged in the cupboard under the kitchen sink and took out the Semtex that Tom had given me. There was enough to disable Himmler Tower and cause chaos.

I pushed the detonator prongs into the Plasticine-like bars and attached them to an electronic timer. This was not the home-made lash-up that I would have expected, but a piece of specialist American military hardware.

I set the detonator for 10.00 by twisting the plastic dial. Then I pressed the arm button. A red LED blinked twice, and a countdown began on the liquid crystal display. The explosives could now not be disarmed or tampered with unless a deactivation code was entered on the mini keypad. I started work at 07.00, which would give me less than three hours to plant them and exit the building before they exploded. Three hours sounded a long time, but this was one of the most secure buildings in the world, full of highly trained soldiers and secret agents, with an advanced electronic monitoring system and an atmosphere of extreme paranoia.

I put the explosive devices into an A3-sized Jiffy envelope and covered it with some official papers.

I experienced a sense of belonging to the resistance that I had never felt towards the Gestapo, yet I still did not know whether I could follow through with their plans. They expected me to kill colleagues I had been working alongside for months.

At 06.30, I put on my uniform. On my way out, I noticed that somebody had put a letter under my front door. On the envelope in neat handwriting, it read, *Only open this if you are having doubts.* I felt taken aback. Who had put this here, and how did they know where I lived?

I resisted the temptation to open it. I put it in my briefcase and left for work. I parked in the basement and passed through security with minimal fuss, attempting to remain calm.

I walked to the central elevator and felt a hand on my left shoulder. I spun around.

"Father," I said in surprise. "What are you doing here?"

"What do you think?" he replied. "You know what's happening today."

"Do I?"

"The attack? By the Americans?"

"Oh, that."

"What else did you think I meant? Anyway, I just wanted to say that I'm very proud of you. Oberregierungs Weber isn't easy to please."

"Thank you."

"Your mother says you must come over for dinner soon."

The elevator arrived with an electronic chime. We stepped inside.

"Which floor do you need?" I said to my father.

"Fifty-four," he replied.

I pressed the button and the one for my own floor. The doors closed and the elevator rose to the thirty-second floor. The doors slid open onto the central gallery, overlooking Hitler's bronze shoulder.

"Good luck for today," said my father. "It's going to be a long one."

"You too," I said awkwardly, exiting the lift, aware that I was sweating profusely.

✠

I sat down nervously at my desk. Fred came over.

"You okay?" he asked.

"Worried, if I'm honest. I didn't sleep last night."

"That's understandable. What the Americans have planned could plunge us into World War III. I imagine it was hard to switch off."

"Absolutely."

"Are you sure you're okay? You look ill."

"I think I'm coming down with something. On today of all days."

"There's a departmental briefing at 08.00 sharp. I've got some Voltaren if you want some."

"I'll be all right. I'll see you there."

I wiped my brow. It would be so easy to tap in the deactivation code on the keypad to disarm the bombs and dispose of them in the Thames. I had memorised it – 33758. I could carry on living a lie, pretending that I was a loyal employee of the Gestapo. Bumping into my father changed things. There was a substantial probability that he would die in the explosion.

Fred was halfway across the office floor. "Fred," I shouted.

He turned around. "Yes?"

"I need to speak to you," I said nervously.

Fred walked back to my desk. "Make it quick. I've got a meeting with Sutton."

"I feel that I may have missed out some information in my report on Ost-Bereich. Regarding Thomas Jordan."

"And?"

I looked around at my colleagues, tapping away on computers or talking earnestly on the phones. Many had pictures of their children in frames on their desks.

"Well, come on, Stephen, I've not got all day."

"This is going to be tough to explain."

43

20th September 1993

STEPHEN TALBOT

"You said that you'd missed out some information," said Fred. "At this late stage? Is it vital?"

"It's about… I…"

"I'm not being funny, Stephen, but can this wait? Let's just get the next few days out of the way, then you can have my undivided attention."

"Sure," I said, relieved. I thought of Tom. He would be well into his own mission now.

Fred headed back towards Sutton's office.

I opened my briefcase and took out some papers. Nestled amongst the sheets of A4 was the manila envelope from the unknown sender. I had no idea what it contained, but I knew that I *was* having doubts. I prised open the flap and took out a crumpled piece of notepaper. It was handwritten, on behalf of Tom.

> *I know that you will be having doubts because you are human. That's why I love you so much. One of our contacts within your organisation has dug out some interesting information. You will not like it, but sometimes we have to face the*

truth. I hope it helps you make the right choice. Please know that I have no wish to hurt you, but this will be painful.

PP Tom.

There was a number written at the bottom of the paper. I recognised it as a central computer database reference assigned to an individual case file. URN/1433/08/1988 – 49983412, with an accompanying password.

I was surprised that the resistance had moles within the Gestapo. I wondered who they were. In this instance, it would need to be somebody reasonably senior to have clearance to examine archived files like this, a *kriminalrat* at least. Did they know what was going to happen today or would they be collateral damage?

I logged on to my terminal and typed in the reference code into the clumsy text-based R-UNIX system. There was a pause before the slave terminal prompted me for the password, which gave me access to the restricted file. The screen slowly filled with green text.

<Subject: Phillip TYER> <Interrogator: Edward TALBOT>

FILE STATUS – CLOSED

CONCLUSION: Subject charged and convicted. D11 issued. Subject deceased before arrival at labour camp. Died as a result of injuries sustained during interrogation. Next of kin informed.

Press <ENTER> for detailed case notes.

I felt nauseous. I recalled the wreck of a human being that I had witnessed in the car park. A crime committed by the man who had convinced me that he had saved me from a slow death by calling in favours.

However, the fact was that killing people was not something that came naturally to me. This revelation only added to my confusion. It certainly made me hate my father and the system he represented, but I still did not know if I could go through with bombing my colleagues.

My briefing was in a few minutes. Fred emerged from Sutton's office and came over to my desk.

"You look like you've seen a ghost," he said.

"Perhaps I have," I said, hurriedly switching off the computer screen.

"You'd better get a move on. Briefing is about to start."

✠

I sat in the briefing room, listening to Oberregierungs Weber barking orders in his thick accent. Those around me listened intently, hungry for some action and focused fully on the task ahead. In contrast, my mind wandered. I did not care any more. I was more concerned that time was ticking. I was unsure whether to deactivate the bombs, but if I did go through with it, time was running out for me to get a safe distance from the building.

Fred nudged me and whispered, "Pay attention."

I focused for the last few minutes. Afterwards, I signed out my firearm from the armoury and returned to my desk.

Fred was waiting for me. "What's wrong with you?" he said crossly. "Kriminalrat Sutton just had a real go at me. You were paying no attention whatsoever in there. If you're ill, just go home."

"Leave it, Fred."

I put my briefcase on top of my desk.

"Our personnel carrier leaves in fifteen minutes," he said.

"Do you trust me?"

"What do you mean?"

"Do you trust me?"

"Of course."

"I've sat at your kitchen table with your family, played football with your children, shared good times and bad. You're a good man. One of very few in this place."

"What's this all about?"

"Come with me."

"Where are we going?"

"To my car. In the basement."

"We don't have time for games. We're about to—"

"Trust me. You'll want to hear this."

✠

We took the service elevator to the basement and got into my Golf.

"What's all this about?" said Fred.

"I need to tell you something," I said, reversing out of my space. The guards at the entrance opened the barrier, and I drove out onto Embankment, accelerating hard.

"Slow down."

I took the car up to eighty kilometres per hour, overtaking the slow-moving traffic, before braking and turning onto Waterloo Bridge. It seemed like an ordinary working day, with Routemaster buses and black cabs trundling along the riverside. Like those on board the *Titanic*, nobody knew that disaster was imminent.

I sped over the bridge, flashing at cars to move out of the way. Once across, I joined Höss Straβe and parked the car as close to the river as I could.

"We'll walk from here," I said.

"You'll get us both sent to Ramsgate. You can't just walk out of the office and go on a joyride on a day like today."

We walked up a cobbled street to the granite wall on the bank of the Thames, overlooking Himmler Tower on the other side. It was a clear day, with blue skies and the autumn sun low on the horizon, rising from behind us, glinting against the glass-and-steel skyscrapers of the rapidly burgeoning skyline, as London reinvented itself as the world's third financial centre.

"I have to ask you something, Fred. Did you know?"

"Know what?" said Fred impatiently.

I looked him directly in the eyes. "That Weber and Sutton instructed the other agent to kill me."

"Don't be ridiculous. Why would they do that?"

"Their original plan was for me to eventually kill Thomas Jordan. Then, I was to be discovered. Their other agent, a man called Bill, was going to kill me to prove his loyalty to the BLA and regain the trust of the Army Council. All part of Weber's grand plan. It was only thanks to the fact that the resistance uncovered Bill and killed him that I'm still here today."

"You're shitting me?"

"Don't fuck with me, Fred. I just want to know the truth. Did you know?"

"Of course I didn't know. If I did, I would have objected, and duty or no duty, I would have found a way to tell you."

"Are you sure?"

"Yes. I swear on my children's lives. You shouldn't have even needed to ask me."

"I believe you."

"Good. Because it's the truth. They never would have disclosed something like that to me. Apart from the fact I'm too junior, they know about our close friendship. How did you find out?"

"The other agent confessed."

"Confessed to who?"

"His captors."

"Under torture?"

"Yes. Carla – the girl in our cell – told me."

"And you believe her? Wake up and smell the coffee. They're playing you."

"No. I considered that possibility, and you're wrong."

"Face up to it. They've turned you against us. They've got inside your head. I wish you'd been more honest with me. If you were having second thoughts about your role over there, I could have helped you."

"You helped me more than you could know. But you must choose what side you're on today."

"What do you mean, what side I'm on? I'm on the same side I've always been. The side you're on, I hope."

"I know you're not one of them," I said, pointing at Himmler Tower.

"What on earth do you mean?"

"You're not one of them any more than I am. I see it in your eyes. The self-loathing when you carry out your orders. The battle between obedience and the desire for morality. They spent decades trying to brainwash you, to eliminate your conscience and make you like them, but I see the inner Fred Stanning. The man who cuddles his children when they cry. The faithful husband and loyal friend. They've not driven all of your humanity from you."

Fred sighed. "This is dangerous talk, Stephen. I know you're pissed off with Weber, which is understandable, but what you've just said to me could land you in a correction facility."

"Pissed off? That's a slight understatement."

"You know the business we're in. Even if this whole story about you being killed by our other agent is correct, we all have to be prepared to make the ultimate sacrifice. That eventuality should have been drummed into you at training school."

I turned away from him towards the Thames. "Look at the building we work in. How it towers above the cityscape. Dominating the skyline, lit up at night, visible for miles around. A symbol of ultimate state power. Understand me, I'm doing this not just for myself, but for the next generation. So that your children have a chance to live as free men and women."

Fred took his gun out of its holster and pointed it at me. "You understand that I have to arrest you."

"Of course you do. I've put you in an impossible situation."

I looked at Himmler Tower in the distance. I knew that it would be any second now. I glanced at my watch.

"Put your hands on your head and kneel down," said Fred.

As he spoke, a massive explosion ripped through Himmler Tower. I heard the sound of shattering glass and steel beams collapsing, along with numerous alarms and sirens drifting across the Thames. There was a smaller secondary explosion a few seconds later. I could see smoke billowing out of the middle floors.

"Your work, I presume," said Fred. "Given what you've just told me, and your urgency to get out."

"Yes."

"My God, what have you done?"

"I made a choice. As you must do now. I chose to follow my conscience. What will you decide?"

"You've spent too much time in Ost-Bereich. Don't you see? You've been radicalised. It's an insidious process; you're not the first to fall for it. It happens when you're undercover, but we can help you. We can enrol you on an intensive therapy course at Heydrich House. The psychiatrists there are among the best in the world. You'll soon be back to normal."

"I don't need therapy. The resistance has liberated me. Tom has liberated me."

"You're wrong. Tom is a terrorist, a murderer. He's corrupted you. We underestimated him."

"No, he has set me free. Don't you see, Fred – the Americans will prevail. Soon Nazi rule will be over. Weber, Müller, the cronies and hangers-on – the lot of them, they'll all be under arrest within weeks. This isn't a dream. It's happening as we speak."

Fred lowered his gun.

"I'll give you a ten-minute head start," he said. "Then I'll report you."

"You have no choice."

"God help you. God help us all."

"The Americans will win."

"You hope. I'm hedging my bets. Which is why you must punch me in the face. As hard as you can."

I hit Fred in the jaw, and he fell to the ground. He was still conscious, but hurt.

"God, that hurts, fuck, fuck, fuck…" he cried.

"You're a good man, Fred. I hope I'll see you again."

I left him writhing in pain, ran to my car and sped off, my tyres screeching on the tarmac. I headed towards the *zwischenwand*. I knew that I had clearance for today's operation, so I expected to be allowed through, and Tom had arranged a hiding place for me once I was on the other side. I felt a mixture of guilt and excitement. My adrenaline levels must have been sky-high because I was trembling involuntarily. I thought about my father. The bombs were not huge; they were designed to disrupt rather than maim. I really hoped that he had managed to escape. Whatever he stood for, whatever he had done, I still loved him.

At the border post, I wound down my window, handing an SS guard my warrant card.

"Have you heard the news?" he said.

"Himmler Tower being bombed?"

"What else?"

"If I'd left five minutes later they would have got me too. My father was in there when the bomb went off. The bastards."

"Get us some payback," said the guard, waving me through.

"I will," I said, winding up the window.

I drove for about ten minutes and parked the car on a potholed side street. I opened the fuel cap, took a handkerchief from my pocket and stuffed it inside, so it soaked up the petrol from the tank.

"Easy come, easy go," I murmured as I struck a match and watched the flames lick over the petrol-soaked fabric. I quickly walked away, tossing the car keys into a drain. After about a minute I heard an explosion. I ran towards Bethnal Green Tube Station, discarding my cap and ripping off my Gestapo tunic.

44

20th September 1993

THOMAS JORDAN

I sat in the control room with our hastily recruited production team, looking at the screen, which showed John and Maria behind the news desk, just as usual, except that I had removed the RT logo and swastika. Luke had printed off a Union Jack onto a piece of A3 using a colour inkjet printer, with the words *British Liberation Army Television* underneath.

The building's power had been cut, but there were emergency generators which had enough diesel to last a few days if we were careful, so we turned off stuff we did not need, including the air conditioning. It was like an oven with all the studio lights.

Through the building's external cameras, we could see that tanks were circled around us, with their turrets pointing upwards. I knew that they would think twice about destroying this facility. A soldier stood holding a placard towards one of the cameras, with the message: *SURRENDER NOW, AND YOU WILL BE PARDONED.* It was about as believable as the acting in *The Peelers*. We all knew that the only way out of here alive would be if the Americans came good.

My worst fears came true when there was a loud metallic ring, like the sound of a ship's hull buckling. They had fired a missile at the shutters, but the uroferranium alloy was holding. It did not even dent under the impact.

We were playing for time, and we had hostages acting as a human shield. The Nazis were evil bastards, but they would think twice about killing hundreds of regime loyalists in the building. Unfortunately, I also knew we could only push them so far before they would cut their losses.

I thought about Stephen. If he had followed through with the plan, the bombs would have been planted and would detonate any minute now, creating mayhem and a highly visible symbol of defiance to Londoners.

The countdown started for the 10.00 news. I believed that the presenters were on our side, but I could not be sure until I heard them speak on live television. If they betrayed us, I would have no option but to shoot them both. This would hardly be a winning blow for our cause, watching two of the country's national treasures sprayed with bullets on live television. The news theme music started and the *LIVE ON AIR* sign illuminated. I took a deep breath.

The stand-in director, a man called Bob, spoke into a microphone to Cameraman 2.

"Zoom in slowly to John," he said. This image was going out live all over the country.

"Good morning, Britain," John said. *"And I use the word 'Britain', as in Great Britain. The birthplace of the Industrial Revolution, the nation that invented democracy and once ruled three quarters of the globe. Not Region 6, which the German invaders have chosen to call us. I'm John Jeffries. You're not dreaming, and it isn't 1st April. This is British Liberation Army Television, covering the revolution currently sweeping through our country, without censure*

and with impartiality. For once, I'll be speaking the truth, not toeing the party line."

"And I'm Maria Thorpe. If you're just joining us, then you should be aware that this is a momentous day in our history. I, too, speak of my own free will. The television station is under the control of the BLA, but under siege by government forces, so I am unsure how long we will be on the air, but I hope that you will stay with us for as long as we can keep broadcasting."

As they spoke, I could not help but imagine the shocked faces of those who would be watching. This was unprecedented.

"The resistance has asked all those who support us to engage in a general strike," said John. *"Don't go to work. If you are there already, please go home and stay inside. Assistance is coming."*

"The resistance – and I use the word 'resistance', not 'terrorists' – have asked me to read this statement," said Maria, unfolding a piece of paper.

> *"My fellow citizens of our once-great country. This is a frightening time for all of us. You have watched this news station for years, with the truth hidden from you. It will be both shocking and painful when you see the images that will shortly be shown. You must not blame yourselves. Very few of you know the truth. You have been indoctrinated from the moment you were born.*
>
> *We, the BLA, have been cast as terrorists. Murderers of men, women and children. The loss of any life is regrettable, but we hope that you understand that we are fighting for a just cause. To liberate our country from the German invaders, who have taken away our freedom, massacred millions, and continue to torture and persecute so many.*

For decades, you have been drugged into apathy via the water supply. We have now removed this chemical. You should be feeling different already. We ask that you keep an open mind, and support us by joining in a general strike across the country.

The Americans are on their way to help us. We honestly have a fighting chance to throw off the yoke of occupation and realise our potential as one of the greatest countries in the world.

The next few days and weeks will be difficult. The Nazis will not hesitate to kill indiscriminately. They will threaten and torture, it is the only thing they know how to do, but I assure you, their days are numbered, and they will soon face justice. We are playing to win, and I believe that we will."

"The note is signed using a pseudonym: General Charles K, member of the British Liberation Army ruling council."

"Thank you, Maria," said John. *"Some words for us all to dwell on, there."*

"Breaking news just coming in," interrupted Maria, fiddling with her earpiece. She spoke urgently. *"We're getting reports that Himmler Tower, the headquarters of the SS and Gestapo, has been bombed. We're receiving some footage now."*

A news crawler scrolled along the bottom of the screen, as the production staff in the office fed stories into the computer, live as they happened.

People watched the news on the enormous screens at Piccadilly Circus, on the mini screens on the Tube trains, and in their homes. They were free of the effects of DHPA, and they were, at last, being shown the truth.

John Jeffries spoke: *"I have sat in this chair for nearly thirty years. It would be hypocritical not to admit that I have had a blessed life, but there comes a point when one has to ask oneself, What are my values? Am I a journalist or a politician? Today, I saw pictures that I am confident are not fake. They have been examined by our own experts at RT. These images are so shocking that I could no longer in good conscience continue my job in the same way."*

"We were given a simple choice: tell you the truth, or remain loyal to the regime and sit this out in the safety of the floor below," said Maria. *"At risk to our own lives, we chose to tell you the truth. Please believe me when I say that I had never seen these images before today. You will be shocked. It won't be easy to accept the kind of society that we are part of. Perhaps we collectively suspected, but we just didn't want to know or contemplate. It was easier for all of us to keep our heads down and turn a blind eye to our inner feelings. I can't prepare you for what you are about to see or how you will react. Some of you will feel overwhelming guilt; others will no doubt deny the truth. The fact is that we are all guilty of collusion. I leave you to pass judgement in the privacy of your own minds."*

One by one the graphic photographs were displayed, with Maria and John providing explanations for each one. The forcibly starved African children, the tortured faces of identical twins experimented on at Auschwitz Birkenau, the crematoria and macerators in Vorkuta and Auschwitz 5, the three-storey-high hermetically sealed gas chambers in Tripoli and Cairo. This was the first time most people had seen the images. Automated mass murder on an industrial scale.

Just as it was a powerful recruiting tool for the resistance, we hoped it would create a tidal wave of opposition to the regime. The impact was better than we could have ever prayed for. People publicly broke down in tears. There was a riot in Piccadilly Circus as people watching the screen started to attack the police when asked to move on.

Many were persuaded to support us. Of course, there were the small bands of ultra-fanatics, who believed that nothing was off limits to further National Socialism. Then there were the disbelievers, those who would or could not believe their eyes. Perhaps their denial was down to guilt. Guilt that their whole comfortable existence was based on a foundation of mass genocide.

We had managed to keep broadcasting for an hour so far. Helicopters circled the roof of the building, but James had managed to boot up the building's defences and shot one down, causing the others to back off. That kid was a geek, but I was glad that he was on our side. I knew that the American Marines would be entering the Docklands soon. We just had to hold out for long enough.

✠

It was at midday that American tanks were seen moving through the streets of London. The government had made a catastrophic mistake in concentrating so many troops in Liverpool. The capital city was poorly defended, the Gestapo and SS were in chaos, and command structures further broke down due to the Americans' advanced jamming technology, which disrupted radio and electronic equipment.

Operation Achaeans' Revenge was progressing well. In our case, the Trojan horse was a cargo ship returning from the Grenadines with a shipment of bananas. Except there was no fruit. Just tanks and five battalions of elite trained men, pissed off that their countrymen had been murdered on Flight AE539. American technology was way more advanced than the Nazis', and they were armed to the teeth. The Americans aimed to gain control of Euston Airport, which, if captured, would enable them to fly in thousands more troops, tanks and supplies.

The attack had taken the Nazis by surprise, and American forces moved across the capital, surprisingly swiftly, towards the airport. The Nazis, hopelessly unprepared, scrabbled around for reinforcements. Initially, resistance was light and many regular army conscripts surrendered without even firing a bullet, but this was to change.

Ost-Bereich was completely liberated in a matter of hours. The Americans were welcomed with open arms. Striking workers waved British and American flags and cheered the troops as they marched through the streets, securing district by district and digging in defences. They brought food, medicine, and toys for the children, and in return were welcomed into people's homes as heroes.

Conscripts were one thing. Unfortunately, the hardcore SS were a different story. They were determined to fight to the bitter end. Soon, the streets of London became scenes of fierce fighting. The Nazis dug in around the approach roads to the airport and blockaded Autobahn 40, knowing full well the consequences if Euston Airport fell.

Realising their mistake, Nazi troops were ordered back south to defend London. However, American missiles had blown up sections of the northern autobahns, hindering their progress. American F16 fighters were far superior to the Luftwaffe's Messerschmitt-Z1 jets, a design that dated back to the early 1970s, and it was evident fairly early on in which direction the air battle was heading.

The ground war was a different matter. Once German troops eventually reached London, it seemed that every inch of land was going to be fought for at great cost. No matter how well trained and equipped they were, American troops still only numbered a few thousand, against the might of the Wehrmacht. It was going to take a miracle to win.

45

22nd September 1993

THOMAS JORDAN

At the television station, we were all exhausted and hungry. We were into the third day of our siege. We had taken it in turns to sleep, including John and Maria. The canteen food had run out, so we smashed the vending machines and distributed the contents among the staff, along with our own rations. We knew that we could not survive on chocolate, crisps and fizzy drinks. The fatigue combined with the hunger had made us irritable, and it was a challenge to keep everyone motivated and focused on our task.

The Nazis had shot down the cameras monitoring the outside of the building, so we were blind. They tried cutting through the uroferranium shutters on the ground floor, but backed off when James started the automated machine guns.

They were keeping up the pressure on us, and we were at breaking point. They were getting messages inside the building, promising leniency. I knew this was bollocks, but some of the RT staff were naive, suggesting that we should consider surrendering.

American troops halted at the *zwischenwand*, a fair way from Euston Airport, and were outnumbered, but holding their position. Having overcome the guards, they were now using the wall as a defensive barrier, supported by the American Air Force. We could just about hear the air-raid sirens and the sonic booms of jets, through the shutters.

✠

Another twenty-four hours passed. We kept transmitting news, but around 14.00 hours on Thursday, the Germans managed to damage one of our satellite dishes, taking us off air. Some of the technical staff tried to boost the power to the transmitters but were unsuccessful.

There was nothing more we could do from here, except sit it out. It was frustrating, but since we were no longer a threat to the regime, we were a less important target, and the firing had stopped. They knew that we would soon run out of food and water. It was only a matter of time.

I still had radio contact over a secure channel with my compatriots, and James had enabled the telephones on our floor. I had allowed the staff to make calls to their families, while there was still time. I could see many of them sobbing, trying to explain their actions, but what was touching was the number of times I heard the words 'I love you' whispered in those conversations. It brought it home to me that this may be the last time they ever spoke to their loved ones. If we lost, and sadly, things were not looking too good, everyone in this office would be executed for sure.

To save power, we switched off the studio lights and cameras, and being so high up with no heating, the office quickly became cold. You could see our breath condense. Maria and John came into the main office, looking shattered.

"We did what we could," said Maria.

"We've thirty years to make up for," said John.

"At least when they take me to the gallows, I'll know I tried to put things right," said Maria.

"Nobody here is going to the gallows," I said. "Least of all you."

"If it's not the American gallows, it'll be the gas chambers," said John grimly.

"It's not over yet," I said, feigning optimism. "The Americans are putting everything into this."

"But without the airport, it's over before they've even started," said John. "Even with control of the airspace, how long are a few thousand troops going to hold out against the Wehrmacht?"

46

24th September 1993

THOMAS JORDAN

The office was freezing cold. The carpet was soaked from the sprinklers, which made it smell mouldy. Some of the staff had huddled together in a group to stay warm. Others were slumped over desks, trying to sleep. Two of the auxiliary generators had run out of diesel, and the last was struggling, so the emergency lights dimmed and flickered pathetically, like a candle running out of oxygen. The computers were off too. We had run out of food, the water cooler was empty, the taps in the bathroom were not working, the toilets did not flush, and the phones had been cut off. It was unhygienic and demoralising.

At midday, General K radioed me. Everyone looked at me hopefully.

"The Americans have captured the airport," I said, not knowing whether to punch the ceiling in excitement or cry. Instead, I just looked down in relief and took a deep breath.

There was applause and cheers. The mood changed in an instant.

"Are you sure?" said John Jeffries.

"Absolutely," I said. "That was a member of the Army Council."

"That must have been a battle and a half," said John.

"It wasn't all down to the Americans," I said. "We had agents working undercover in the terminal building." I shook my head sadly. "We've lost a lot of colleagues, and hundreds of American soldiers died. But it wasn't in vain. Euston's in American hands now."

"This is it," said Luke excitedly. "Surely we've won now. The Americans will move in reinforcements."

"It looks like it," I said anxiously.

Mark patted me on the back. "Tom, this is what we've been working for all these years. Why the long face?"

"It's Stephen."

"You mean… he's been…?"

"I don't know. General K said he doesn't know his status. For all I know, he could be dead, or worse."

Mark looked at me seriously. "He'll make it. He has training. He's a survivor. Trust me."

"I know, but what if—?"

"Fuck off," said Mark. "Don't even think about it. Besides, I've ordered a new hat."

"What are you on about?"

"For the wedding, stupid. By the way, if you need a best man…"

I laughed drily. "You're such a prick."

"Seriously though, mate, keep it together. He'll be okay. Focus on the mission. This lot need you to lead."

I put horrible thoughts out of my mind and raised my voice to address the office.

"We just need to hold out for a few more hours," I said. "The Americans are on their way. They need this facility."

I looked around at the collection of weary faces. We had hope. Maria offered me a cigarette.

"No thanks. I don't smoke."

"Maybe you should start," she said, lighting up.

✠

The Americans quickly took advantage of capturing the airport by flying in masses of troops, who had been secretly based in supposedly neutral Ireland, flown in on passenger airlines over the last two weeks, disguised as tourists.

After losing Euston, the Nazis decided to cut their losses and destroy it. They fired V17s at the runways, but the Americans had an advanced anti-missile system called Patriot, which shot them down before they hit their targets. None got through.

Soon, tens of thousands of soldiers were moving out from the airport, taking defensive positions around London, digging in with heavy weaponry. It was at that point I really believed we were going to win.

The second prong of the American attack started shortly after the airport was secured. American warships that had been anchored near the Strait of Dover entered the Thames Estuary and made their way along the river towards the Houses of Parliament.

By 18.00 we realised that we were in for yet another sleepover. We had managed to get some water from another floor, but we were all hungry, cold and tired, and tempers were flaring.

47

25th September

THOMAS JORDAN

My experiences at Ramsgate had prepared me for dealing with the lack of sleep, but the others were on the verge of cracking up.

One of the RT staff had found a transistor radio. We listened to an American station reporting the progress of their armies. Overnight they had moved gradually westwards, backed up by formidable air power. The troops in Ost-Bereich had blown up large sections of the hated *zwischenwand*.

It seemed that the Luftwaffe was already overstretched defending the Reich's African interests, and unable to compete with superior American technology. A correspondent said, "*This war is showcasing how sophisticated American weaponry is. It is like the Reich military has fallen asleep at the wheel. Lack of investment because of a failing economy has taken its toll.*"

The Governor General and Prime Minister had fled by helicopter, but were intercepted and captured by the Americans. Their arrest had been broadcast on the radio, their voices clearly identifiable when asked for their names. That was a major coup.

Later that afternoon, our last pair of batteries failed, the radio went dead, and once again we were cut off from the outside world. We could hear gunfire on the streets below, and planes flying overhead. We sat there, mostly in silence, reflecting on our own fate and that of the world. We had all become part of history, but whose history would that be?

✠

At 16.10, the Americans finally arrived at Television Tower and cleared the immediate area of the few remaining regime troops that had not deserted their posts.

The power supply was swiftly reconnected, the emergency lights extinguished, the main lights came on, and the office became full of the noise of whirring computers as they rebooted. We were no longer under siege.

James deactivated the building's defence mechanisms. I squinted as the shutters opened, letting in the bright sunlight.

When the Americans entered the office, they were met with cheers. They brought us food, water and hope. I briefed a lieutenant on the situation in the building. All personnel outside of our floor were arrested.

The revolution snowballed quickly. The general strike was being observed. The Americans fixed the damaged transceivers, and we started broadcasting again. The Americans provided us with videotapes, which we broadcast, of swastikas being ripped off buildings and statues being torn down. The Nazi flag was removed from the roof of Buckingham Palace, and the Union Jack hoisted in its place. The swastika banners were cut down.

Maria Thorpe described it as *"the symbols of tyranny being dismantled"*. The statue of Adolf Hitler, towering in front of the Houses of Parliament, was toppled by a crowd who had surrounded it with a rope. It crashed to the ground to claps and cheers. People set about it with hammers. I wished

I could be in the Reich Chancellery to see the expression on Goebbels' puffy face.

Other scenes showed the people rising up in the northern cities. Regional party offices were in flames. Crowds marched on the streets with home-made weapons and petrol bombs, torching SS cars.

The Americans provided air support, but their ground troops had not reached this region yet, and there were already reprisals. Squadrons of Death Heads opened fire on unarmed crowds, killing women and children indiscriminately. Any hopes of this being a bloodless revolution were dashed early on. It was going to get very nasty, and a lot of people were going to die.

Like all of us, poor John and Maria must have been exhausted, but unlike them, we did not have to sit in front of the nation. They soldiered on, taking our message to the public, kept awake by coffee and adrenaline. The production team had hastily designed new graphics for the rebranded station, with a British Liberation Television logo – a stylised figure of a man holding a tall pole with a Union Jack waving in the wind, which when shown was accompanied by an instrumental verse of *Rule, Britannia!*

I imagined the government ministers must have been furious, knowing that they had been taken in by the false intelligence we had been feeding them. Their parasitic lives of leeching off the rest of us were over.

The Nazi armies in Liverpool were hopelessly exposed when they retreated south. Alliance submarines concealed in the Irish Sea launched missiles using information from spy satellites. The American attack was devastating; they even sent us images of their missiles with inbuilt cameras closing in on their targets. It was the first time that we had seen warfare in this way.

Maria spoke: "*Churches across London are ringing their bells in unison. People are enjoying their first taste of freedom for four decades. A provisional government has been formed by the Americans to ensure a smooth transition of power. More on that later. We now cross over the Atlantic, where President Turnbull is making a live public address at the White House.*"

The picture showed the US President sitting at his desk in the Oval Office with the Presidential Seal behind him.

"*My fellow Americans, and peoples of the free world – and from today, that free world just got a little bigger. I bring you a mixture of news. First, it is with great satisfaction that I can report that our military operation against the Third Reich in Great Britain is progressing well. The capital city, London, has been liberated. Our troops are currently shoring up their defences. The enemy has taken heavy losses, but they are fighting on. We expect the battle for the rest of the country to take many weeks, if not months, but I can promise you this: good will always triumph over evil – we will prevail.*

"*I commend our troops, who have acted with professionalism and bravery. Our losses have been acceptable for this kind of operation, but the loss of any life means that American families will be without fathers, brothers or sons. My heartfelt condolences go out to them. They have not died in vain; they died defending liberty and American values.*

"*We also commend the British resistance, who not only provided us with the intelligence for such an operation to succeed, at significant personal risk, but have also died fighting alongside us.*

"*Great Britain is blockaded by sea and air. Our overwhelming air, sea and land superiority means that the Nazis will be unable to send in reinforcements. We urge Chancellor Goebbels to bring this to a swift conclusion and order German troops to surrender, whereupon they will be treated humanely in accordance with the Geneva Convention.*

"Earlier today, I spoke with Princess Elizabeth, who expressed her delight at the course of events. A provisional military council has been appointed as a caretaker administration until the constitutional monarchy is restored and a democratic civilian government can be elected. All Nazi laws are herewith struck from the statute book. I urge all Americans to join me in prayer for our soldiers. Lastly, I quote from Churchill's final address before his arrest in 1943: 'This is not the end, it is not even the beginning of the end – but it is perhaps the end of the beginning.'"

"*Inspiring words from the American President,*" said John Jeffries. "*Chancellor Goebbels has issued a bellicose statement, demanding what he describes as an American invasion force to withdraw immediately or face the consequences. In an interview earlier today with the German news agency, Die Wahrheit, he refused to rule out the use of tactical nuclear weapons. We'll keep you abreast of all the latest developments as they occur.*"

The use of the word 'nuclear' sent shivers down my spine. We all knew what the Nazis were capable of. They were trapped in a corner, and that made them unpredictable. Hitler had used the atomic bomb without hesitation. The question was whether Helmut Goebbels would be mad enough to do it and risk the nuclear reprisals. His statement had certainly dampened the mood.

Some more American soldiers entered the office. A colonel came up to me and shook my hand.

"Great job," he said warmly.

"Thanks," I said. "How are things on the ground?"

"Pretty much as you've been reporting it," he replied. "Hell, they're not going without a fight, but we know they are overwhelmed. And they've got their hands full in Russia and Africa."

"Excellent."

"People no longer believe in the thousand-year Reich," he said.

"Do you think they'll nuke us?" I said.

The colonel shrugged. "Who knows? I'd like to believe that it's just bluster, but if they did, there would be reprisals. The whole goddamn world would go up in flames. I don't think that motherfucker Goebbels is that dumb."

"Fuck me, I hope you're right."

"You should go home and get some sleep," he said. "My driver can drop you back."

"I know the team here will need to rest as well. There's only so much coffee you can drink."

"I'm here to sort that out," he said. "We've got people on the way."

I walked back into the office and thanked everyone for their help, then Mark and I followed a US marine into the elevator.

The outside of the building was ring-fenced by sandbag trenches, with gun turrets manned by US soldiers. Carla was standing under the remains of the glass canopy.

"Hey," I said.

"We did it," she said.

"We did."

She gave me such a tight hug, I nearly suffocated. "I bloody love you," she said.

"I love you too."

✠

There was an armoured Humvee at the end of the road. A marine drove us through the deserted streets towards the East

End. The crowds had been evacuated while American special forces mopped up the SS snipers. I noticed how clean the air was, now the factories were closed and the traffic banished.

We headed towards the remnants of the *zwischenwand*. The checkpoints and guard towers were deserted. We crossed into the East End unhindered.

"I never thought I'd see the back of that bloody wall," said Carla.

"Just think," said Mark. "There's nothing to stop us walking all the way to Buckingham Palace. No border posts, no travel permits that take months to get. It's going to be amazing."

"This is just the beginning," I said. "You wait. I reckon in a few months, the Tube stations will be reopened. The city will be reunited."

Then I saw a man walking on the pavement near to us.

"Stop the car," I shouted to the driver, who slammed on the brakes.

I jumped out and stood still, frozen to the spot. I squinted at the man, who was wearing a Kevlar vest and helmet. "Stephen?"

He started running towards me.

"For fuck's sake, Stephen – it's really you," I shouted.

I started running too. We collided and embraced.

"God, I love you so much," I said, holding him tightly.

"You too," he replied. "You've no idea…"

We stood there intertwined, wanting to kiss but aware that we had an audience. We looked into each other's eyes longingly.

"What the fuck are you wearing?" I asked.

"The Americans issued it to me. They've set up an operations base in Mile End Underground Station. I just had to get out for some fresh air and light."

"I'm so glad you're okay," I said, starting to sob. "I didn't know if I'd ever see you again."

"Me too. I mean, I'm glad you're okay as well as glad I'm okay," he said clumsily. "And I haven't stopped worrying about you."

"I can't believe you actually blew up Himmler Tower."

"Neither can I."

"Why don't you come back to my house? There's no need to hide any more."

"I've got a better idea. Would your driver mind taking us back over the *zwischenwand* to my place?"

"I'm sure he won't."

"We might as well take advantage of my apartment, while I've still got it."

We got into the Humvee. Carla beamed at Stephen.

"I knew you'd come good," she said.

"No you didn't," said Mark. "You said he'd blab."

"Fuck off, carrot top," said Carla. "I said no such thing."

"No sense of humour, that one," said Mark.

I chuckled.

Carla ignored him and spoke to Stephen. "Make sure you look after Tom, or you'll have me to answer to."

"He looks really scared," said Mark sarcastically.

"I will, I promise," said Stephen, ignoring Mark.

After we had dropped off Mark and Carla, the driver took us to Hampstead, which was eerily deserted.

48

25th September 1993

STEPHEN TALBOT

Tom and I walked into my apartment. I gave him a quick tour. To my mind, it was pretty ordinary, but Tom, who had lived such a sheltered life, was awestruck.

"It must be worth more than all the houses on my street put together," he said.

"It's only rented. It's not like I deserve it."

"It's still amazing."

"It's all right."

We went into the kitchen. I put my hand into my pocket and found my warrant card. "Shall I keep it for posterity?" I asked.

"Nah," said Tom. He took it from me and tossed it in the bin.

"I guess I'm unemployed now."

"Don't dwell on the past."

I ran my hand gently down his rugged face. He was dishevelled and in need of a shower, he had a week's growth of stubble, and his eyes betrayed his fatigue. I shed a tear. I pulled him towards me. We hugged each other tightly.

"I didn't know if I'd ever see you again."

"Ditto," he replied.

The euphoria of the past few days' events evaporated as I thought about my father. I gently detached myself from Tom and looked down at the floor.

"What's wrong?" he said.

"I'm worried about my father. Did you know that he was in Himmler Tower when I blew it up?"

"I thought there was a good chance that he may have been. That's why I got that note to you."

"I wonder if he got out?"

"From what I saw on the news, most people got out safely."

"I hope you're right."

"I'm sorry to have put you through this."

"It's okay. It was my decision." I hardened my heart. "At the end of the day, he's killed and maimed enough people."

"He's still your father."

"Yes, I know. And despite everything that he is, I do love him." I wiped away a tear. "You know, I'd rather not think about it at the moment. What's done is done."

"You did something courageous that could help win this war. And unlike Wertheim, this was a military target."

I nodded sadly. "It wasn't an easy decision. It's not only my father; I had colleagues working in that building. Colleagues with children... wives..."

"I know."

"Do you?"

"Yes, and you have to believe me when I say that I understand. I wish I could say, 'Never mind, it passes' but, like me, you are going to have to live with yourself."

"Can I just say something?" I said, changing the subject. "Please don't be offended."

"What?"

"You absolutely stink," I said, pulling away from him.

"Fucking charming. But in fairness, I've not washed for days. Not to mention the sewers."

"Come on, let's get you showered."

I led him into the bathroom. We took off our dirty clothes,

and I followed Tom into the shower cubicle. I turned on the taps, and soon the bathroom was steamy. I put some shampoo in my hands and began to massage it into his scalp. His hair, usually freshly cropped, had two weeks' growth. It suited him. Soon we both smelled pleasantly of lemon-scented shower gel. The water beat down on our skin. I gazed into his eyes. He pressed himself against me.

"You've no idea how good it is to see you," he murmured.

"I feel the same."

"Do you think, once this is all over, being a homo might be, you know… legal? Like it is in America or Australia?"

"I know that it couldn't possibly get any worse. That's not what I've risked my life for. Besides, we could always emigrate."

"You used the word 'we'."

"Aren't we a couple, then?"

"Of course we are. I've just never… thought of it like that."

"Neither had I, until then."

We hugged and kissed under the shower. Unlike in Ost-Bereich, the hot water did not run out in a couple of minutes, and Tom said that he had never felt so clean. I turned off the shower and flung him a fluffy white towel. Tom brushed his teeth, and we dried ourselves off. Then he took my hand and led me to the bedroom.

I lay on my back, and he climbed on top of me. We kissed for ages before he took the towel off me, and we made love with the sound of gunfire in the distance.

Afterwards, Tom rolled over and fell asleep. I gazed up at the ceiling, deep in thought. I could hear shelling in the distance. I did not know if the Americans would prevail, neither did I know what would be my fate, but I savoured this beautiful moment to the full. Whatever the future held, Tom and I would face it together.

Region 6 Timeline

12th March 1938: Germany annexes Austria.

15th March 1939: Germany invades Czechoslovakia.

1st September 1939: Germany invades Poland.

3rd September 1939: France and Britain declare war on Germany.

April – June 1940: Most of Western Europe falls to the Nazis during the Blitzkrieg, including Denmark, Norway, Holland, Belgium and France.

10th May 1940: Winston Churchill becomes Prime Minister of Great Britain.

10th July – 31st October 1940: The Battle of Britain. Germany loses.

27th September 1940: Germany, Fascist Italy and Imperial Japan sign a Tripartite Pact, creating the Axis Alliance.

22nd June 1941: The Axis powers launch an attack on Russia.

7th December 1941: Japan launches a devastating attack on the US Navy in Pearl Harbor.

8th December 1941: America enters the war on the side of the Allies.

4th March 1942: The Japanese defeat the American Navy at the Battle of Midway.

23rd August 1942: The Battle of Stalingrad begins.

2nd December 1942: The Allies push back the Axis powers in North Africa.

3rd December 1942: German troops unexpectedly retreat from Stalingrad. Stalin orders victory celebrations.

14th December 1942: The Germans drop a twenty-five-megaton atomic bomb on Stalingrad, causing devastation.

15th December 1942: Joseph Stalin makes a defiant speech accusing the Nazis of genocide and stating that the Soviet Union will never surrender.

29th December 1942: The Germans drop a thirty-megaton atomic bomb on Moscow, wiping out the Politburo.

3rd January 1943: Stalin emerges from hiding, and in a radio broadcast urges the Red Army to fight on to the bitter end.

6th January 1943: The Germans drop thirty-megaton atomic bombs on Leningrad and Novosibirsk. Stalin is believed to have been killed.

8th January 1943: German infantry advance on Moscow, mopping up light resistance.

11th January 1943: Nikolai Voznesensky, the most senior surviving member of the Soviet government, unconditionally surrenders to the Germans.

19th January 1943: The Germans attempt to drop an atomic bomb on Birmingham to destroy many of the nation's munitions factories. The aircraft is intercepted by the RAF at Dover, but the pilot manages to detonate the bomb, which wipes out most of Kent and parts of South-East London.

20th January 1943: The second Battle of Britain begins. With Russia defeated, the Luftwaffe are able to devote all of their resources to wiping out the remainder of the RAF. America has become bogged down in the war with Japan.

9th February 1943: The RAF have been decimated and the Luftwaffe control British airspace. The Americans offer little support. The British public live in fear of a nuclear attack.

12th February 1943: Field Marshal Walther von Brauchitsch launches Operation Sea Lion against Great Britain, threatening nuclear devastation if Nazi forces are defeated.

13th February 1943: American aircraft carriers retreat out of range of German bombers and focus on the war with Japan.

14th February 1943: The royal family are evacuated to Canada.

16th February 1943: Hitler refuses to share the secrets of the atomic bomb with Japan, leading to a split in the Axis.

23rd February 1943: The Allies collapse in North Africa. The Germans take the Suez Canal.

26th February 1943:The British government unconditionally surrenders to the Germans. Winston Churchill is arrested for war crimes and deported to Berlin to face trial.

2nd March 1943: Germany and America agree to an armistice. Hitler promises not to invade Ireland.

2nd April 1943: Following a show trial, Churchill is publicly executed in front of the Brandenburg Gate.

1944 – 1945: America is still fighting a costly and arduous war with the Japanese Empire, which now includes most of the former British Empire in the East including Burma, Malaya and India. The Chinese have driven out the Japanese from their country, but are still officially at war with Japan.

7th February 1945: Chief nuclear scientist of the Third Reich, Werner Heisenberg, defects to the USA via Ireland.

8th April 1945: Heisenberg is assassinated, slowing development of the US atomic bomb.

12th April 1945: Franklin D. Roosevelt dies after suffering a major stroke. He is succeeded by his Vice President, Harry S. Truman.

4th September 1945: America drops atomic bombs on Hiroshima and Nagasaki in Japan.

6th September 1945: Emperor Hirohito unconditionally surrenders to America.

9th September 1945: Hitler calls a final end to hostilities between the USA and the Third Reich, stating he has no further territorial ambitions in Europe and wishes to concentrate on colonising Russia.

12th September 1945: Hitler, Mussolini and Truman attend a summit in Tehran to discuss ending the war.

30th September 1945: A peace treaty is signed between the USA and the Third Reich, formally ending the Second World War.

Key details:

– Ireland and Sweden to remain neutral.
– The former Soviet Union and Europe to remain under Germany's sphere of influence.
– Libya and Egypt to remain Axis colonies, but the American Merchant Navy is allowed access to the Suez Canal.
– All remaining British overseas territories gain independence, including India.
– Japan to fall under American influence.
– Italy, Spain and Portugal to remain independent fascist states.

12th April 1946: On the anniversary of Roosevelt's death, Harry S. Truman claims in a lengthy address that the former President's biggest regret was abandoning the Allies to a fate under Nazism.

11th July 1963: After remaining out of public sight for two years, it is announced that Adolf Hitler has died of natural causes at the Berghof.

14th July 1963: Heinrich Himmler dies in a car crash in Bavaria.

15th July 1963: Joseph Goebbels is appointed Chancellor of the Third Reich.

4th August 1963: Hitler receives a massive state funeral attended by world leaders. Goebbels announces that a mausoleum will be built next to the Great Hall in the German capital, Germania.

16th October 1969: Chancellor Joseph Goebbels dies from pancreatic cancer.

28th October 1969: Helmut Goebbels is appointed as his successor.

Thank you to John Scotney
for his patient and invaluable guidance.